Who Is Teddy Villanova?

Other novels by Thomas Berger

SNEAKY PEOPLE (1975)
REGIMENT OF WOMEN (1973)
VITAL PARTS (1970)
KILLING TIME (1967)
LITTLE BIG MAN (1964)
REINHART IN LOVE (1962)
CRAZY IN BERLIN (1958)

WHO IS TEDDY VILLANOVA?

THOMAS BERGER

DELACORTE PRESS/SEYMOUR LAWRENCE

Library of Congress Cataloging in Publication Data

Berger, Thomas, 1924–
   Who is Teddy Villanova?

   I. Title.
PZ4.B497Wh   [PS3552.E719]   813'.5'4   76–42227
ISBN 0–440–09546–8

To Charles Rydell and Colline du Vent

We are all celebrating some funeral.

—BAUDELAIRE,
"On the Heroism of Modern Life"

I

Call me Russel Wren. A secretary named Peggy Tumulty
was my unique employee, and at the moment I owed her
a fortnight's pay. In arrears on the rent for my apartment,
on the door of which the churlish super had posted a notice
that tended to humiliate (and which, ripped away, was
soon reborn in more blatant advertisement), I had lately,
stealthily, moved, auxiliary underwear and socks in an ex-
Downy carton, into my office.

For another ten days I was a tenant in good standing in
the five-story structure of superimposed lofts on East
Twenty-third Street, where my neighbors were little novelty firms, agencies for obscure services, and, in the second-
floor rear, an after-hours social club for persons of Medit-
erranean mien and attire.

I was a licensed private investigator, but I possessed
an unlicensed firearm, a tiny Browning automatic in .25
caliber (pressed upon me once, and then forgotten, by a
client who, suspecting his wife had taken a lover, had
worked a ruse-suicide attempt that, owing to a hair-trigger,
had cost him an earlobe). I keep this pistol in hiding;
against any arm more formidable than a penknife it would

be outweaponed; and in New York, defending oneself against attack not only is in heinous violation of innumerable ordinances but might well provoke the frustrated assailant to bring a successful suit for damages.

Finally, before we make a flying cannon ball into the murky waters of this narrative, I should say I am a bachelor of thirty (but heterosexual, as some have said, to the threshold of satyriasis). I took a B.A. and M.A. amidst the thronged anonymity of State, thereafter served at the same institution, for a niggardly wage, as instructor in English; was released as redundant and tried to write a play; and after having been photographed in intimate conversation with someone else's wife, was given employment by the private investigator, himself a grandfather, as cameraman as well as technical adviser on contemporary illicitness. Eventually he turned over to me the transom department of his business, going himself into the more lucrative assignments in the detection of shoplifting. I opened my own agency a year later.

I was metaphorically on my uppers, though literally dozing at my desk, on that late-April morning when Peggy signaled me by interoffice buzzer. My latest job had ended two weeks earlier. Crying "Room Service!" I had induced a married man to open the door of a hotel room for which he had registered under a false name with a woman not his wife. His legal spouse was my client. I was alone, not needing a friendly witness, because the wife wanted me at this time only to serve as a threat to his composure and not to collect evidence for litigation.

In this assignment I failed. He was a short and slight-built man—a figure very common among satyrs, incidentally—but could laugh as robustly as a worthy of twice his bulk. Lowering his chin at last—he had been guffawing at the chandelier, a hippodrome for silverfish—he said: "Tell Gretta that it isn't Gertrude." He repaired into the bathroom, could be heard mumbling, and soon brought out a remarkably obese woman, nude above but toweled below the navel. "Speak your piece," said the man. In a voice of thin timbre, suggesting Shylock's "squeaking of the wry-neck'd fife," she said: "I'm a prostitute."

"That was Gertrude all right all right," said Gretta, when I delivered my report. For this job of work I received $100. Easily earned, no doubt, but it represented my entire income thus far in April.

It had been so long since I last heard Peggy's signal that it quite startled me now: I came to full life with a scowl and a shudder. To ask about her wages Peggy would way-lay me if I passed through the outer office; for this reason I tended more and more to stay holed up until she went home at five, not seeing her person all day. For rou-tine communications—arrival, lunchtime, departure—she cracked my door an inch and shouted in, though the stri-dent voice she assumed for such a purpose was a squander of energy, as was opening the door, given the thin plywood that divided my half-loft into two rooms.

Since I had set up housekeeping in the inner office (per-forming my toilet at the deep washbasin that I had in-herited from the predecessor photographic lab; mixing my freeze-dried Taster's Choice and Cup-a-Soup with hot water from the tap, which owing to the rust of vintage plumbing drooled already dark as beef broth from a de-generated rubber aerator fixed on its nose, a device I suf-fered to remain because I could not bear to touch it), Peggy had never penetrated that space. She was twenty-nine, a Queens Irish spinster of the type I should call relentless, and unless she had lost her *fleur* while compet-ing in the high hurdles as a parochial schoolgirl, she was yet in formidable possession of it. My theory was that Peggy believed her entering my chamber might be con-strued as a suggestion, even though she carried a file of unpaid bills, that in reciprocation the temple of her body might be invaded.

Peggy had an elaborate pair of breasts, but quite near and flanking them were always, even on winter days when the heat invariably fled the corroded old radiators, crescents of sweat stains in the armpits of the oysterish or pale-beige blouses she doggedly favored. She had rather more ample hips than those that attract me most, yet a slacker behind, and withal plump calves, notwithstanding which she wore skirts which cleared the knee. Only under certain freakish conditions of light could her hair be seen as not absolutely black. I dote on pale blondes.

Her voice was off-putting as well. When she raised it she could loosen the hardened putty from the window-panes, and though sexually a prude she was coarsely candid about truly impolite functions. "Got to hit the can!" was her shout as preface to a visit down the hall, if indeed her name for that facility had justice: toilet, basin, and unshaded light bulb, the door unmarked as to sex and usually left unlocked by the denizens of the rear loft, who, I suspected from the name of their operation, The Ganymede Press, printed pornography of the pederast persuasion. Winos sometimes found their way to the water closet and went peacefully to earth within—until routed by Peggy's howl: she was self-righteously fearless at such encounters.

Back, finally, to her summons. The phone company's intercom arrangement was, like all the offerings of that extortive monopoly, too expensive. We had our homemade rig—Peggy's work, actually; I am maladroit with pliers: a little push button on her desk was connected to a long wire that traveled, stapled intermittently, over hill and dale and windy moor, I mean under the door, along the base of the wall and then, turning at right angles, straight across the carpetless floor and up the back wall of my desk to a buzzer half the size of a cigarette package and powered by two penlight dry cells.

At the sound I picked up Ma Bell's jet-black baby from its cradle, a simple extension from the one on Peg's desk.

"Are you free?" she asked, and when I responded without chaff—I never wisecrack with Peggy when I owe her money—she said: "Will you see a Mr. Bakewell?"

She was bright enough to turn away bill collectors without consulting me; therefore I asked for two minutes, and put my dirty coffee cup in a drawer and scraped the English muffin crusts and crumbs into the waste can.

I was on the point of entering the noose of an already knotted tie when I realized I was wearing a soft knitted shirt of Ban-Lon. The blue hand-towel hanging from the lip of the washbasin was damp but of too dark a dye to show dirt. I swung its clamminess around my neck and fashioned it into a makeshift cravat. I found my tan corduroy jacket and punched into it; even when new that garment had an abused look, but worn with an insolent carriage it would, I hoped, escape the downright crestfallen. Finally, I seized from the couch the Indian blanket under which I had slept the night, its fringes up my nostrils, and pitched it behind the waist-high trap door of a disused dumbwaiter, the little rising stage of which had fortunately last halted, and frozen there, at my level: it served as the only closet in either room.

I limped, my left thigh exuding the pins & needles it had collected during my doze, to the door, which I opened as deliberately as, given my hunger for a client, I could, and saw Mr. Bakewell seated on both the camp chairs which with Peggy's desk comprised the furniture of the outer office. At least I saw *him:* the chairs had to be assumed to be supporting his vast body, as he occupied the place where they had been, and he was in the position of sitting. I estimated his weight as a good 300 and, when he rose, adjusted this upwards. I am, with expanded chest and rigidified tendons, just, or at any rate not far from, five feet ten. He must have risen to six-six or -seven, and as he plowed towards me, as if wading through knee-high slush, I feared he would never negotiate the entrance to my inner office, which was of both a height and width somewhat less generous than the standard, owing to my having taken the advice, as usual to my detriment, of Sam Polidor, my landlord, and hired for its fitting the building-super, an ancient winesoak, so feeble he could scarcely lift a saw let alone cut steadily with it. Though no cabinetmaker, Peggy took over finally and got the thing to hang in approximate agreement with the jamb, if to do so the former had to be reduced in longitude by three inches, in width by four.

"Good morning, sir," I chirped, stepping through with dipped shoulder and torsioned trunk—and my current weight was 157 in anklets and smallclothes. "My officesess being remodeled," I added in an anxious lisp. "Shall we converse in the corridor?"

I took a step towards the outside door, to dramatize my suggestion, and then quickly took another to avoid being humorously, inexorably trampled into the scarred old floor boards. So distracted, I did not see the maneuver by which, incredibly, he passed through the strait gate of the inner room, but it must have been as marvelous as the glide of rich men into heaven. When I turned back I could see nothing through the frame but an expanse of suit: this was all the more remarkable in that he was actually some distance from the door. As it happened I scraped my head on my own entry.

He spun about to face me, in as swift and deft a movement as that by which he must have cleared the doorway. I had not yet had time to react to his visage, which was appropriately large, but also, in its upper half, unexpectedly delicate. He had especially lustrous eyes, long-lashed, almost girlish, and a nose of sensitive modeling. But his mouth was small and mean and set above jaws that came forward from behind flat ears to join in a dimple the lobes of which were as big as baby's kneecaps.

He spoke in a singular manner, scarcely opening his oral aperture; yet I suspected, from the swelling above and below, that his upper row of teeth was nowhere near the lower; that is to say, not in the malocclusion of the "tough" style of address, but in the uncertain suspension of poorly fitted dentures. It was impossible for me to estimate the age of a man that large.

"Oorillpuh—" he began, and then, confirming my suspicion, probed his mouth with a parsnip-finger, and started again with a clarified version of the same phrase: "You little punk—"

He employed his massive hand once more, now not for the resituation of his dental plate but, formed into the claw of an earth mover, to grasp the entire bosom of my knitted shirt, which had it not been of elastic synthetic would thereby have been ripped from my quailing chest, revealing the grayed but recently laundered T-shirt beneath. That the latter clung to my skin despite his grasp suggested either the surgical delicacy of his fingers or the imprecision of his rage: it was yet too early to determine whether he intended to hurt, or merely to warn, me; and naturally I clung to a hope for the milder, despite a profound, probably masochistic conviction that favored the worse.

I had fenced some in college: if I could get down the hall to the toilet, where a filthy old mop was cached, I might fend Bakewell off with its splintery handle. As an idea this was much less farcical than one would be in which I designed an attack on him with my bare paws. Speaking of bear paws, he had now lifted his other one, clenched, to a position near the tremendous boss of his right shoulder cap.

I had probably been uttering unarticulated sounds of dismay—*someone* was gasping and grunting—but now, though no less desperate, I managed to deliver a statement so banally reasonable it could not but assume the form of a cliché.

"I don't know you from Adam."

Nevertheless his fist, having reached the limit of its upward travel, came forward. The movement, however, was as yet oleaginously slow, quite unlike his mode of slipping through constricted doorways. He was therefore a complex man. And, understanding that, I believed I was no longer unarmed.

"Very well," I said, throwing my opened palms colateral with my hips, shrugging to the extent allowed by the taut Ban-Lon. "I'll take my punishment. Then perhaps you'll tell me what it was for."

I was wrong about his complexity, at least in this regard. He took me simply at my word. The bludgeon of his balled hand continued towards me until it obliterated the world. An instant of darkness, then one of brilliance, though I felt the actual impact not at all. I had no consciousness of my backward velocity. When I saw him next, he was yet where he had been, but the edge of the couch seat was fitted neatly into the small of my back, my nape was against the rear pillows, and my knees were just off the floor, with my calves and feet compressed precisely, painfully, between.

He had struck me in the forehead, that helmet of protective bone, an impractical stroke even for such stout fingers as his, had he not turned his hand on edge and presented to my skull the resilient karate blade that swells out between the base of the smallest digit and the wrist:

in his case, the size and consistency of the fleshy side of a loin of pork.

He continued to loom there while, shaking my head, I put my vision, which for a moment was as if through shattered glass, in order. I was pleased that the first punch, whether by design or poor coordination, had been relatively harmless, but I could not count on receiving a succession of such favors—not that this hammer blow was utterly undamaging, for that matter: the surf surged regularly in my ears and in the intervals of its ebbing left me with a throatful of wet sand. My loafers were in a position just ahead of his coal-barge brogans, a yard from where I slumped; meanwhile, my feet, twisted on their edges and crushed under the crease between thigh and buttock, were only stockinged: he had knocked me out of my shoes!

I should have liked to learn to walk erect again by stages, beginning with the infantile, but suspecting his next assault might catch me with his foot in my mouth, I instead drew myself warily up the face of the couch and when my rump reached the level of the seat, shot it back. My hips now descended into one of the cavities made by long use of what to begin with was a cheap piece of furniture, feebly sprung. My knees rose high as my clavicles. My gun was concealed behind the books on the shelf four feet above and at least two to the left. Funny that when standing, with some chance of reaching it, I had thought rather of the mop in the hall toilet.

But it did occur to me now to cry for help. "Peggy! Call the police!" If indeed, bless her soul, she had not already done so: my fall against the couch must have shaken the entire floor of the old building.

At my appeal the giant broke open the lower, nasty half of his face and laughed, not with the volume and depth one would have expected, but rather as if he were whispering a series of *f*s.

"Schmuck," he said then. "She went to lunch."

Dumb bitch. I was more bitter at her desertion than by reason of his attack.

"You pack quite a wallop," said I, choosing the vernacular as the proper idiom for obsequiousness. "I don't intend to fight back. In a word, I'll *co-operate*."

He closed his eyes briefly and widened his mouth, as if uttering a silent prayer to the god of chagrin.

"Of course," I went on, "it would help enormously if you told me what it was I should do. I wasn't lying when I said I did not recognize you, and surely your appearance is unforgettable—" It was a mistake to sound this note. He was now definitely scowling. In haste I applied corrective adjustments: "I mean, I have a remarkable memory for faces, and as it happens—"

"Shut your fucking flytrap," he growled. "Gonna say one thing once, and ain't gonna say it again, so get it straight the one time I say it, because you ain't gonna hear it any more."

I made a mental memorandum on his tendency, only now revealed, to be redundant: it might be his usable weakness.

"I'm listening," said I. "I need only to hear it once."

"Well, you better," said he, taking a ponderous step in my direction, "because I ain't gonna chew my cabbage twice."

"Of course," I said, subtly inserting the tip of the wedge with which I might eventually cause him to topple, "if your statement proves unusually complex, there might well be some advantage in repetition, using alternative terms and varying syntaxes, not only for the sake of sheer verbal charm, but also with an eye to the state of affairs in the English language, in which, as one authority asserts, the only exact synonyms are 'furze' and 'gorse.'"

He seemed to reflect on my suggestion for a moment,

and then he asserted that on further interruption by me he would kick me so vigorously as to bring my mouth and my rectum into juxtaposition, though to be sure he used different locutions to construct that vivid image.

He concluded with: "Listen to this here: you tell Teddy Villanova to lay off Junior Washburn."

I repeated these names *sotto voce*, and then, because I detected no quickening of elephantine leg in preparation for the lifting of mastodon foot, I said aloud though not very: "Yes, sir. Yes, I will—if ever I meet Mr. Villanova I shall convey that message instanter. In fact, even before saying 'hi,' if at all possible. But—and please don't feel it necessary to strike me again—I do not now know that gentleman, or in view of your apparent feeling towards him, that scoundrel. Nor have I had the pleasure of Mr. Washburn's acquaintance. I have in fact never before heard either name."

This assertion, accompanied by every toadying embellishment of gesture and fix of face, had no effect upon him.

He lifted the hand with which he had chopped me and, having pondered for a moment, went to the sink and washed it quickly though with care. The mountain of his body approached me again. Once again I had had time to go for my gun, but now I had squandered it in reflection: no, the names meant nothing to me. I do have an excellent memory, and I had not had that many clients to forget. Since leaving college, I have had no male friends.

"Look here," I said. "I don't wish to offend you, but this is surely a case of mistaken identity."

He pointed at my throat with a dripping hand. "Gimme that towel."

At any rate, my emergency cravat did not fool him. I unwound it and handed it over. He dried his fingers and threw the towel in my face. I was blinded for an instant. When I removed the clasp of wet terry cloth he was gone, having once more slipped through the narrow doorway as deftly as a perch fins among subaqueous rocks.

Now I did go for my pistol, removing from the shelf the two-volumed Complete Plato, boxed, and taking the weapon from the thick dust behind. Automatic in my besmirched hand, I dashed through the outer office and into the hallway.

The big man was nowhere to be seen.

We had but one elevator, for both passengers and freight, and its door was just opening. Peggy Tumulty emerged, carrying a white bag, with stridently colored logo, of the nearest Blimpie Base, which was her alternate source of lunch, the other being a Chinese take-out sweatshop on Lex.

She waved the bag at me. "Fancy meeting—"

"*See him? Where'd he go?*"

"Don't have to bite my head off," said she, disregarding the questions, anguished movements, and gun. She huffily jerked her shoulders and marched into the office.

I raced to the stairway door, situated between the toilet and The Ganymede Press. I seldom encountered the personnel of the latter because they invariably used the steps rather than the elevator, perhaps for discretion—though in truth one in good condition could make better time on foot than on the old lift.

Descending, I heard nothing but my own dampened footfalls on the ancient stairs. I was still in my stocking feet, picking up the odd splinter from the desiccated wood. One penetrated my big toe: I limped down the last flight.

Sam Polidor, the landlord, stood in the wretched lobby, if it could be called that, picking at the scabbed wall near the rank of mailboxes, not built-ins but rather separate black-tin containers of the old-fashioned style used formerly in small towns like the little village, dreaming on the banks of the Hudson, in which I was reared. These current examples were frequently rifled by derelicts, first among them, I suspected, the super, and it was not unusual to find a pool of vomit on the floor beneath.

Without turning his outsized horn-rims on me, speaking in response to my footsteps alone, as was his wont, Sam said: "Be happy to know a paint job is in the offing. Not today, and not tomorrow, but soon."

"Did you see a great big man come down here?" I asked, gasping between each second word, not so much because of the physical exertion as in delayed rage at having been so savagely and undeservedly used in my own office.

"Never," Sam said negligently. He looked at me now, first at my nose and then at my pistol. "You'll murder me because the elevator's out of order?"

"Oh." I lowered the gun, which had been pointing at the swollen knot of his cerise necktie. His shirt was striped with puce over a ground of jonquil. "Do these names mean anything to you? Teddy Villanova? Junior Washburn?"

I had decided that the man could not have gained the street in the moments since he had left the third floor. Therefore he must be lurking somewhere in the building above. Now my anger began to recede. Whether he had damaged me enough to justify my shooting him after an office-to-office search was in doubt. I am not accustomed to premeditating violence.

Indeed, I was already at the point from which I might have retired in embarrassment had not I been irked by the insolent grin Sam now displayed.

"I assure you this is no joke."

"I assure you I'm shitting in my pants," cried Sam, thus identifying his expression as hysterical. He continued in the same state for some time after I had deposited the gun onto the dirty handkerchief in my back pocket.

"I had too many pistols pointed at me!" he howled.

I tried to pat his shoulder, but he recoiled even from

that gesture of compassion. "Sorry," said I. "I forgot about the Nazis."

"I'm native-born," he wailed. "It happened to me in midtown."

I realized that it was definitely useless to look further for Bakewell if I had not the stomach to shoot him. The gun, so little that three-quarters of it vanished in even my medium-sized fist, was not, if merely displayed, that formidable a threat to a man of his quantity. I had the awful feeling that he would nonchalantly crush it inside my hamburgered hand and pile-drive me again with the other fist.

The aftereffect of the first blow now, in my static situation, began to assert itself; also, my pierced toe smarted. Sam's image registered on my retinas as if I were staring through lenses of lemon-lime Jell-O in which banana rounds were embedded. My neck seemed to support a beer barrel, and my thorax was a construction of pipe cleaners. Only mixed metaphors will serve here: I was a chrestomathy of them at this juncture. I sought support against the leprous wall. My hand brushed one of the mailboxes, and the tin container quavered on its rusty nail, then dropped clattering onto the floor.

Even in my vertigo I was worried about Sam's reaction. Mean as he was about building maintenance, he took it very ill if a tenant so much as extinguished a cigarette under heel on the premises or lost one Planter's Dry Roasted peanut from the package, crying "Fire!" or "Rats!" as the case might be. He had an especial, and negative, concern about the wretched mailboxes, "Government property!" and used that technicality as an excuse never to have them replaced or even rehung firmly. The damnable thing was that despite the injustice of his attitude, his persistence in it tended to cow me. I have never been able to cope with the self-righteous, self-pitying assurance of indigenous New Yorkers.

Therefore although any decent mailbox should survive such a slight graze, I knew guilt in dislodging this one, said, "Sorry, Sam," and prepared nevertheless, in my faint condition, to hear a complaint.

But Sam was silent. . . . No, as I ascertained with a slow revolution of head, seemingly in my dizziness the full 360-degree circuit, traveling the inside wall of a fishbowl, no, in fact Sam had vanished. The door of the cellarway was ajar and still trembling.

I did not immediately plunge to retrieve the fallen container, fearing I would be too weak to rise thereafter. Being careful this time where I placed my wrist, I supported myself against the wall and inclined my head, bringing my eye very near the hinged lid of another box—my own, in fact. One end of a long envelope protruded from it. I found the energy to curse Peggy again, one of her few duties in this period of nonbusiness being at least promptly to fetch the mail.

Annoyance being with me always a source of strength, I pushed myself erect and removed the envelope. Without looking at its face, I tore it open and extracted the single sheet of paper within. I read the following legend, typed flawlessly, the spellings *sic*.

Dear Teddy,

I'm not going to push the panick button. I have my weaknesses, as you are the first to know, but I keep a stiff upper chin when the cards are down. I won't knuckle under, show the white feather, and I don't intend for a moment to run away with my tale between my legs. Under ordinary circumstances I would

take my medicine, but there is something rotten in the
state of Danemark. Be careful the tables aren't terned
on you.

Yours firmly,

/s/ DONALD WASHBURN II

I then inspected the front of the envelope and saw the
by now well-known name, for the still mysterious personage: MR. TEDDY VILLANOVA. Followed only by the number of the building, my own name not in accompaniment;
and there was no return address. Why had it been put in
my box? Who *was* Villanova? *Who*, besides being a master
of received idioms, was Washburn? Just as a tissue of
clichés did not, these days, rule out a Harvard education,
his Roman numeral was not necessarily a suggestion of
good birth: that sort of thing had already become a popular affectation among the lower middle class in my child-
hood. My high-school friend, son of a private refuse
collector, called himself Dom Mastromarino II.

I scanned the designations on the remaining mailboxes,
for Sam Polidor was never to be trusted when asked for information about the other tenants; not that he was consciously discreet: he neither read nor heard attentively. He
had referred on occasion to my nearest neighbors as the
"Gung-Ho people," and to the Wyandotte Club, the after-
hours establishment on the second floor, as "those Wyoming guys." In my own name, simple as it is, Russel Wren,
he often transposed the vowels and called me Run, and
though Private Investigator was printed on my rent checks
and also on the card Scotch-taped to the face of the mailbox, he persistently believed me a salesman of novelties,
once showing me a rubber puppy dog he had purchased
from a sidewalk vendor—pressing the bulb that formed
one terminal of the tiny hose from which it depended in-

flated and ejected its pink tongue—"Should take on such a cute item in your line, Run."

No Villanova was listed on any mailbox. I did not expect to find Washburn. *He*, after all, was writing *to* this address, not *from* it.

I made my way, still giddy, to the directory board on the wall between the outer and inner doors of the entry-way, a foul six square feet of sticky tile and the oppressive stench of urine, and looked through every name on the roster, there being only eight for the four stories above the street. The ground floor, aside from the loathsome little lobby in which I stood, was occupied by a greasy-spoon, ptomaine-terror-type of lunch counter, with its own entrance next door.

The first thing I learned from the directory board was that the white-plastic letters for Fun Things, Inc., the actual novelties firm with whom Polidor confused me, had as usual been rearranged by a nonperfectionist wit into FUCING, to do no more than which the original vandal, perhaps the same individual, had jimmied the lock on the protective glass last year. Sam of course never made a repair. He had in fact not noticed the alteration until I pointed it out, and even then he said: "Oh, yeah, Foosing, they went under and moved out, owing me a bundle." From time to time I had idly reassembled the letters in their proper sequence, but my unknown competitor soon made amends.

I went through the rest of the board: *Alpenstock Industries*, 2A, whatever they were; *Custer's Last Dance*, 5B, a rock group who used their loft, thank God the far rear one on the top floor, as practice hall; *Corngold & Co.*, 4A, who I believe dealt in costume-jewelry findings, giving Polidor the pretext for a rare bon mot, "for costumed Jews," he having the habitual New Yorkish derisive regard for his own folk.

After these, and *Fucing*, the unused letters from which were confettied pathetically at the bottom of the case, came: *Natural Relations*, 5A, some sort of marriage-counseling service or perhaps a computer-dating agency, Sam being unclear as to the distinction, and for this lack of clarity I should defend him.

Next was *Newhouse, E.*, 3A, a name I had never noticed before, but then I had never before scanned the board with such care; and *Nice Nelly Fashions*, long defunct and replaced in 3B by, these six months, my Ganymede neighbors, who as yet, typical of Sam's negligence and perhaps of their own, unless they had good reason to avoid publicity, had no listing.

The *Wyandotte Club* was the last-named, the penultimate being myself—or rather WERN R. I had been too busy mending Fucing to check on the sequence of the letters in my own name—and had earned the inevitable punishment of the meddler.

Transposing the *R* and the *N* was the work of a moment, but a moment more distinguished by two other phenomena: one, I realized that the unknown Newhouse was registered as of the same office number as my own, 3A, and erroneously so unless Peggy had assumed a pseudonym —or had lied about her real name from the first: I was a bit paranoid from the blow on the forehead, but dismissed the feeling as I became conscious of the second event now in progress: the elevator was descending with its noise so suggestive of the trappings of Marley's ghost, i.e., as if hung with chains and cashboxes.

Had Bakewell lain doggo in the third-floor toilet and only now, the coast cleared, taken the descent to the street? I clawed for my gun but found only the wadded handkerchief, as moist as a flayed peach: at some point I must have mopped my brow.

I was frantically searching the rest of my person when I

heard the elevator thuddingly arrive at its ground-floor terminal. I had propped open the inside door of the entryway so that it would not slam and lock behind me. My keys were on my desk top upstairs, next to a half-eaten bar of Cadbury's mint-filled milk chocolate. Sam had of late disdained the truth that a commercial building should be accessible during business hours, and if by locking the door he excluded some criminals, he must surely have discouraged some customers as well, there being no intercommunication system from lobby to offices. (Which consideration produced another question: how did Bakewell get in?)

Not being able to find my gun, I went to kick away the wooden wedge that held the portal open, and then, having provided at least that pitiful, temporary barrier against pursuit (all but useless, for the door of course was never locked against departures—but this is the reflection of a tranquillity that was remote from me at that time), sprint for the policeman who sometimes directed traffic at the adjacent intersection (but only if, at Friday rush-hour, there had been an accident involving more than one car— if you can think clearly after a savage assault by an eight-foot brute, who is furthermore en route to give you more of the same, I applaud you).

However, having foolishly inserted the peg, with its crude, hand-carved serrations, too firmly at the outset, I could not quickly free it now. Rejecting the first clause of my plan, then, I turned to run—but was suddenly struck by the failure of Bakewell, if indeed it was he, to leave the elevator. The door had slid open, as I could see from my extreme angle, ten feet away, but no passenger emerged in the now more than adequate time for such egress.

All in all, I think this was rather intrepid: my face warming from retained breath, I gingerly approached the facility, broadening and deepening, as I went, the portion of the cab available to my vision. When I could see about a quarter of the interior, a tremendous shoe, sole at right angles to the floor, came with it; at a third, I had all of one enormous leg of trouser and most of the other; they were horizontal and diagonal.

When I was full face with the open car, I saw him in his entirety. His trunk was vertical in the far left corner. His expanse of florid face was impassive. His eyes were closed. I knew he was Bakewell. I thought he was dead.

2

I stayed in the hall and examined the body by eye, having a horror of corpses and also being well aware of the injunction, enunciated in first-aid manuals and on TV police shows, against the civilian moving of the victim of any disaster—and I certainly should have had to disturb his body in a search for what brought him down; no symptom was visible.

Everyone knows, after one visit to a funeral parlor—and, alas, as a child I was dragged on many—that even an embalmed body will be seen to breathe under the fixed stare. Therefore I assigned Bakewell to my peripheral vision, first on one side, then the alternative. If he was not as dead as the cold lasagna on which the tomato sauce has begun to darken, I was a Dutchman. The gaudy and, in the absence of blood, inappropriate metaphor actually came to mind at the moment, as a willed ruse to lure me away from panic—the fundamental purpose of most caprices of language, hence the American wisecrack—but it failed.

It was as if some giant, even larger than Bakewell, seized my shoulders and shook me as though I were an empty suit of clothes. I was helpless in his grasp and under his gasp, and the eventual understanding, when he proved silent to my entreaties, that I pleaded to an apparition created by shock, did nothing to arrest my frenzy.

How long I continued to quake I cannot say, but eventually I discovered that I had simultaneously retreated across the hall and through the inward-opening door of the cellarway and now stood among the trash cans on the landing there. Sam had presumably gone down the communicating stairs. I called to him, but got no response.

Remembering his late agitation under the muzzle of my gun, I cried: "I won't shoot you! I lost the pistol anyway!"

His distant answer was heard: "I know. I took it and threw it away."

"Come on! There's been a new development." He remained silent. I started down the steps.

"Stop!" he screamed. "You got a knife now? I got a club!"

"I'm unarmed!" There was nothing for it but to descend all the way and confront him in his refuge behind the corroded boiler.

Indeed he brandished a baseball bat, a rare instrument to see anywhere in Manhattan, where stickball, played with a broom handle between the sewer covers that serve as bases, is exuberant youth's most popular game after the brutalizing of candy-store owners. Sam demonstrated that he was no athlete by holding it cross-handed, in the fashion that one is assured as a child will break one's wrists.

"Listen," said I, straining to see him in the gloomy corner, "now be serious. There's a body in the elevator. I suspect it is dead. It's the great big man I asked you whether you'd seen."

Sam emerged slowly, clearing me from his projected route by threatening to use the bat as cattle prod. "So you found the gun?"

"Forget about me except as victim! *He* savagely beat *me.*"

"So he's the one who's dead?"

I sighed. "He left my office alive. I didn't see him again until his body came down on the elevator—dead, I believe. I do not know. I am not a physician. What does one do when not certain? Call the police or an ambulance?" Observe my lack of true concern for Bakewell; I confess I was relieved to see him downed. "And, listen here, as long as I've got hold of you: who's the E. Newhouse listed on the board as occupying my office, 3A?"

"So many questions!" Sam complained, lifting both arms, the bat still in hand. I seemed however to have allayed his fears, for he proceeded to put his back to me and smite the old boiler with a mighty blow of the Louisville Slugger. "Loosens interior rust," said he as if quoting the language of an instruction manual, "which if allowed to accumulate clogs the valves, hence discoloration of water."

It took me some minutes to induce him to return to the ground floor, any sound from which was obscured, while we were below, by the clangor of wood striking galvanized steel, for he gave the boiler a succession of blows.

On the way up, I asked him, over my shoulder, still another question, my attraction to trivia having survived thus far in the unfolding adventure: "You've never hurt your wrist with that grasp?"

"An old wife's sale," said he. "Gives more power: you can hittem outaduh park, like Teddy Villanova. He always used crosshand."

Had I not at that moment reached the garbage cans on the landing, I might have fallen backwards upon him.

"Teddy Villanova! I just asked whether you had heard that name. For God's sake."

He gained the top stair. "Gonna let me up?" I stepped into the lobby, my back towards the elevator.

"He's a ballplayer?"

"Years ago," said Sam, shrugging. He lifted the lid of one of the cans. "Before your time. When the Dodgers were still at Ebbetts." He peered into the container. "Who eats all the Blimpies? I should get me some franchise. Orange Julius! The coloreds drink that like water. But if I did, no nigger'd be thirsty, shit on me."

"I want to hear more," I said. "But first, look at this body." I turned and went to the elevator. Went in the elevator and walked unobstructedly about the entire floor of the cab. Bakewell was neither there, nor, as admittedly unlikely as that would have been, on the walls or ceiling; the trap door in the latter was firmly fixed, the turn buttons sealed in place with verdigris.

"I got one answer," said Sam, grimacing and rubbing the bald spot on his crown, across which he futilely directed strands of the canescing hair, barbered long for perhaps that purpose, from his temples. "Don't call neither police nor meat wagon. Call the loony bin."

"I tell you he was *here*."

"Your winos come and go like a fart. You can't count on them. That's why I lock the inside door. See, it's open again. You people never listen to nothing." Indignantly Sam marched to the entrance, deftly kicked out the wedge that had defied me, and pulled the door to.

I dogged him. "Where'd Villanova go after the old days? You sure you've got the right name?"

"Household wade," Sam said impatiently. "Went to hell

second year inna majors, hit minus two hundred. Spring training the next, in Flaridar is killed by a shock inna water."

"Shark?"

"Electricity," said Sam. "That was before the portable radio took over the plug-in set. His fell inna tub while connected to the one-ten from the socket."

"A long time ago, then."

"Thirty-five or -six. A man named John Nance Garner was Vice President of the United States." Showing vanity about his command of historical detail, Sam began to name the other members of Roosevelt's cabinet: "Harold Ickes, Interior; James J. Farley, Post Office . . ."

I tuned out. My, or I should say rather Bakewell's (and Washburn's), Villanova must be the son or grandson of the ballplayer, if indeed there was a connection. Still, it was none too common a name. But it was comely, no doubt Italian, *Villanuova* originally, the *u* having been discarded for the convenience of American orthography. Slight variations would occur in the other languages derived from Latin: *Villeneuve* for a Frenchman, *Villanueve* to a speaker of Spanish; *Vilanovo*, if you wanted to go as far as that, in Portuguese. I was once a formal student of languages and have continued as an amateur, with a smattering of many.

With Bakewell gone, and Sam disbelieving in his existence, there would be little point in summoning the police and of course none at all in calling an ambulance. I had only the name to go on, if indeed I wished to pursue this as yet totally absurd affair. . . . *Villanova.* In German it would be *Neuhaus.* In English—

I seized Sam's sleeve, getting the French cuff, which was fastened with a link in the form of eyeball, a souvenir of his wife's ophthalmologist brother, a horrible, cold ceramic thing to graze.

"*Newhouse!*" I cried. "Who *is* he? *Why* is he listed at

three A?" I had Sam's shirt but not his arm: the fabric was strained as he made evasive action. I let him go.

"Thanks for that," said he, for some reason adjusting the other sleeve, that one I had not grasped. "I got news for you: I never heard of Newhouse. But I wish he *was* in three A, or anybody else instead of you. You stopped some time ago being my kind of guy. You want outa the lease, you just ask."

Notwithstanding these and like protests, I forced him through the inner doorway and pointed at the board.

Not only was NEWHOUSE now gone; the names that preceded and followed it in the file were so closely arranged as not to allow an intervening space where it could ever have been. My first reaction was to ascertain whether FUC-ING and WERN were back, establishing a pattern of nomenclatural vandalism perhaps only coincidental with the Bakewell-Villanova-Washburn affair—but they were not.

After this experience Sam washed his hands of me—literally, with air—and left by sidewalk, though not without giving me his plan for lunch: "I'm going for chinks." Which was to say, chow mein. He added that, hoping to eat in peace, he would not disclose which of the local Oriental establishments he headed for. He was safe: I don't care for toy provender.

I returned to the third floor by elevator, still staring around the cab; and of course I had adequate time for wonder, the conveyance rising with the speed of a backlash of taffy.

Peggy was exploring her teeth with her finger as I entered my office. The crumpled Blimpie bag was before her, and a can of Tab, by now surely empty, stood at her elbow. If I knew her feckless habits, this rubbish would stay in place till she went home—three days from now. That sort of thing annoys me, though Lord knows I am guilty of it myself, but I am not a—I was going to say *girl*, but the feminist propaganda of a few years back had got to me (I am now consistently rude to women at doorways)—I am not an employee. Such neglect implies a lack of regard for the person who pays the salary, the mention of which reminds me that I hadn't paid hers and therefore the point, otherwise a feasible one, must be dropped.

"Gawd, I'm still hungry," she said, with the same righteousness as that in which Zola penned the memorable *J'accuse*. "I couldn't afford Blimpie's Best. I had to take Number One, all roll."

"I haven't had the leisure for lunch, myself," said I. "I was savaged by the gigantic hoodlum you nonchalantly admitted. I called for help, but—God's blood!—you were already gone."

"I don't have to take that type language," she asseverated in her fire-siren voice, her plump breasts bouncing. "My brother'd pound you to a pulp if he heard you." I didn't know to which brother she referred, the sanitation-union functionary or the one who was a petty timeserver in Queens Borough Hall, sans power to fix a traffic ticket, or perhaps merely the inclination to exert it: earning him, at any rate, a deafening blow on the ear from an offended cousin at one of the Tumulty family's Thanksgiving Donnybrooks.

However the statement suggested something. "You don't have a relative who's a cop, by chance?"

She was immediately mollified by the personal note. "How about a fireman?"

"What I need, you see, is somebody to assist me in an investigation."

"So call the precinct."

"Remember that detective who came last year when your typewriter was stolen?" This had happened when she was down hall at toilet, I in back office on phone—the crime, I mean; the syntax however refers to that of the dick, who had said little else, sneeringly disregarding me, leeringly studying her bosom; he had never been heard from since. What I meant now, to Peggy, was that he had been useless. "Anyway, I don't want this on record, at least not yet."

A smirk was peculiarly unattractive on Peggy's visage, which was rather pretty when totally, egglike, without expression, and nearly beautiful when truly lugubrious, probably in imitation of the *Pietà*, an ever available model for Catholic women and greatly preferable to, say, a motion-picture trull.

"I thought"—she simpered here—"I thought he was kinda cute." She soon frowned. "He was wearing a wedding band."

In her sexual attitudes Peggy dated from a bygone age. Despite the public harangues of polymorphous perverts and their tracts on venereal liberation, she still looked first at a man's third finger and not at the swell of his groin. My fancy could not cope with the image of Peggy at the act of darkness—though my mind's eye could easily enough depict her in the shower, shaving her calves, or trimming her toenails.

"I gather," I said, "that you have absolutely no interest in my troubles of the preceding twenty minutes."

I must have expressed this with a feeling more plangent than the skin-deep sardonicism I intended, for Peggy, who like nurse or nun ignored mere peevishness but rallied round at the suggestion of weightier agonies, gave me a gathering of eyebrows and the pursed mouth of formal compassion.

"Aw, Russ . . ."

She had first-named it from the beginning, even when I paid her regularly, even when I tried calling *her* Miss Tumulty.

However, the current display of sympathy was enough

to use as a cue for bravado. "I've taken my knocks before. I'm not down yet. I've only begun to fight." I realized I was speaking in the hackneyed idiom of Washburn's letter, but it proved an effective one with Peggy, who looked at me with an admiration I had never before identified. For my part, on the instant I began to find her desirable.

"Have your eyes always been bright green?" I asked.

But this was the wrong string to pluck. She quickly drew back in spirit, while leaning forward, like a hungry truck driver at a lunch counter, on crossed forearms.

"Why," she asked, "are you giving me that bull?"

"This is serious," I quickly barked. "I've got three identities to track down. Get your pencil: Bakewell, Christian or for that matter Hebraic or Islamic name unknown. Had you ever seen or heard of him before he lumbered in that door?" A misapplication of verb; when passing through portals the man was, as we know, as adroit as an eel undulating through seaweed. "Don't rely on memory: check the files. Next, Teddy Villanova." Pronouncing that name had begun to give me a weird thrill. "There was a baseball player by that name in the nineteen thirties. Call one of the newspaper sports departments and find out whether he had a son who would be alive. A grandson would not be out of the question. Criminals begin young these days: I know a girl whose wallet was filched in a supermarket and swears she had been near nobody but a child in a stroller. The ballplayer incidentally was accidentally electrocuted in the bathtub. He played for Brooklyn."

Peggy had put pencil to paper as ordered. Now she raised the former, put the eraser to her lips and withdrew it with an osculatory sound. "That was Eddie Villiers," said she. "If a Teddy Villanova ever played for Brooklyn, I never heard of him."

"You're a baseball fan?" But already I had the awful conviction that whether she was or not, she had exonerated

Teddy V. from the charge of being a professional athlete—
to my taste, a very grave one. Sam and his tin ear!

"Fanatic," said she, "a real nut on the subject. A buff."

"O.K., then forget Villiers," which I could already see,
upside down from my perspective, on her notepad. "Check
our files for *Villanova, Teddy*. Also *Newhouse, E.*, which
may be a translation of it."

"Of what?"

I had to explain in some detail. Scholarship, unless applied to some practical end, had never impressed her in
the past. She was skeptical of its value now.

"But maybe it isn't."

"All *right*. But do it. The last name on my list is Donald
Washburn the Second." I watched her pencil. "No, don't
write 'the Second.' Make a Roman numeral Two."

But she thought she had me there. "You say 'Second,'
though, on the phone, don't you? 'Two' sounds snobbish."

"The call was supposed to be about Villanova. As he's
not the ballplayer, you don't have to make it." I said this
with less exasperation than I felt, for she might have
bridled at much acerbity. "However, it would be a good
idea to search the phone book, in fact all the directories
for all the boroughs including Staten Island—especially
Staten Island, now that I think of it: a traditional lair for
Mafiosi."

"Then Jersey too."

"Jersey absolutely! You're picking up the rhythm now."

"Though Bakewell and Washburn aren't wop names by
far."

I had put Washburn's letter in my right rear pocket,
transferring the damp handkerchief to the left. Oddly
enough, in view of the recent disappearances, the folded
missive was yet there.

"What do you make of this?"

Peggy pushed it to arm's length: at twenty-nine her

vision was middle-aged, but she was too vain to wear glasses.

"It's certainly well written, I'll say that. From his way with words, I'd say he's a college professor or newspaperman."

"Perhaps," I said. "But here's my hypothesis, as of now: Washburn is a kid, by which I don't mean literally a child, who may or may not be of good family, but he ran up quite a gambling debt with Teddy Villanova, which must surely be the name of a mobster. He cannot pay it. Therefore Teddy has threatened him. Bakewell might be an old retainer of the Washburn family, a butler or the like, but formerly wrestler or strong man in the circus— perhaps a hired goon, but in this theory Washburn would be too broke to hire one. Bakewell at any rate comes here to warn Villanova to call off the hounds. He gets to my office by mistake, or by some cunning misdirection— there's a mystery there, all right." I told her how "Newhouse" had come and gone from the board.

She threw her open palms at me, the pencil secured on one with a crossed thumb. "That's a P.R. delivery boy does that."

"That's *your* theory, anyway," said I.

"I've seen 'em at work."

"Done nothing?"

"Get a switchblade in my breadbasket?" Peggy horse-laughed at her stolid Tab can.

"Anyway, assuming that I was in the employ of Villanova, Bakewell delivered his threat to me, driving it home with a hammer blow to my cranium."

Peggy's lip curled. "What good is that gun of yours, then?"

"How do you know about that?" I was furious. "How dare you sneak around when I'm away. Yes, *sneak*! You won't set foot in that room when I'm there. I suppose you think I'll throw you on the couch?" My anger with a woman often takes a sexual turn, of its own energy as it were, whatever inspired it. "I've got nothing better to do than rape a frigid spinster from Queens?"

Peggy had closed her eyes and composed her face into a pious mask, maintaining it until I finished, which was immediately thereafter that below-the-belt remark, unforgivable from employer to employee, whether or not she herself respected the hierarchical code.

"Please forgive me," I said. "I don't know what I'm saying. I was ferociously assaulted only twenty minutes ago. I may have a concussion of the brain."

She was coolly smiling in what seemed blatant vanity. "But you were asking about the gun. I saw it once when looking for a dictionary. Knowing you as I do"—she had the effrontery to waggle a finger at me here—"and I certainly *do* know you, I know that it's legally registered. You're an obedient little boy when it comes to the rules of society, though you're immoral with girls."

No one likes to hear from even a virgin—especially a virgin—that he is no swashbuckler. Actually, I am a complete maverick in the bourgeois world and in no way conform to its mores and norms.

However, when viewed dispassionately, as I realized later, Peggy's assessment of me was dead accurate. The only real maverick is the criminal, and like most people I am but the occasional breaker of minor ordinances. And now, though Peggy seemed to be related to no policeman, her familial connections to the Department of Sanitation were official enough to give me pause.

"Certainly I have a permit. What do you think." At the moment of course I did not possess the gun, which Sam had picked from my pocket and discarded, by his own admission, probably in the waste cans at the top of the cellar steps. Good, let it be. In fact, to the devil with this whole business. . . .

"Say, Peggy. If that guy ever shows up here again—I'm talking about Bakewell—you give me three short buzzes, and I'll call the police."

I threw up my thumbs, disposing of the matter and with it the burden on my spirit. I have that kind of resilience. It compensates for a certain deficiency of stamina. I had arrived at a similar conclusion on the day I put aside my play. I tried to tell as much that evening to the liberal-lawyer's wife I had met in playwriting class at The New School, who believing I should soon make my mark in the theater fed me frequently at French restaurants of the second rank (her husband was likely to be found in those of the first), but she monologized endlessly on the lore of the grape, learned in the wine-tasting course given by the Société des Avaleurs (e.g., the inscription on many a cheap Burgundy, "bottled in our caves," is meaningless), and then dragged me away to the hotel room in which the investigator cornered us a quarter-hour later, she still in her bra and I in my Reis boxer briefs of burnt orange.

"Sure, Mike," replied Peggy, never averse to passing up a job. She ripped the page from her pad, balled it, withdrew her calves from the kneehole of the desk, and used the waste can which, concealed there, must have crowded that area and provided a useless reminder to Peggy to keep her thighs joined.

"And while you're at it, the Tab can and the Blimpie bag," said I, pointing serially at each. Her response was a silent snarl.

I ducked into the inner office and found that reality ineluctably opposed my capricious decision to forget about Villanova, *et al.*

Bakewell's tremendous body covered my studio couch.

His nape was applied to one end-bolster; at least two feet of shoe and shin protruded beyond the other. He seemed even deader than before: a small hole had been punctured between his eyes, and a filament of red ran from it along the bridge of his nose, collecting in a pendulous drop at the tip. His coat was open to display the belt buckle over the dome of his belly. A small automatic pistol lay at the top of his fly.

I picked it off. Its muzzle smelled of ignited gunpowder. It was very like my own weapon, of which, alas, I had never written down the serial number. I removed the clip and determined that one shell was gone from the stack that compressed the spring in the base.

I returned the clip to the gun that was either mine or not, and having made certain that the safety was on, put the weapon on my desk and covered it with two weeks of unopened junk mail and the fragment of Cadbury milk chocolate, mint-filled, hitherto mentioned: I had no sweet tooth at the moment. I put my keys in my pocket, having a premonition that I might have need to leave the building soon.

The telephone proceeded to ring several times. Peggy Tumulty was presumably gone again. I picked up the instrument. Peggy always answered by giving the number: a rude practice, by my lights. I utter a hopeful "Yes?" But now I was humiliated to hear it emerge, owing to stress, as a susurrant whimper.

"Teddy, we're gonna ice you," said a voice the timbre of which suggested it came through jaws that could have chewed hickory nuts in their shells.

"I'm not Teddy Villanova!" I managed to say, or croak. "I'm Russel—" But already I addressed a dead line.

}

I decided thereupon that any further delay in summoning the constabulary was likely to prove ruinous and was about to dial—alas, now that I needed it, I could not recall the emergency number of the local force, instead remembering, ridiculously, WHItehall 1212, from some bygone thriller concerning Scotland Yard. To dial Information, these days, was to incur an additional charge beyond the quota of message units—I would almost rather be murdered than lose another sou to the phone company, those swine who could have, in their monopoly of wires, made the cops as simple to dial as C-O-P. (I am a man of words, not arithmetic; for the weather I call WENCHES.)

While I was so frozen—ironically, in an attempt to evade being "iced"—who should suddenly penetrate my inner office but two policemen! Beetle-browed, black-eyed, prominent-nosed, blue-jawed, they were both also of the same height and stocky build. One wore a handle-bar mustache, and one was clean-shaven.

He with the bare lip said to me: "You're busted." And to the other: "Give him his rights."

The other seized his navy-blue crotch and said: "I got your rights right here."

"Now wait a minute," said I.

After a cursory glance at Bakewell's body, Mustache asked: "So where's the piece?"

Not familiar with their jargon, except for the unconvincing version used by actors, I failed to get his meaning as quickly as he wished, and in obvious disapproval of my lethargy he seized my Ban-Lon bosom and, unlike the late

Bakewell, got a handful of pectoral as well in fingers stern as tongs. He was of about my own height but considerably more burly than I. He gave me a backhanded stroke to the mouth and then returned the palm smartly across my nose.

Holding my face, though spreading the butts of my hands so that he could hear and be without motive to punish me for obscurity, I said: "Oh, you mean the gun that was used to kill him? Oh."

"Oh, yes, fag, oh!" he burlesqued me in a still higher falsetto than mine, then thrust his kneecap into my groin. I buckled, clutched, hovered, and finally fell to the floor as if in several parts.

A leather sole, looking quite new, its buff color scarcely besmirched, descended to within a centimeter of my left eyeball, the right being compressed against the floor boards. No threat could have been more effective.

"The desk," I sniveled, for my nose was running from the slap it had accepted.

They proceeded to remove the drawers from that furnishing and empty onto my body, from a height, the contents thereof, including a Scotch-tape dispenser with a leaden base. From the weight of its blow on the side of my calf, I, being lean of leg, suspected the bone might well have been cracked, but owing to the dominant agony in my testicles I could not be sure.

They ignored the pile of junk mail, and even in my wretchedness I was pleased to see that I had been right about something, though typically of something without profit, for I should only be beaten further until they found the pistol.

Therefore I was forming my sore lips to say "Desk top" —when suddenly they abandoned the search.

"Fuck *this*," said the mustachioed patrolman. "It don't matter. Let's haul the garbage."

The clean-lipped cop dropped the final drawer—the

double-sized one, for files; happily now empty—onto my head, which given the respective angles received only a glancing blow, and went to Bakewell's feet while Mustache repaired to the shoulders. I managed to sit up, assuming the simulated lotus position of the yogi who fakes, and watched their remarkable show of strength.

It is a general rule that two large men are hard put to tote even a small drunk between them, the difficulty owing to the density and not the weight itself—sober and tense, he might be lifted as easily as a plank. But the rigor had not yet claimed Bakewell's corpse. He looked better than 300 pounds and of the consistency of sacked sand.

Yet in one coordinated effort they raised him from the couch and carried him through the contracted doorway. From my squat I could see them until they cleared the outer room and turned into the corridor.

At this point I crawled to the desk, fished out the gun from beneath the mail, crawled to the dumbwaiter, and burrowing under the crumple of my clothes on its platform, found the space beneath (through which I had lost the odd sock), and pushed the pistol into the shaft. I could not hear the report of its striking bottom in the cellar, four levels down; for one, my ears were muffled by the heap of clothing in which my face was buried (the odor of which reminded me that I was overdue at the Laundromat); then too, it could be supposed that a cushion of rubbish lay at the bottom of the shaft, a veritable midden the lowest level of which might well date from the turn of the century and contain whalebone corset stays, celluloid collars, and desiccated French letters discarded by fornicators long dead.

But as yet I was scarcely scot free. Surely the police had not, despite the insouciant obscenity, brushed away the matter of the gun. Also, as I now reflected, a dumbwaiter shaft, especially one in disuse, is a notoriously classic place in which to dispose of a murder weapon. Nor had I remembered to wipe from its smooth blue barrel my dirty, sweaty fingerprints—add bloody to that series: what had seeped from my nose was red.

I decided I had better volunteer to give these officers a full account than to wait for them to return and beat me mute. While their hands were literally full of Bakewell was a splendid time for my purpose.

I got on my feet, though it would be frivolous to say I could yet stand fully erect, and hobbled—yes, as if my shoes were laced each to each; I had by the way reassumed them, unconsciously, while trying to remember the phone number of the police, which of course I could now, not needing it, recall with crystalline clarity as 911—I stumbled to the outer office.

Where Peggy, back again now that all was quiet, said in disgust: "For pity sake, Russ. At *noon*, already?"

"I suppose you didn't see or hear anything again!" I cried, lurching towards the hall, but the effort to top her indignation cost me dearly: the floor rose in serrations, and I missed the first illusionary stair-tread and fell to my poor knees.

"I've seen you tipsy before"—a lie—"but never low-down and dirty drunk! If you think I'll put up with this!" But immediately after concluding this scream, which no doubt marked the crest of her rage, she descended to, and wallowed in, a trough of the maudlin. "For heaven's sake, Russ, call A.A. before it's too late. Their program really works. They were my brother's salvation. They'll give you something to believe in. With God's help you'll be a man again one day in the foreseeable future. You'll—"

In supreme exasperation I managed not only to ignore this but also to rise and stagger through the doorway and look along the corridor. The police and Bakewell's body were gone, this time not mysteriously: the elevator hummed. I was in no condition to negotiate the stairway.

I turned back and said to Peggy: "Get this, and get it straight: I'm suspected of murder now. I was savagely worked over again. Call the police and say that I want to make a statement voluntarily."

"Why didn't you tell those cops I just saw getting on the elevator?" Peggy asked suspiciously.

"You did see them then?" I needed this confirmation; thus far I had been all alone and lonely except for my brutalizers.

"They were carrying that great big man who came in here this morning. Remember, you asked about him? Was he back there drinking with you all along? He *was*, wasn't he? He was stinking drunk also."

"He was dead," said I. "I don't know who did it, except that it wasn't me. Now get on that phone."

She dialed 911. "Russel Wren wants to make a full statement." She covered the mouthpiece and said to me: "They want to know about what?"

"About the Bakewell murder."

She passed this along. Then, to me: "They said to hold on."

I collapsed in one of the camp chairs. After some moments Peggy heard something that made her say: "I agree," and hung up.

"What was that?"

She twitched her nose. "They said there wasn't any such murder reported. They said you were a crank. They said there are a lot of them who tie up the line while the victims of real crimes can't get through and the perpetrators escape apprehension. They said—"

"Oh, shut your stupid mouth, you halfwit."

Without another word Peggy took her purse from a bottom drawer and her dun cardigan from the back of the chair, and left the office in a martial stride. Head in heels of hand, I sat there for as long as it took the elevator to rise at her summons, her to climb aboard, turn and step out, and return.

"There's blood all over it."

"That's funny," said I, staring at my groin, from which the excruciation had now gone, leaving as it were a great humming nullity between waist and knees.

"Well," said Peggy, "not if he was murdered it wouldn't be funny."

"Uh-huh."

"It's really only a few drops, come to think about it," said Peggy. "He might of had a nosebleed." But at my display of teeth, she backed away slightly and said: "All right, all right. I believe you. O.K.?"

Actually, I had been gnashing my incisors without reference to her. It was rather the reaction to my having understood, suddenly, that the policemen were bogus. Real cops don't carry away the bodies of victims. There are ambulance attendants for that, and they employ stretchers with zippered covers. Many a time I had observed the real thing on TV news, though never in the plain air.

But if the worthies who had savaged me and borne away Bakewell were not authentic patrolmen, who were they?

Otherwise unfurnished with advisers, I applied to Peggy, expecting little but the usual boneheadedness, which however might provoke, by contrast, my own powers of reason.

But she surprised me. Not only did she accept my theory that the cops were probably fakes, but went along with the rest of it, yet unvoiced: that they were mobsters, as well. She took the chair alongside mine, and having pointlessly (given our relative positions) pulled her skirt over the knees, said: "They looked Italian to me, and I know Italians when I see them. My best friend at Saint Dottie's was Treese Conigliaro."

I blenched at the nasty sound she made of what in the Old Country would have been pronounced *Tay-ray-sa Cone-eel-yah-ro*, a very lovely name, though surely Peg had learned to say *Cunnig-laaroh* from good old Treese herself.

"You think these 'cops,' then, were mobsters? Mafia types? That would fit with 'Villanova.' " I began to count the points on my fingers. "Bakewell was obviously Villanova's enemy—not personally, but acting in Washburn's interest. After threatening me, the great big man did not leave the building—Sam Polidor was in the lobby all the while. What happened was that Bakewell realized I had nothing to do with this affair. How—I mean how he realized that, when he had not earlier on, remains among the ponderables."

"What?" asked Peg.

"No matter," said I. "Maybe he simply ran into Teddy Villanova himself, whom he recognized. Teddy's response to the threat was to shoot Bakewell between the eyes." I sighed in despair. "With my gun." That made no sense. "But how would he come to be carrying my gun, which I had lost only minutes before?" I saw an exit. "Wait a minute. . . . Teddy brings his trash down to the cans, finds my gun in one of them, and thinking it would be handy in his profession, takes it along when he goes back upstairs, meets Bakewell en route, hears the threat, and impulsively kills him. Then, his rage having cooled, realizes he's stuck with a corpse and a pistol recently fired. He looks for and finds an open, empty office—mine—and puts both body and gun in it." I was excited by the sheer logic of this progression. "How's that sound?"

"I don't know, Russ. That's pretty farfetched."

"*Nothing* can be farfetched in view of this incident," I said with heat.

Peggy held her hand opposite her chin and flapped its loose fingers. "Too bad there's no money in it."

I narrowed my eyes, playing a part mostly for my own benefit. "Maybe there is . . . maybe there just is." Repeating the phrase with slight variations, I actually began to believe in the possible validity of the vague scheme, half-formulated, of which it was a shadowy expression. But first there was another troublesome detail to piece into place: the visit of the fake cops.

"Villanova's bravoes, of course," I said, and went on, ignoring Peggy's raised eyebrows—she read nothing but *The National Enquirer*, which however for my money uses a much more exotic vocabulary than is at my disposal. "But what baffles is how they just happened to have two policeman's uniforms, instantly available for such a stunt as this: unless they pull similar ones often. Beyond that, why take away the corpse when, if left there, it would embarrass me and not Villanova? That apparently was his original plan. Why was it altered?"

"There's one reason, and only one reason alone," sententiously said Peg. "Bakewell had something on his person that they wanted, something that to look for they wouldn't have time, because they might be interrupted meanwhile, and also so small it would take time to find because it would be so little and tiny."

I record this utterance as literally as I can remember it, to demonstrate that despite the brothers Fowler bizarre syntax is often as perspicuous as the king's English. Peggy's supposition was also perspicacious. Her elaboration of it, however, proved preposterous.

"Maybe a microdot, a tenth as large as the head of a pin, pasted on his chin like a pimple."

"That's from a spy show," said I. "Not likely with mobsters."

"All you know." Peggy moued. "There may be a link between the Syndicate and the Commies." From which I judged she had lately T-Viewed a movie from the 1950s. "Or the dot could contain a list of all the Cosa Nostra bosses for the whole nation, including Canada and the Caribbean, and a list of their legitimate covers, like diaper services, chinaware distributors, sporting-goods stores, and—"

"Protestant houses of worship," said I, and before she could react adversely, gave some sensible alternatives as aims for Villanvoa's change of plan: "Realizing that I could prove myself a respectable citizen and that the police wouldn't long suspect me of murdering a man whom I didn't know and that, on the other hand, Bakewell had threatened Villanova, Teddy had second thoughts about leaving the body on my doorstep. His own activities would soon enough come into question when the name 'Washburn' emerged. Therefore he sent his bullies here to collect the corpse and no doubt strip it of identification and bury it in an isolated marsh on Staten Island."

"Or Jersey," Peggy added, with her bias, old news to me, against the Garden State. Whenever a foul odor came through an open window, or for that matter an insect, she theoretically traced its origins to New Jersey, in which, she brazenly admitted once, she had never set foot.

For some time the Wyandotte Club, physically in the second-floor rear of my building, had been creeping in the abstract into the ratiocinative area of my brain. Its comers and goers—few before midnight; most, moving in duets and trios, between 3 and 4 A.M.—were of Italian pigmentation and mien. I had once or twice shared an early-morning elevator with them, though my peregrinations during those hours were rare. I hadn't recently had enough money to stay that late at a public place of entertainment, and am no nighthawk in the most prosperous of times.

But now and again, having to leave my current girl's place in the wee hours, owing to the return of her roommate, who frequently got the sudden boot from a boy friend's bed in the middle of the night (he being seemingly a certifiable paranoiac), I had come back to my office building and encountered Wyandotters. They were good neighbors, Manhattan-style, neither looking at nor addressing strangers (the chummy, in New York, are invariably perverts, panhandlers, or footpads), nor, for that matter, each other. They might have been two or three persons, coincidentally Italian, who by pure chance found themselves rising simultaneously in the shabby elevator of a seedy commercial edifice sometime before dawn, then, the fortuity still at work, deboarding at the same floor and applying for entrance at the same portal, which was opened by an individual who made no sign of recognition but admitted them without ceremony—as I had seen beyond the slow-closing door of the lift which eventually took me to the floor above.

Whatever went on inside, it was either quiet in both conception and development or insulated by good sound-proofing.

Sam Polidor, who was fearlessly rude to my face, and probably worse behind my back, became so craven at the mere mention of the Wyandotte Club as to refuse even to speculate on what went on within its walls, beyond sending his eyes up into his frontal sinus and saying: "Parcheesi. Don't ask, ya live a rife old age."

"Mafia, maybe?"

"Everybody has to be Jewish?"

It was obvious to me now that Teddy Villanova likely had some connection with the Wyandotte Club. My fecund response to Peggy's despair that there was no money for me (and thus none for her) in the Bakewell killing, my "maybes" now can be interpreted as referring to an inchoate, a dim inclination, hardly yet a true plan, to penetrate a roomful of gangsters and, isolating him who was probably Mr. Big, shake him down for a generous fee in return for which I'd stay mum about the corpse.

Alas, I have the kind of fancy that conjures up subsequent scenes: Teddy laughs with two rows of pasta-choppers, fells me with an exhalation of garlic fumes, and says: " 'ey, Mario, Gino, beat the shit outa dis bum and trow him downa airshaft, huh?"

Nonetheless, I leered at Peggy, so violently that, probably taking it as an expression of lust, she left the neighboring chair and put the desk between us. Now, however, when to do so would have been practical, she failed to lower the hem of her skirt, and through the kneehole— this piece, which I had purchased from Goodwill Industries for a song, was not equipped with a so-called modesty panel; perhaps that had been extracted by some previous voyeur—I could see the seam made by the compression together of her robust white thighs until eventually it was terminated by a portion of embedded slip.

I began my cunning proposal: "Say, Peg . . ."

"Knock it off, Russ."

"No, no. Listen!" I exposed my theory of the Villanova-Wyandotte link. I proceeded more cautiously in regard to the shakedown, of which I now had a perfect formulation. "Bear with me for a moment. Since the Middle Ages, Italians have had a very special attitude towards women—"

"Boy, don't I know that from Treese Conigliaro's brothers!" Peggy cried with heat. "Roman hands, I call it."

"*Illuminatio dei*," I proceeded relentlessly, "the reflection of God. Dante finds Beatrice in heaven, on one side of the Lord, with none other than the Virgin on his other hand. Think of that, a trinity in which two of the elements are female!"

My torch was failing to ignite Peggy, who showed no spark even at the reference to the Madonna, which I had always assumed surefire. "O.K.," said I, "look: remember when Joe Columbus was shot on Italian-American Unity Day at Colombo Circle? . . . Uh, reverse those terminal syllables. Anyway, prominent gangland figures were quoted as doubting this was the work of a rival, because *women* and children were present—and it is the law of the underworld that families are sacrosanct. You might well say, 'What hypocrisy,' but all the same . . ."

She wasn't saying anything of the sort. She had instead begun early on to fix me with a grim stare. And what she said was: "You got another thing coming, brother."

"Oh?" Like many persons who are habitually obtuse when dealing with the mundane, Peggy proved she could penetrate the exotic, the unprecedented, with the ease of a Roentgen ray passing through fatty tissue.

"Yeah!"

"I guarantee that Teddy wouldn't lay a hand on a woman." Except a gangland doxy; but I didn't add that. "I think we would be within the realm of reason if we asked ten thousand, 'ten big ones' in his parlance, which perhaps, in the interests a show of authenticity, we should adopt. A melon, my dear Peggy, we would split right down the middle. That's one-three-*five* to go into your now battered, soon to be replaced purse. New cardigans for you as well, cases of White Owls and Seven Crown for your brothers, a rampage through Korvette's for your mom, et cetera. Heck, *new cardigans!*" In its previous employment this term had not scored. "Heck, a pilgrimage to Lourdes!" A shrewd touch, she being literally Margaret Mary Bernadette Tumulty.

"Russ, now you hold it right there," Peggy said levelly. "I have no intention of going now, or never, to the Wyandotte Club and trying to blackmail Teddy Villa-whoozit."

I abandoned the scheme, at least her role in it. I am like that. "But you do agree that he would likely be found there?"

"I couldn't say."

"What do you think are my chances of getting killed if *I* go there?"

"Two hundred percent."

"That bad, eh? But look, how about if I protect my rear, so to speak? You know what I mean." I put authority into my voice. " 'I'm not acting alone in this. If anything happens to me, my associate will go to the police.' "

Peggy again picked up her sweater and purse. "I've got a bellyful of you, Russ, and I don't mean maybe. You want to get us both killed. I don't work for you now, and I haven't ever held this position." She was on her feet. "I'm willing to swear to that."

I waved her down. "Can't you take a joke any more? Do I look like a blackmailer? It was just something to clear the air, Peg. To play for time. I've got to work this thing out. A human being has been killed, and the police won't believe it."

Reseated, Peggy yawned cavernously—as usual, unless a lascivious detective was present, without covering her mouth. "Gee, who cares?"

"Well, really!"

"Well, really," said she, "when I was little it used to be two people per day were murdered in this town. Now I think the rate is twice that. Everybody knows this is a cesspool of humanity. So what? You're stuck with it."

"Then why not move?"

Now she grimaced horribly. "And go to the sticks?" Another bit of typicality. For many years Peggy hadn't experienced more of Manhattan than could be encountered within three blocks of whatever office she worked in. In the morning she came by subway from Queens, and in the evening returned, neither trip without an aboveground detour unless there was a fire en route to the station. She lived with her parents in a rabbit-warren apartment house that was one of thousands of such structures set fifty feet apart on the concrete plain that began at the East River and continued through half of Nassau County, with only an occasional pause for cemetery, oil-tank farm, or airfield. Her acquaintance with the heart of Gotham, its cultural treasures and pleasure palaces, began and ended with Radio City Music Hall, where on some birthdays as a child she was conducted to witness Disney on the giant screen and the terpsichorean precision of stage.

Since having begun regularly to depilate her legs, Peggy had probably not been north (aboveground) of West Twenty-eight Street, where prior to her employment with me she had worked for a wholesaler in cheap neckties.

"Well," said I, working the self-righteous vein, "*I'm* concerned, having, as you pointed out, a highly developed social consciousness—"

"I said nothing of the kind. I said you were scared to break the law."

I gave vent to my spite. The Wyandotte project had been a damned good idea, and only she was blocking it at this point. "Do you know why you will be only a sporadically paid secretary all your life? Never a true gal Friday? You have no sympathy."

She wailed in disbelief: "Why should I feel sorry for *you?*"

"I don't mean that. I mean you are incapable of cooperating. You have no sense of *team*, something of which you are a part but not the whole, working for a common cause."

"Oh, what do you know." She upended the Tab can and shook the remaining drops into the hopper of her outthrust lower lip.

At this moment, through the doorway, which despite the events of the morning I had not closed—no door in Sam Polidor's building would long have delayed a desperate character, and, the street windows being shut against the black snowfall from nearby incinerators, ventilation must needs come from the hall—striding vigorously over the threshold came a handsomely attired, splendidly fit, and nobly profiled chap of about thirty.

Soon giving me the tapered back and flared tail of his subdued houndstooth jacket, with its long double vents, he drew up before Peggy's desk, lowered his blond head, and spoke in the mixture of slur and precise enunciation that must eventually be proved British or Northeastern American.

"I believe this is Mr. Russel Wren's office—I read it backwards on the door!" Though I could not see his face, he seemed to be asking for some amused award for this feat. In Sam's building all doors opened out; my own was folded against the corridor wall and held there by a fire bucket full of sand studded for the last six months with the same cigarette butts.

Peggy was vaguely hostile, as always with visitors of some distinction in clothing, countenance, or carriage. Only to obvious undesirables was she immediately genial. She had probably dripped all over the grotesque Bakewell.

She winced suspiciously. "Yes? . . ."

"May I see Mr. Wren?"

Now Peggy's response became openly offensive. Elaborately raising the one eyebrow visible to me—I could see exactly half her face: a strange effect, suggesting that when her visage was again whole it would belong to a stranger—

she began her stare at his crown and lowered it slowly along the length of his body available to her search, coming to a halt at groin level.

Stunned by this for an instant, I continued to sit in silence behind him.

When Peggy finally spoke, however, her tone was routine. "Whom should I say . . ."

"Don Washburn," the man answered vigorously.

"That wouldn't be the Second?"

"It would indeed! How nice to be expected."

I hurled out of my paralysis and addressed his back of golden head.

He swung his sparkling teeth around. He thrust a hand at me. He had a walnut tan, in April. His jacket was unbuttoned. He wore fawn-colored trousers of luxuriant cavalry twill, the kind that has a dull silken gleam; a self-belt closed these at the lean waist. His fly, however, was open, and a view of a naked, small, seemingly withered phallus was offered.

Peggy's demeanor was thus explained. As he approached me, she darted frantically from the office.

4

Rising quickly to the occasion, this being one I could manage, having been a man since birth, I pointed and used the vernacular for a statement so suited to it. "Barn door's yawning, my friend."

"Good gravy!" he exclaimed, looking but not immedi-

ately taking measures. First he assumed an air of mock
indignation and cried, from a head that swiveled to survey
the room: "All right, who did that?"

To ease the moment I joined him in a jovial chuckle.
When finally his fingers fell to pluck at the tiny Talon tab,
I saw I had suffered an unprecedented trick of the eye:
what showed from the groinal aperture was not his virile
member but rather a fragment of harmless beige shirt-
tail.

"Good job it wasn't fouled in the teeth," said he, disposing of the twist of fabric and causing the peculiar
scream produced by a zipper when rapidly closed.

At this point, Peggy being absent again, I should not
have been surprised by his drawing some deadly weapon
or felling me, by means of the hand that rose inexorably from his fly to seize mine, with a judo throw. But he
did nothing of the sort. Displaying his palate to the
dangling uvula, those perfect incisors and canines fencing
the foreground, he expressed concern that, through
thoughtlessness, he had routed my "girl," actually saying
"gull."

In relief at his pacific manner, I made a jocund play on
words: "I have never succeeded in gulling her into being
my girl, as it happens."

He put his lips together and frowned his immunity to
this jape. He was handsome again; he had looked a bit
foolish with an open mouth. He was one of those persons
who should limit their facial mirth to the wry indentation
of dimples.

"I assure you, I did not come here to jest."

"You *are* Donald Washburn the Second?"

He took out an elegant notecase and offered me a
driver's license and a selection of credit cards from expensive emporia.

I fended them off in polite horror and, warning of the

constricted doorway, led him into the inner office, where, after the briefest inspection with flared nostrils, he sat down on the couch, avoiding the well of collapsed spring, and crossed his long legs, one jodhpur boot, of the hue of antique brass, dangling.

"I was obliged to move into this shambles while my own suite of offices was being redecorated. Little did I then know of the ways of feckless plasterers, and the electricians are scarcely better."

"Still," said he, "pigging it can have its charms."

"Yes, it can," I admitted with a stage guffaw. "I must remember that." I lowered my brow. "Well then, to the matter at hand. Before hearing your account, I think it would be of some service to relate the extraordinary events of my morning." I gave as concise a narrative as I could, eliminating any expression of the emotions to which it gave rise, though he, if willy-nilly, bore some responsibility for them.

He listened soberly, perhaps even gravely.

When I had finished, I said: "Naturally, I have a number of questions. But I'll reserve them until I get your response to this series of—to me, at any rate—bizarre events."

He frowned. "I don't mean to be rude, but are you possibly an Englishman?"

"No, I'm not," said I. "I'm from upstate, a drowsy little hamlet, dreaming on the Hudson shore, as it happens."

"Ah."

"Be that as it may, would you like to tell me about Mr. Bakewell? Now departed but, frankly, not lamented by me."

Washburn gave me a generous quota of cerulean eye. "I never heard of the man."

"Perhaps a false name? He was a good six-seven or -eight and a bad three hundred pounds . . .?"

Donald Washburn II shook his head decisively. "*Niente.* He said he worked for me?"

"In so many words. It was presumably on your behalf that he gave me the warning to forward to Teddy Villanova. *There's* a name to conjure with. Have you ever heard of *him?*"

Washburn continued to profess total ignorance, and nothing in his immaculate saddle-leather face suggested he was lying. Indeed, he began to smile. "I was not aware that it happened in real life—mistaken identity, not to mention a disappearing corpse."

I was not amused. "Didn't you see blood in the elevator?"

"I took the stairway. I welcome opportunities for exercise." He clapped his knee. "Well then, shall we press forward in this business about Teddy?"

"You *do* know him?"

"*Him?* I mean *her.*"

"Teddy is a woman?"

"No, I told you I don't know Teddy. I said 'Freddie.' "

"His name is *Freddie* Villanova?"

Washburn's smile turned oversweet. "My dear fellow," he said, "I assure you you are persisting to no purpose in that direction. I have come to you because of my wife, whose name is Frederika Washburn. I suspect she is having an affair. She seems to speak in code language when she answers certain phone calls. I've found more than one cigar butt in the ash trays when I've come home. And swarthy hairs in my power comb. Imagine someone with the gall to brush his head with my property. Freddie's hair is red, incidentally."

"That's the only reason you've come here, to employ me for an investigation?"

He raised his fair eyebrows onto his tanned forehead. "Isn't that the sort of thing you do? I found you in the Yellow Pages."

I had not forgotten about the letter. In quest of it I went into my back pocket. It was gone. I prowled the rest of my person unsuccessfully, then dashed into the front office and looked there, with results quite as nugatory. The fake policemen must have taken it from my supine body, though at no time had I lost consciousness.

I returned to Washburn and explained.

"I have never written you a letter," said he. "I never heard of you before coming upon your name in the classified directory this morning."

I stared at the cracked ceiling over my desk and quoted one remembered cliché from the letter that was certainly apposite to the whole bag of worms: "Something is rotten in the state of Denmark." An as it were photographic reproduction of the actual epistle was projected onto my screen of memory: "Danemark" had been the spelling there given. Were an umlaut furnished to the first *a*, this would be the rendition of that geographical term as written by a German.

"Excuse me for what might appear as impertinence," I said to Washburn. "But does your wife happen to be Teutonic?"

"Too *tonic?*" he replied in what seemed genuine bewilderment. "Your queries have now, I'm afraid, taken a definite turn towards the cryptic, Wren. I suspect you as yet haven't recovered from the singular events you described to me a moment ago. If I were you, I'd put these mysteries in the hands of the police." He returned to his own narrow interest, as even people far poorer than he tend to do unless they are hypocritical: I had not escaped the cynicism of New York. "You will take my case?"

My own interest, a desperate one currently, was of

course in making an income, lost corpses notwithstanding. I gave him my terms: a hundred dollars a day, one-fifty in advance, three hundred guaranteed, plus expenses to be submitted and paid every five days, he to accept my own accounting throughout, which however would be modest. He must also sign a form giving me immunity from certain types of litigation—for example, a suit charging invasion of his own privacy; far from an outlandish provision, incidentally: I had been so threatened by the first client I had ever had, and settled by reducing my fee.

He met these obligations without argument. He did better: he put three hundred-dollar bills into my hand. In view of this generosity it would have been in poor taste to press him further about Bakewell, Villanova, or for that matter, Newhouse.

Along with the money he gave me the following information about his wife. "Freddie is a tricky woman. It's possible that those calls she seemingly answers in code are fake—by which I mean real enough for the caller, who might be an encyclopedia salesman or whatnot on routine business. And herself collects cigar butts in some public place, *ugh*"—he portrayed disgust, an expression that came easily to him, who had been halfway towards it since entering my inner office—"brings them home and strews them around." His face cleared. "Even smokes them herself—in that case, starting with fresh cigars, naturally."

"What would be her motive for such an imposture?"

He threw his wrist towards his shoulder. He wore a dull-silver watch no thicker than a Necco wafer. He was expensively accoutered in every respect.

"To get her stiletto in me."

"I'm neither priest nor lawyer," said I. "But since I do act in a confidential capacity, the more I know the better

I can perform. Can you tell me why she might torment you in such a fashion?"

He gave a further burnish to his forehead. "She's a cold woman. She is aroused only by cruelty. I'll tell you frankly: that's why I have never bought her a pet—except a bowl of Japanese fighting fish."

When he had risen to pay me and sign the release, the superb fabric of his jacket smoothed of its own luxurious weight; this was true of his trousers as well. Mine, when I stood up, had to be plucked free from the nether cleft. I hadn't been able to afford first-quality attire for many years—since birth, indeed. But now I held his three hundred dollars.

"I was admiring your clothes," said I.

"I simply throw on anything I find on the floor in the morning."

"I suppose they're custom-made."

He waxed apologetic. "I've no choice, with my weird body. I'm indecently deformed. My legs are a good inch longer than those of the average person my height, and my waist is out of kilter with the chest, thirty as opposed to forty-three. Really grotesque."

"Strange complaint," said I, awed by these Greek dimensions, with my own thirty-two-inch belt and suits in thirty-six regular.

"But see here," he said, "they could do really a good job on a well-built chap like you, if you're looking for a tailor: Hallam and Tennyson, of Burlington Gardens."

"You're speaking of London?"

"They do of course pop over here in spring and fall, which is outrageously convenient for me. I don't get to England every season."

I folded the bills and put them into the side pocket of my twenty-nine-dollar double knits. I took a ball-pen from

dicament. The cuckold is, or was once, at least, a stock character in the farces of France and Italy, but in America he has always played a dreary role, because seldom even for native Catholics has marriage been considered seriously sacramental; thus whatever pain comes from its miscarriages is merely private, with no reference to social arrangements designed in heaven. Perhaps this explains why I, a student of traditional cultures, have never wed.

Beyond this observation I might note that my professional services are sought almost exclusively in financial and not emotional interests. If money is not in question, it is a rare spouse who as an exercise in pure masochism hires an investigator to confirm a suspicion that his or her mate is errant.

"Do you mind telling me," I asked Washburn, "who controls the money in your family?" I naturally assumed it was exclusively he; dependents are in no position to be aggressive in collecting evidence of betrayal, and that a gigolo should wear horns is almost a moral impossibility.

Thus I was amazed to hear him say: "Freddie does." He pinched his right earlobe. "I'm a flunky, let's face it." But the admission seemed to cheer him; he began to smile again. "It's been a damned good six years, though, and well worth the trouble for the perquisites alone." He winked. "Vintage vino and fine fodder. If it's over now, I'll have to go back to the top of the chair lift and see who comes up."

"You're quite the skier?"

The question provoked him into outright jocosity. "Apparently I look like one when I wear a boot on one foot and a cast on the other."

Confessions of charlatanism are ingratiating. His served to distract me from undue envy. I shouldn't have minded being wealthily espoused myself, my tastes having been thus far in life indulged, so to speak, by pressing my nose against the wrong side of plate glass. They had been acquired by collecting the vintage lists provided on liquor-shop counters, and reading such manuals as the Penguin *Posh Food.* I also eye the well-dressed (insofar as they can be found any more) on foot and in advertisements, and I watch revivals of drawing-room comedies of the 1930s, since the end of which epoch elegance has not been represented in public entertainment.

My simulation of epicureanism served to dupe the liberal-lawyer's wife, who was raised in the commercial class of Great Neck, but, owing to my habitual lack of access to true luxury, would scarcely pass muster with a Frederika Washburn. Washburn himself, if false as a sportsman, displayed what seemed the natural grace and/ or insouciance of the gently reared. Even the indifference to his open fly, on entering my office, suggested that; as did the bone structure of cheek and jaw, his leggy carriage, and also his eyes, which were rather smaller in circumference than those of the average plebe. (This theory may attract scoffs, but it is my contention that the wellborn often have little eyes, in the paler range of coloration.)

"But you, yourself, come from a good family?"

"If you mean money, you're right," he said. I was relieved to hear this, my speculations having this day been so often proved in error. "But my father has arranged so that I can't get any of it, even though he dies, until I'm fifty years old. I was raised as virtually a raga-muffin. I wore hand-me-downs from an older brother. I was sent to public schools and then for two years to a shabby little community college that occupied the buildings of a disused insane asylum. I had to work as a common handyman around the place during most of my child-hood. While the proper caretaker sat in the tool shed drinking beer and leafing through stroke magazines, I cleaned out drains, waxed floors, and the like, and my wages were two dollars per week. The idea of this was to build my character. The result was that I acquired the ambition to become only a parasite when I left home."

Washburn's spirits had fallen again in the course of this account.

To cheer him, I said: "In that you have succeeded, I gather."

He brightened slightly. "It wasn't till I met Freddie that I really ever was able to do what I wanted."

"Which was?"

"Spend money!" His shout, given volume by his vehemence, based on experience—delayed, perhaps, but still gained early enough: he looked about my age—now made it impossible for me to withstand the onslaught of envy. Also, I suddenly had to urinate.

I quickly took his phone number—though of course without a profession he had no office, he had a private line at home and an answering service which took messages when he was absent—and blurting a promise that he'd hear from me before the week was out, I ushered him through the front office, past Peggy's stare (for she had returned), along the hall to the elevator—the floor of which, incidentally, showed no blood drippings—and saw him inside. Then I hastened to the lavatory.

I was within six paces of it when the door to The Ganymede Press was flung open, a little man in black hat and black raincoat dashed out, leaped across the corridor, and plunged into the water closet, throwing the bolt violently. That sort of thing being routine in New York, I saw nothing especially sinister in this example. And with Washburn gone, I returned to the stoicism with which I had survived the years of denial, inconvenience, and discomfort that are the habitual lot of commoners and kings in this metropolis: even visiting Prince Philip had been trapped once in midtown traffic; well-kept Washburn would ride back to Sutton Place in a filthy taxi, his elegantly trousered hams prodded by broken springs, an empty Fresca can rolling against his boots.

The door being wide open, I looked into the Ganymede office for the first time ever. Sitting at a desk was the middle-aged woman I had briefly glimpsed in the hallway from time to time, and had always been somewhat astonished so to do, given my assumption as to the nature of their commerce. Sometimes she had been accompanied by a man of the same years. He was not in evidence now, and it had not been he who beat me to the toilet. The office was a far cry from mine: the floor decently carpeted, the windows Venetianed and maroon-draped.

Soon noticing me, the woman smiled and nodded in a maternal fashion I had not seen since leaving my little home town, where it was not unusual for someone else's mother to be amiable to a boy. When I answered her greeting in kind, she beckoned me to enter.

"Would you like a homemade brownie?" she asked, extending towards me a china plate on which a dozen or more cubes of that confection were mounted pyramidally.

I found myself simpering, an effect that comes over me involuntarily when in the presence of women of her age and demeanor, i.e., "nice ladies."

"I'd just hate myself for spoiling such a pretty arrangement," I cooed, or to be exact, said with a set of lips and teeth that might have been used to imitate a dove though no *oo* sound came literally into play. I think I picked up this style from my father. In many ways, my little town was one that time forgot. But so was Queens, if one could judge from Peggy.

"Mmm," I continued, squirreling my teeth for the first taste, taking it, then speaking through my munch, "goor, delisha! Made these yourserf?"

"Oh, no," said she. "They're from the Homemade Bakery, over on Second Avenue."

Names of course have no real referents in Manhattan, where fish shops sell "fresh" frozen mackerel, "local" vegetables come from Pennsylvania, and "egg creams" are concocted without either cream or eggs, but in fact the brownie that crumbled in my jaws was quite O.K., rather better than those of yore, from which my aunt seldom had been precise enough in eliminating shards of walnut shell.

I have earlier mentioned my suspicion concerning the business of the Ganymede folks, the lovely Greek boy of that name having been brought to Olympus by Zeus to replace ox-eyed Hera in the marital bed, as anyone can read in bawdy Ovid among other places. That a gray-haired lady, her glasses secured by a neck ribbon attached to the temple pieces, might have a conscious role in the dissemination of literature for those who crave male children was, if not to be encountered daily, neither outlandishly beyond possibility in this Sodomist time and Gomorrhean place.

Nonetheless, it was kind of her to give me the brownie, and I thought the least I could do in return was to voice a pleasantry.

"How's business?"

She grimaced and made the so-so gesture with a fan of fingers in a half-turn of wrist, bosom-high.

To the left was a door that no doubt led to the private office of the man I had usually seen with her; again, it was of good quality, not like mine: blond wood, chromium knob. My glance was cursory; I didn't want her to think me a snoop. Their trade did not require my approval. The most culturally resplendent era in the history of man, the time of Pericles, when more philosophers, poets, and heroic sculptors were extant synchronously than have been accumulated by the twenty-five centuries since, was also the Golden Age of Pederasty. Far be it from me to find a message in this state of affairs. I am immune to the lure of catamites. In fact, I abhore children of either sex.

Notwithstanding these sentiments, however, I could not see a book or periodical on the premises. The outer office was smaller than Peggy's, and because the back lofts in Sam Polidor's building were much larger than those in front, it could be presumed that the space beyond the private door was more generous than mine.

I suppose my inspection took longer than I thought. When I looked again at the woman, she wore a different type of smile, one I can only call, owing to its glint, a leer.

"Have you something particular in mind, or would you like to wait for the boss? He'll be back from lunch soon." She rolled her chair away from the desk and stood up, lowering her spectacles to hang from the ribbon. "Why don't I just let you browse inside, in peace?"

I have a horror of disabusing courteous strangers of their expectations. Taken as a floorwalker in more than one department store, I have forthrightly directed women to the counter in question, insofar as I knew which, or, failing that, pretended it was beyond my jurisdiction and pointed to the authentic functionary.

But to be taken as having a lust for lads, to be admitted to an inner sanctum where I was expected to linger loathsomely over the pictures of naked striplings, such as those displayed on segregated racks marked ALL BOYS in the corners of peep-show anterooms, was too vile a misapprehension not to correct, with brutal candor if necessary.

However, before I could produce the words that the scowl of indignation yet withheld, she had got to the door, inserted and turned a key, and thrown one switch that ignited, in the hesitant two-stage blink of fluorescents, a series of ceiling fixtures, the lines of which were so extended in distance as apparently, in the well-known effect, to converge. There was much more space back there than I had realized. . . . And no pornography of any sort. The long room was ranked with tables holding pots and pans.

I recovered quickly. "You people are in housewares? I thought you were some sort of publishers."

Instantly she fingered out the lights, closed and locked the door. She returned the glasses to her face, enlarging the hostility of her eyes, then gave me a wrinkled nose and marched in silence to her desk.

"Well," said I, "you call yourself a press, after all."

Seated now, she took a deep breath and said: " 'Press' is the boss's name!" She winced incredulously at me. "You know, in ten years *nobody* ever got that wrong? I mean, that's dumb!"

I must have taken the second brownie at this point, though unconsciously. "*Ganymede's* his first name?"

She rolled her eyes behind the lenses. "Ganymede's another thing. There's a story there that's kinda cute. It's the pressure cooker, you know. . . . No, I guess *you* don't. Well, we distribute it exclusively, and our name being 'Press,' well, figure it out. But many years ago"—she assumed a maudlin purse of mouth—"the teeny little daughter of the president of the pressure-cooker makers, sitting in her high chair at mealtimes, banging her tiny little spoon, would try to say, 'Give me meat!' But what it sounded like, you see, was, 'Ganymede!' "

Her dirty look returned. "Now you know, and now I've got work to do." She turned to the typewriter on the metal stand at her right elbow and began to punch its keys.

I had consumed half the brownie before her final speech, her back to me, made me realize that I had so much as lifted it off the plate: "Next time, buy your own lunch. That's the cheapest trick I ever saw."

As I stepped into the hall, I reflected that at no time had she recognized me as a neighbor, which might mean that my appearance was even less distinctive than I thought.

I had exulted too soon over the absence of nutshells in the Homemade Bakery's brownies. With my final bite of the one I held, I almost broke a tooth on some small adamantine object.

I spat it into my hand. It was a tiny cylinder of metal, with a rounded-conical tip. It was a slug of lead. It was very like a bullet that could have been fired from a .25-caliber Browning automatic.

5

As it happened, the woman with Ganymede (which I still thought a damned deceptive name) was correct: the brownies were the only lunch I ate that day.

When I returned to my office, Peggy was yet there, from which presence I gathered that nothing untoward had occurred. I showed her the slug and told her where and how I had come upon it.

At first she foolishly insisted it was rather the tip of a ball-point pen. I realized I held it too close to her eyes, and pulled my hand back to accommodate her aging vision.

"You really should get glasses, you know."

"When you get a toupee," she riposted in sheer Irish

spite. My temples had not receded nearly that far. She still squinted. "I wouldn't know a bullet from . . ."

While she groped for a word sufficiently preposterous (and found it: ". . . ballot"), I said, maintaining the low voice I had assumed so that I might not be heard down the hall: "Would this suggest the Ganymede people were involved?"

Peggy put her hands flat on the desk top, her attitude of sweet reason, and said: "Russ, I ask you, what connection could there possibly be between some hoods and some people who sell pressure cookers?"

"You were always aware of the nature of their business?"

"Why wouldn't I be? The name's certainly obvious enough." She made her nose and mouth into the momentary mask of wryness. "And it so happens we have a Ganymede cooker at home, Mr. Smarty." At this point she pursed her lips in the same fashion as the woman next door and began the same sanctimonious tale: "Do you know the cute story of the name? It seems this little baby used to call for her food—"

"I know it," I said curtly, and kept repeating the phrase throughout the narration, which she continued relentlessly notwithstanding.

When she had finished, I said, rolling the bullet between thumb and forefinger, "The plot thickens. But no one else has been slain, to my knowledge. And, more importantly, I've got work!" I put a hand into my pocket, separated one of the hundred-dollar bills from the other two, and brought it forth. "And a nice retainer. Run down to the bank and change it, and you can keep half."

Peggy seized the greenback and, unbuttoning the collar of her blouse, dropped it into her bosom. "I'll keep it all, thank you, sir! You now owe me only two hundred and seventy-five bucks as of last Friday."

"Hey, hey!" I protested.

"You're lucky I don't demand the other two hundred Washburn gave you."

She had of course listened through the plywood partition, but what baffled me was that neither he nor I had mentioned the amount he had generously deposited in my palm, as opposed to the one-fifty I had asked.

Furthermore, she added even more smugly: "I'm on poor Mrs. Washburn's side. *He* looked pretty"—she leaned forward and pantomimed the twisting of a television dial —"*you know . . .*"

"The man simply neglected to zip his fly. That could happen to anybody."

"If it happens with *you*, you'll never see *me* again."

"Peg, I'm going out on this assignment. I won't be back till tomorrow. Eventually, in fact quite soon, you'll get all of what I owe you. At the moment I need the rest of the money on hand to get into my apartment again."

She cocked her eye. "Two months in arrears at two seventy-five per? How far will two hundred bucks get you?"

"At the moment, all I need is ten, maybe a twenty, for the super. The building's owned by a gigantic absentee company. It takes forever really to evict anybody in this city, especially when you stay on good terms with the functionaries actually on the premises. You have to use New York's inefficiency and anonymity for your own benefit, Peggy. It's also morally better to think in terms of the individual. You don't get nearly so bitter if you regard bus drivers, cabbies, and so on as persons like yourself, much put upon by the pressures of urban life, but for all that human undernea—"

Peggy slammed a drawer shut with a report that effectively terminated one of the little efforts I made from time to time to sweeten her world view, on the rare occasions when my own had got less acrid.

"I'm taking the afternoon off, also," said she. "It's the first time in weeks I could afford to."

I didn't argue with this solipsist logic. "With my compliments," I said. "It's been a strange day, and God knows I took enough punishment, but money's the best bandage for any wound." Toying with the bills in my pocket, I also felt the cold little bullet I had put away there.

My gun lay at the bottom of the dumbwaiter shaft. The giant corpse had vanished without a trace, along with the two fake cops who had borne it out. My client Washburn denied being either the person referred to by Bakewell or the person of the same name who had signed the letter, which had also disappeared. A raspy voice had addressed me as "Teddy" on the telephone. "Newhouse" was the English translation of "Villanova." Finally, a slug had been found in a brownie.

I resisted making another hasty decision to dismiss the Villanova affair altogether; I merely moved it out of the foreground. Riding the down elevator with Peggy, who when the door closed backed into a corner of the cab and pressed her palms against the walls, I looked again for bloodstains and again saw none.

Then I asked, "Why are you standing like that?" She had an inevitable way of doing things that irritated. Now it was as if she feared being goosed.

"It's crazy, I know," she admitted. "But I have a tendency to motion sickness."

At the corner outside we diverged as she headed for the subway and I towards my apartment building, which was but several blocks south on Third Avenue. Not having answered the natural need that had asserted itself in the final moments with Washburn, I stepped up my pace, penetrating the sidewalk congestion oblivious to the individuals who made it up, each the hero of his own tragedy or farce, most no doubt involved in both at once, as I

believe it was Schopenhauer who stated in a Teutonic bon
mot. Elsewhere he deplores the cracking of whips heard
in the streets of his day, then the implements of coachmen
and not exclusively the furniture of S & M get-togethers.
As I used to tell my students, a work should be read in the
context of its time.

Between my apartment building and the sidewalk was
a yard-wide fragment of lawn behind a margin of box
hedge too stunted even at the peak of its luxuriance to
need trimming—and thus a jurisdictional dispute among
the maintenance men was avoided: in snowtime no doorman would so much as scrape the threshold with the side
of his boot, and the certified janitor could never be found.
In this strip of pasture a large animal now grazed, a great
Dane to be specific, no doubt the pet of a small person
who lived in a tiny apartment, though no owner was in
evidence at the moment. As I swung jauntily in off the
public sidewalk, under the canvas canopy with its old
L-shaped tear that blew back in rainstorms and admitted
water to flow down the neck of him who awaited a cab,
the tremendous beast, assuming the middle-distance stare
of canine preoccupation, hunched itself and defecated
abundantly. The wind changed, and I was swept into the
lobby on a stream of fetor.

The doorman, who emerged only to rout toy poodles,
sat inside on the shiny pea-green couch otherwise seldom
used—it was in fact banned both to residents and their
guests, and of service only to building employees and
the postman, who, having hidden his cart full of week-old
mail, would loaf there and glower at tenants.

The doorman was feeding on a meatball hero sandwich
and leaning at an extreme angle so that the tomato sauce
would drip on the couch and not in his lap. Thus he did
not mark my entrance, and I gained the elevator in a feat
of eventlessness. He and the colleagues who manned the

portal on the other shifts were often distracted: either that was the explanation or they themselves had stolen the remainder of the lobby furniture. When I had moved in, two years before, the couch was flanked by matching end tables bearing tall lamps of false copper with a fake patina; and a mirror, framed by the raptorial wingspread of a gilded (and deformed) eagle, had hung on the parallel wall above a chair upholstered in glossy maroon plastic.

I deboarded on the fifth floor and took the route, with its three turns, to my quarters, 5K, behind the elevator shaft, in the far right rear of the structure. I had what in New York is called a studio apartment, i.e., one room, in this example fifteen by eight, with a kitchenette counter behind louvered doors, and a compartment in which basin, toilet, and bath were such close neighbors that I was obliged to open its door to bend for the toweling of my body below mid-thigh.

Still, it was home and not having used it for two—no, almost three weeks, I looked forward to reclaiming it, especially to using its water closet, which was exclusively mine—quite a valuable possession, as one who has had to share a sanitary facility is soon brought to understand. Speaking of which takes me back to my childhood, when our bathroom was controlled by my sisters; and when they were physically absent, the place was festooned with their wet underwear.

New Yorkly, my portal was locked by three arrangements from outside and a fourth, a chain, when one was in residence. Now that I had fled its humiliating message, the advertisement of my delinquency in rent had vanished, leaving four shiny little diagonals where the Scotch tape had been fingernailed off the matt-black surface of the door. I keyed the trio in series—standard latch, Segal deadbolt, and Police, and reached around the jamb and lifted from its floor slot the inclined iron brace of the last-named, and pushed in.

I was prepared for a musty odor. Instead, soon as I had closed the door behind me I smelled a sweet, almost sickly bouquet.

Well, that mystery could wait at least until I visited the bathroom, opening the door to which I was assailed and almost overcome by a cloud of the same scent. The top of the toilet tank was cluttered with bottles, jars, and vials. And there, so near as to brush my shoulder when I stood in the current attitude—wide Bakewell, that human mountain, would have to stand outside the door to perform the manly act—were my old bugbears: articles of female underwear hanging wetly from the rod of the shower curtain.

So again I retained my water, spun around with such energy that my flailing elbow hooked the clammy, clinging cup of a brassiere and brought it along four feet into the outer room, before it fell to the Rya rug just ahead of the sling chair of rust-colored suede, impeccably maintained for twelve months (by never being used) but now defaced with a dark, sleek-surfaced stain, free-form, probably oil, forever ineradicable.

Against the eastern wall, across the room from the windows that offered a close-up of the ruin of the neighboring building—still at the stage at which it had been arrested by a strike of the demolition workmen four weeks before —my convertible couch was opened to the double bed ordinarily secreted within its bowels by this time of day.

Even before marching to my only closet, throwing open its door, and seeing my extra shoes, habitually arranged by pairs in the forefront, now heaped in the rear to give ground to a white-hided valise the like of which I had never owned, and hanging from the rod various garments all in gayer colors and most of more delicate fabrics than my own clothing, which had been ruthlessly bunched to the far left, I began strongly to suspect that another person than I, and of another sex, had recently been on the premises.

I needed a drink. When last at home, I had washed down my meager repast (a length of pepperoni, a doorstop wedge of rattrap cheese, seven green grapes) with a glass of Almadén Mountain White. The rest of the bottle should be yet in the fridge: turned to vinegar, perhaps, but I had no alternative.

I repaired to the kitchenette and opened the half-refrigerator tucked under the Masonite counter. My modest California plonk, necessarily lying on its side owing to the narrow space between the wire shelves, had been transformed into a bulkier bottle with a protuberant mouth swathed in metal foil. I withdrew its heavy, dark-green, moisture-beaded body. The label too had been altered: it now read *Veuve Clicquot*.

Inspecting the rest of the interior, I saw I had been robbed of: an encrusted jar containing a quarter inch of Mr. Mustard; a blob of butter already rancifying three weeks earlier and in addition once melted and subsequently congealed in its greasy paper; a slice of dark-edged liverwurst. These were but all I could remember; no doubt there had been other items of like quality.

The thief had made replacements: beluga caviar in glass and a tunnel-tinned loaf of Strasbourg *pâté de foie gras*. These delicacies were as yet untasted.

Now, it was my kitchen, in my apartment, and an intruder had used it freely without my permission—yet the kind of chap I am, though loving nothing more than caviar unless it's *foie gras*, and worshiping champagne above all fluids, I put all of these away after my salivating inspection. The fridge might be mine, but the comestibles were not. I might have dipped into them had they instead been pressed ham, egg salad, and a bottle of Bud. I was even conscious of taking a kind of toady pride in the usurper's superior tastes. Drinkless, I returned to what should have been the living area but was yet the bedroom, and looked for a place to sit other than the stained suede, seeing which I was flooded with indignation again and concomitantly remembered my need to urinate.

I strode to the bathroom, coming upon and picking up the damp brassiere, nasty thing, en route. Having to free my hands of it before I proceeded with my own business, I hung it up again, alongside the underpants and other items of damp lingerie hanging from the rod above the tub. I habitually kept the shower curtain (a rather vulgar one, left behind by the previous tenant, of shiny plastic imprinted with orange water lilies against a background of Prussian blue) closed even when not showering, because of the condition of the tub, the porcelain of which was badly pitted by the pox of use and stained by a rust against which scouring powders were impotent.

It occurred to me that if my bathroom was to be used, without my permission, for hanging wet laundry, the latter might as well be dried more efficiently: given such ventilation as was available in a tiny compartment without a window, i.e., not plastered against plastic. I took the articles from the rod and hurled the curtain away with a clatter of its rings.

Bakewell's body lay in the bathtub.

"Lay" is a poor verb for the work it must do. The tub was considerably shorter, of course, than my office couch and inserted tightly within two right-angled walls, allowing no overhang at either end. His knees were therefore pointed towards the ceiling, his chin embedded in his chest. Surely the rigor had set in by now. I did not probe him to confirm this assumption. Nor did I entertain any plan to dispose of the body discreetly.

I went out to the phone, a wall-mounted instrument over the kitchenette counter. I discovered I still held the moist underwear. I flung it away with some difficulty, the wet fabrics being tenacious. I spun the three digits of the police emergency number—and heard nothing but the raspy revolutions of the bent dial. I remembered then that I had had the service disconnected when I made the decision to live in my office till the wind changed.

I sprang to the lobby-intercom apparatus on the wall beside the main door, held my finger against the signal button for an eternity, and at length heard the doorman's brutal grunt.

"Call the police," I said, "and send them to five K."

"Why?"

"There's been a murder."

"That ain't humorous, sonny. You just wait for your mama to come home."

I realized that I had been affected vocally by the shock, and endeavored to lower my voice. "I'm a grown man. There's a corpse in my bathtub. Please go to an outside phone and call the cops."

After a moment I heard either a vigorous exhalation or a downright Bronx cheer. "Whyn't you go fuck yourself?" He hung up.

I gave him a furious shot of the buzzer and when he came on again I cried, commanding in my desperation an idiom that ordinarily was quite foreign to me: "Listen, you rotten little punk, I'm on my way down there to push your teeth through the back of your head." His pregnant silence caused me to go too far and add: "*I'm* the murderer, see?"

He literally whined like the legendary cur. And apparently let the instrument dangle, for I could hear his running footfalls against the lobby tiles. I should not have made that foolish threat. If he had the usual character of a New York doorman—tough *in modo,* cowardly *in re*—and also, with the rest of the population, utterly cynical about the police, he would run away and hide for the rest of the week.

I did not think of the worst consequence: that he would indeed call the constabulary and when they arrived assure them I had boasted of killing a human being.

Thus, five minutes later—impressively proving that the law does act promptly at the sound of the word "murder," at least in my precinct, far south of Spanish Harlem and its Saturday-night sports—my door reverberated with the savage onslaught of revolver butts, and when I opened it a squad of policemen vaulted in, hurled me onto the bed, arranged my body into an *X,* and ransacked its clothing.

They were most of them young men, and almost all wore long sideburns and handle-bar mustaches, with thick clumps of hair protruding from the backs of their caps. They looked very like the actors who represent cops in movies and on TV, which was no doubt the source of their style, but they did not say "Freeze" when pointing their guns at my face, nor did they give me my "rights." Therefore I suspected they were the real thing this time.

When the search of my person was finished and I was, by default, permitted to sit up, I sought to remove the basic misconception.

"*I'm* the person who called you. I'm not the criminal!"

The boys in blue made no response to this information; but when I tried to get to my feet, one of them pushed me down.

"The body," said I, "is in the bathroom. Shouldn't you look in there?"

A sandy-haired policeman, whose name plate read *T. J.*

Muenzer, ostentatiously returned my wallet to me and said: "You got identification?"

"Tons," said I, relieved to have reached a plateau of rationality, and plucked out the sheaf of documents which, with the rest of the race, I must carry to prove I exist. Shaken as I was—though with much rustle of leather and sound of snaps they were now putting away their artillery—I hastily fanned the deck of credit cards, etc., chose a piece of certification that had had to be folded to be of uniform size with the others, namely my private-investigator's license, and handed it to Muenzer.

He peeled it apart, perused it deliberately, and then applied his pale hazel eyes to me. "Where is this Ophelia?"

"Who?"

He fluttered the paper at me. "Duh dawg."

"Dog?"

"This is an attack animal?"

"May I?" I asked, cautiously extending my fingers. He permitted me to take the paper. I studied it. It was a dog license, issued by the ASPCA for the City of New York, registering a female great Dane, named for the poor nymph in whose orisons Hamlet asked that all his sins be remembered, to an owner named . . . *T. Villanova.*

No doubt I blanched. "Believe it or not," I howled, "I do not now own a dog. I have never owned a dog—"

"Sure, Mr. Villanova. You just take it easy. You're all right, see. You got more little cards there?" He now addressed me as if speaking to an idiot child—the fashion in which Matthew Arnold is alleged to have addressed everybody, for what that's worth.

I hung my head. My voice was sheepish as well. "You won't believe this, either, but my name isn't Teddy Villanova."

He smirked significantly at his confreres and shrugged.

Then to me: "If you say so. Maybe you'd like to tell us what your name is?"

"Russel Wren."

"Mind if I look at them other cards you got there?"

I handed them over. He began to read aloud the designation on each, and on all it was *Villanova*.

6

Patrolman Muenzer lowered the handful of "identification"—though it was not mine—and grinning with only his mouth, his eyes lusterless, said: "You picked Villanova's pocket?"

"Someone must have picked my own," said I. "Took my wallet, changed the documents therein, and stealthily returned it."

"It *is* your billfold?" He put his hands at his waist, one just above the gun and the other near a leather sheath, containing two pens, at his left hip. If I had had any doubts as to his authenticity as a policeman, this attitude would have removed them.

I examined the article in question, somewhat embarrassed by his implicit correction of my term: it was indeed a billfold and not a wallet. It had been Peggy's gift to me at lunchtime on the previous Xmas Eve (in response to the collapsible plastic rain hood I had given her that morning, taking her aback some distance, owing to my only lately having denounced the holiday as meretricious; she burst into tears at my charitable treachery; she really has certain fetching ways).

I now lost no time in ripping open the bill compartment. Yes, my seven dollars were still there. Washburn's two hundreds remained in my trouser pocket.

"Well," I said at length, "it certainly looks like my property. . . . Of course, this is a common type of billfold, no? Looks like new. But then so did mine, which was only three months old, and got little traffic, because—ha!— business hasn't been that *good*."

Again I tested him with a rhetorical laugh, but he merely and humorlessly reshuffled the cards of identity.

"Ya know," said he, squinting from them to me and back again several times. "Not one uvem says the name's Teddy. Aluvem just have the letter *T*."

"Before we get into these complex matters," said I, "hadn't you better look into the bathtub?"

"They're *doon* that."

"Oh."

He sighed. "You got *anything* that says yoowaw who you say yoowaw?"

This time I did not respond with "miles" or any other exaggeration. I was too fearful that whoever was ruining my life so deftly as to gain access to my closely guarded billfold would have done an even more thorough job on my apartment, from which I had been absent for three weeks, and into which, with impunity, he or she or they had managed to move an enormous corpse, not to mention a woman's wardrobe.

"If you'll just let me look . . .?"

Muenzer gasped at the suggestion that he of all people might impede me and (in the nonce phrase of our common 1950s boyhood, which has stubbornly persisted) said, throwing his hands off his belt: "Be my guest."

However, neither he nor the other uniformed gentry moved their stubborn figures from my projected path— a disinclination ever to do which would seem another trait of local law-enforcement officers, along with driving through stoplights even when not in hot pursuit of malefactors. Though I am not now nor have ever been a sociopath, I half-expected them, as I penetrated their picket line in a half crouch, to treat me as the victim of a gauntlet run and each administer his peculiar kick or blow to my quailing body. But I am happy, with the thought of the proportion of my taxes that go to pay their wages, to report that this was but the "flight forward," to use Reik's term, of the masochist that perhaps each of us is when confronted by the only municipal employees who legally carry death-dealing weapons.

I had a birth certificate, driver's-license renewal stub, and the like, in an asbestos-lined envelope I had prudently purchased from the catalogue of Sunset House, the well-known mail-order vendors of a thousand and one cunning items for the home and office; and furthermore the envelope was itself enveloped by a Baggie.

This package lay behind the *Selected Thomas Aquinas* on the hanging shelves I had installed myself with those perforated strips and movable supports one buys in hardware stores along with Molly, that fastener who spreads her limbs back of hollow walls. It was this volume I now removed . . . then the Aristotle, then Diogenes Laërtius, the pre-Socratics—but why go through thirty centuries? I simply emptied the entire five shelves, and a crumbling alpine range of books, ranging figuratively from poetry to pushpins, rose high as my kneecaps.

My auxiliary documents of identification were gone. In a way, looking on the refulgent side of this murky adventure, I was relieved that I had not found them and again read the name *Villanova* on each.

While I war employed in this futile endeavor, a number of policemen stepped into the hallway so as to allow room for the entrance of two white-suited men of the black race who pushed in a wheeled stretcher on which lay a withered gray sleeping bag. This duo repaired to the bathroom and fetched Bakewell's corpse therefrom, and I don't like to think about the efforts they must have made to straighten his body; but eventually they trundled the now swollen sack, from which two feet, wearing shoes large as skiffs, protruded to the ankles. I hoped that would be the last I should see of those ubiquitous remains.

The policemen who had gone into the hall did not return, and others left as several civilian-dressed persons arrived, my now old acquaintance Muenzer among the departing. He took no formal leave of me; I had given him no reason for one, being unable to provide him even with a verified name.

He stopped just inside the door to relate whatever he had to tell to a plain-clothesman, a withered young man with a sparse beard and a disorder of facial skin wherever it was visible. This minion of the law was dressed as a lumberjack, in plaid woolen shirt and high-laced boots; but he was much too slight to have worked at that grueling trade, being concave-chested and spidery of limb, and furthermore he displayed a kind of palsy in the grip of which he trembled incessantly. His eyes were running, and he frequently wiped at his prominent nose with a red bandanna. He looked for all the world like Peggy's bête noire, a Puerto Rican delivery boy who spent all his wages on a heroin habit. He was however a detective. At last I had encountered a cop of the new breed. I was soon to find that he was not even Latin, despite the nose, the generous lips, black eyes, and swarthy tight curls that clasped his head.

Swabbing at his nose and eyes, he listened briefly to

Muenzer; then his rickety shoulders climbed as high as his ears, while his body quivered even more violently than before. I thought he might be at the onset of a mortal seizure, but Muenzer correctly interpreted it rather as his own dismissal and left.

The mean little figure approached me, studying the ceiling either for dramatic effect or in some restraint of the mucous membranes as when one tries to inhibit the birth of a sneeze. I was confronted with a pair of hairy nostrils and the whites of under eyes, marbled with scarlet veins—which suggests how far back his head was thrown, for he was a good half a foot shorter than I.

At length his watery irises descended to take a focus on my Adam's apple. He wiped his nose once again and spoke, through the bandanna but clearly enough.

"My name is Zwingli, and I'm a detective. I'll show you my identification, if you'll me yours, as Henry James might say." Then he looked directly at me and I had the strange conviction that he believed his beard to be thicker than it was and that his slight smile was concealed within it; whereas in actuality neither of these assumptions was true, and his expression was quite obviously one of self-satisfaction.

"Zwingli with a *z*?" was, I'm afraid, all I could come up with, though somewhat nettled by his quick boast of literacy.

He immediately became even more overweening. "As with the celebrated Swiss reformer. I understand though there is reason to believe you are Villanova, you insist you are instead Wren, as with the noted architect who built St. Paul's."

" 'If you seek his monument, look around you.' "

In his gloat he went too far: "*Si monumentum requiris, circumspice.*"

"Well," said I, seeing my chance for a lethal thrust,

"that's pretty vulgar, isn't it? To translate back into the original what is already clearly understood?"

He turned plaintive: "It's pretty remarkable for a cop, though, don't you think?"

He did have a point, and I was abashed. Also, he was corporeally a pathetic sight, exacerbating the rash on his nose with that red rag, his eyes oozing, his beard straggly. I suddenly felt protective.

"Do you have an allergy? There's a squeeze bottle of NTZ in the bathroom cabinet and also a few remaining capsules of Allerest, a Sinutab or two as well. I'd get them for you myself, but I'm still queasy. They just took a corpse from my tub."

"Precisely why I'm here," said Zwingli. "I may accept your kind offer, but first I should be in your debt were you to relate this unlucky deed, speaking of yourself as you are and nothing extenuate. Did you cause that man to shuffle off his mortal coil?"

"Certainly not."

"Then we must look for a murtherer most foul? Or could the victim have made his own quietus with a bare bodkin?"

"I believe he was shot."

At last he sneezed, rather modestly given the elaborate prelude. Having scrubbed his nose to a brilliant scarlet, he glanced at my pile of books. "Do I see one or more volumes in the old Boni and Liveright Modern Library, flexible leatherette bindings? You wouldn't happen to have Andreyev's *The Seven Who Were Hanged*?" He plunged to his knees and picked up a little volume. "Ah, Schopenhauer's *Studies in Pessimism*, just the ticket." He thumbed it, found a page, and opened it wide with a binding-cracking sound that made me wince. He read aloud: " 'As far as I know, none but the votaries of monotheistic, that is to say, Jewish religions, look upon suicide as a crime.'" He tossed the book back on the pile and rose.

His entire performance since entering had been sufficiently dramatic to distract me from noticing, until now, that the other detectives were taking my apartment to pieces. One stout fellow in a rumpled suit had been ransacking my desk. He was now in the act of taking from a drawer the script of my unfinished play. Doubting, from his Visigoth expression, that he was equipped to render authoritative judgment on it, I appealed to Zwingli, who in sympathetic response went to him and claimed the double handful of loose sheets, the other surrendering them with a groan of either derision or relief.

Zwingli cocked a skinny buttock and sat on the edge of the desk, beginning to read with discolored eyelids so heavy-looking as to seem closed; it was only from the tremor of separate hairs in his mangy beard, as he apparently vocalized the dialogue in his palate, behind closed lips, that told me he was not dozing. In such fashion he actually read, or painstakingly pretended to read, three pages, without checking the numbers to determine whether they were in sequence—which likely they were not: more than once I had after a brief perusal hurled the sheaf away in chagrin: I won't say why and so nourish the *Schadenfreude* of other would-be dramatists whose scenes, after a vigorous start, founder in the middle as characters desperately ignite cigarettes or spill cups of coffee for wont of pungent dialogue that will get them to the curtain lines which are forceful, e.g.:

ROBERT: Lynne, you're acting like a tart.
LYNNE [wryly]: Oh?
(She being secretly an ex-streetwalker who earned enough to send herself through medical school.)

Zwingli at last lowered the manuscript, which he held in the hand that also clutched the clammy bandanna. He spoke solemnly.

"It's good. It may even be brilliant. There seems to be some direct borrowing from Aristophanes, but that's legitimate enough."

My play was of course never intended to be comedy, but why pick at lint? I was touched. In fact, I was devastated. And while I was in that weakened condition Zwingli whipped a pair of handcuffs from somewhere under his lumberman's shirt and clamped them around my wrists.

With some shame I must admit that while this action seemed unmotivated I did not take it as an outrage, and I made no resistance physically or vocally. No one, not even the liberal-lawyer's wife, had so lavishly praised my work. In fact, but for Daphne Leopold, for such was her name, no one had ever made upon it a judgment that could actually have been interpreted as in any way favorable. The instructor in my playwriting class at The New School, an acrid man who had once seen a one-acter of his own on an Off-Off Broadway run of three nights, had been almost bleak in his assessment of my talent.

"You really think it has some merit?" I asked shyly, my steel-cuffed hands nestling like sleeping puppies in the small of my back.

Zwingli frowned. "It's a pity," said he, "that such a potentially splendid career will never blossom. But he who abandons the pen for the pistol should not be amazed if he is hoist with his own petard." He was caught suddenly by an impulse to sneeze again; but with a violent convulsion of his entire body, which would seem to take more from him than any mere ejaculation of nose, he conquered it.

This passage is very humiliating to detail, in my now

cold blood, but I must further report that I next said: "Why don't you take along the entire manuscript? Perhaps from time to time you could visit me in jail, and then of course you'll be at my trial: we might talk during the recesses. Your criticism would be invaluable. Funny, I wasn't aware of the obvious debt to Aristophanes—though of course you're quite right, and will find even more of it when you get to the second act."

"Say, Knox," Zwingli called to the stout detective. "Mind stepping over here? He's confessing." To me he said: "You have a right to remain silent. You have a right to—"

I was at last struck by our divergence of purposes. "That's a filthy trick!"

"Murder is a dirty business," he stated flatly, abandoning his erudite idiom for the TV cliché. "Some of it rubs off on us, but like they say, 'Next time you're mugged, call a hippie.' "

Knox produced a notebook and prepared a Hardhead Flair for service.

"This is ludicrous," said I. Knox wrote that down, I assume; at least he scribbled something and continued to move his pen as I went on. As succinctly as I could, I related the events of my day, omitting only any reference to my gun. Zwingli listened impatiently for a moment and then, squatting again, returned to the examination of my tumbled library. Nevertheless, I finished my story for Knox's transcription, concluding with a suggestion that a verification of my whereabouts during the time of Bakewell's murder should be sought from Peggy Tumulty; and for the period immediately thereafter, from Sam Polidor, Donald Washburn II, and the secretary of Ganymede Press.

At the last name Knox raised his oxhead and said: "My old lady's got one of them pressure cookers. There's a cute story goes with it. It seems . . ." And so for the third time I heard that sickening anecdote.

When that was done, I lifted my bound wrists off my sacroiliac, making a pigeon chest for a moment in an effort to stretch. It is unpleasant to wear real handcuffs for more than the instant it takes to understand they are not the toy kind which can be tripped open with extended thumbs.

"That's it," said I. "But I'll be glad to answer any further questions."

Zwingli dropped one volume of the three comprising Percy's *Reliques of Ancient English Poetry* and standing erect, literary again, began to recite:

> "Take oh take those lips away
> That so sweetly were forsworn . . ."

His dreamy look then suddenly turned hard. "All right, now tell us what really happened."

I craned my neck and eyed the surface of Knox's notebook, seeing only several games of ticktacktoe, the latest of which he finished as I watched, with a final neat little *X* that was something of a surprise given his burly person.

I then began to shout, and Zwingli winced and raised his wiry hands.

"Once again," said he, "my prayer that a suspect will exercise his right of silence has not been answered." He peered at my chin. "I tend too often to rest in the thought of two and only two absolute and luminously self-evident beings, myself and my Creator."

I suspected this was a quotation from some celebrated thinker, and not Zwingli's own, but I had a greater problem at the moment than the detection of plagiarism.

"Must I go through the whole story again? It won't change, I assure you."

Zwingli continued to study me. "You give up?" said he at last. "John Henry Newman."

For a moment I believed he had mentioned a new suspect or victim. ". . . Oh, you mean the author of the *Apologia pro Vita Sua?*"

"O.K.," he replied, "you got the title. That's half a point. I've been looking through your library, and I don't mind telling you it is pretentious. No so-called light reading is in evidence. These are, to a volume, weighty tomes." Moisture began to blur his eyes again, but he would not immediately remove it. "Frankly, whether you are Villanova or Wren is a matter of small consequence to me. If you killed the great big man, we'll either prove it or we won't. It is quite possible that we will not, for that matter. Citizens are not generally aware that most murders are never solved. I don't have the statistics on that, but they are interesting. . . . But what I can't stand is a bogus intellectual, the type of man who would put up a wall full of highbrow literature so as to get into a girl's pants."

My head reeled. "Wait a minute. You've got too many disparate strings in your knot. First, I've never met a girl who was impressed by anybody's library—"

Zwingli smiled and repeated, "Disparate. . . . I don't think I've ever heard that in conversation, at least not pronounced, correctly I gather, with the stress on the first syllable. You do have a way with words." He scowled then. "But what I want is still more substantial proof. Therefore I intend to give you an oral examination consisting of ten quotations, chosen at random from your own books. For correctly identifying the author of each, you get half a point. Seven points is the lowest passing mark."

Why I fell in with his scheme, which was certainly another violation of my constitutional rights, I don't know.

Perhaps it was because I find quizzes irresistible. Also, I was offended by his doubts as to my sincerity in pursuing the life of the mind. He after all carried only the badge of a New York detective and not the M.A. (Oxon.) of, say, John Ruskin.

"How about *six* points to pass?" I however pleaded. No one, not even Ruskin, could remember every sentence in every volume on his shelves.

He taunted me: "Showing the white feather already?" But he sneeringly nodded his assent, and kneeled at the pile of books, his back towards me so that I could not see which he chose. Knox had sometime since lumbered away. He had found the suitcase in the closet now and was removing from it various items of wispy lingerie and sniggering.

"O.K.," said Zwingli, "here we go. Number One: "Life, I fancy, would very often be insupportable, but for the luxury of self-compassion.' "

I saw no reason why I should be scrupulous, and while mumbling as if searching my memory, I stole quietly near his back and tried to see the book over his thin shoulder. I stupidly forgot to still my murmur when I drew close to him, however, and, though without turning, he up-braided me.

"I knew you were a phony!"

I retreated. "No, I'm not. That's Emerson, *Self-Reliance.*"

"Ha!" cackled Zwingli. "It's Gissing, *The Private Papers of Henry Ryecroft.*"

"Good gravy," I said, unconsciously echoing Washburn. "I forgot I even owned that."

He rustled some pages in a new volume. "Oh, this is priceless: 'Nothing has been so much part of one as that which turns into excrement.' "

But now it was I who exulted, snorting and chuckling

to the degree that he turned and gave me a hairy side of face above which stared a bleak eye.

"*Touché pour moi!*" I gloated. "Elias Canetti, *Crowds and Power.*"

Sourly, silently he averted his countenance. "One full point." Again the susurrus of pages. Then: " 'How much do you think Homer got for his *Iliad?* or Dante for his *Paradise?*—only bitter bread and salt and going up and down other people's stairs.' "

Speak of the devil, that was, of course, John Ruskin, and luckily I owned only one book of his authorship, though his collected *œuvres* comprise something like thirty royaloctavo volumes, an astonishing mass of work for the typewriterless age of Victoria; but I believe he was sexually inept, which is why his child-wife ran off with John Everett Millais, dauber-laureate of the bourgeoisie.

"Ruskin's *Crown of Wild Olive!*" I crowed at Zwingli's nappy head.

He stood up, holding the book, which was closed onto one finger. "We don't have to go any farther. I was ready to swear you wouldn't get a one. I want you to know I played fair and only chose passages you had underlined."

"Ah," said I. "That explains the Gissing. I bought it used, and the markings in it were made by my predecessor."

He wore a strange smile. "That was my surmise. The name 'Gordon C. Rossbach' appears on the flyleaf. Whereas in both the Canetti and this Ruskin, you have written your own name." His smile became broader, showing teeth stained as if with tobacco, though he had not smoked since entering. He flipped open the book he held and showed me. There it was: *T. Villanova.*

Refusing to panic, I held the flyleaf at an angle against the light and looked for traces of the ink remover that had undoubtedly been used to eradicate the "Russel Wren" and date of purchase that I inscribe in every book I buy. Finding none, I demanded that he take the volume to the police laboratory for chemical or ultraviolet examination.

"Why?" he asked. "Why don't you abandon this ridiculous effort to be pseudonymous?" He got out a key and unlocked my handcuffs. "We don't have any evidence that you killed that man. As you say—or did you?—anybody could have a corpse foisted on him nowadays. Good luck with your writing."

Rubbing my wrists, I watched him leave the apartment in his shambling stride. His style seemed eccentric in the extreme, but it was no doubt a gain for society that the stinking cigar, the snap-brim fedora, and the rubber hose were no longer among the inevitable implements of crime detection.

No sooner had I made that tentative judgment, however, than old-fashioned Knox, from behind and without warning, disabled me with an awful blow above the right kidney, and I descended to meet the floor with knees and forehead.

Despite the pain, I was able to reflect that he and Zwingli were practicing the time-hallowed technique of Mr. Good Guy vs. Mr. Bad, which had no doubt resulted in many triumphs of law enforcement over the years. If after Zwingli's praise for my playwriting I was ready to be led off to jail, I was inclined for another motive to cooperate with Knox: as a man of the spirit I respect nothing more than brutal violence.

Before I could make that clear to the stocky detective, however, he fetched me a kick in the fundament that brought me in contact with the floor along my entire length.

Then he bestrode my body and said to it: "One thing I can't stand is a white pimp." He shouted in another direction. "Ain't that right, Calvin?"

An answer came from the region of the kitchenette, in what was obviously a gross and unbelievable parody of a black field-hand's drawl: "Dass rat, massa."

I turned my head to that side and was startled to see that however counterfeit it had come from a black detective.

Knox walked over me and said: "He's worse than I am. All his sisters are in the life." His voice did not have a hint of smile in it; but the Negro laughed until he cried, and added: "You forgot my mama!"

"All right," Knox said to me. "Get up, and if you trip again, don't never claim I touched you." Without understanding that it made a hash of logic, he added: "Or I'll hurt you real bad. . . . The doorman told us all about it. You run this operation for three weeks. You got five-six girls he knows about. Here's the way I see it: the big fellow was a customer. He asks the little lady for something she don't want to do even if she's a whore. She refuses. He gets tough, starts to work her over. You was here, maybe behind them doors in the kitchenette. You come out, but he don't care. He's got almost a foot on you and a couple hundred pounds. You pull your piece and threaten him with it, but by now he's like a mad dog, and you got no choice but to drop him. You might get off on self-defense, but you keep a brothel—and he might be a respectable businessman or something. You're scared. Then the girl runs away. You panic now. You hide the body in the tub. The doorman sees the girl rush out into the street wearing only panty hose"—Knox flipped past the ticktacktoe games in his notebook and peered at the hen tracks on another page—"L'Eggs Sheer Energy, he said the brand looked like. . . . He suspect's something's wrong. He gets you on the house phone. You're rattled, and you confess right away."

This had long since got too preposterous to think of answering in detail. To show my contempt, I turned towards the black cop, who had come over from the kitchenette with the tin of *pâté de foie gras.*

"Sir," I said with conspicuous respect, "do you really think those racial slurs are funny, or could they be only the same old bigotry in a new guise, and even more vicious because—"

He struck me in the mouth, though not, thankfully, with the hand that held the canned delicacy from Strasbourg. No teeth were loosened, but a salty taste seemed to indicate that my lip was split.

Zwingli suddenly appeared again. He had stolen up silently behind me. He put his hand in the crook of my elbow and his mouth so close to my ear that his beard tickled me and I writhed away. But though he seemed in an advanced state of physical degeneration, he was remarkably strong in more than his breath. He pulled me back with such force that I fell onto him backwards, my head on his shoulder. He also subtly twisted my arm so that I could not have moved without spraining it to the shoulder.

The greasy lichen-growth of his cheek was loathsome against my face. For a desperate moment I thought he might passionately glue his lips to mine in the interests of some further filthy ruse, but his hot mouth traveled to my ear, and he whispered: "Trust me."

He thrust his chin towards Knox and said: "The pimping can be dropped: we're not the pussy posse. And I don't know that even Murder Two would stick. The great big man did assault somebody: he's got hair and skin under his fingernails and there's blood on his signet ring, probably not his own. A man that size is a deadly weapon himself. A self-defense plea would probably hold."

Knox glowered and shook his head. "I don't know. I think we should hit this scumbag with everything."

While I was still at the eccentric angle, Zwingli without warning let me go. It took quick measures to regain my footing. He drew Knox aside for an undertoned colloquy.

The black detective showed me the tin. "The key is missing," said he. "And I doubt your regular can opener can get a purchase on a container of this peculiar shape. That's what puzzles me." He snapped his fingers. "Of course: a needle-nosed pliers is your answer. Grasp the little tab and peel away the ribbon of metal."

He had put this nicely, but I decided that he was too willful for me to chance another attempt to converse with him, even on such a morally neutral subject. However, the decision to remain silent also proved impolitic.

He snarled: "Are you so depraved that you cannot even be civil?" He took a blackjack from a rear pocket and brandished it. "I might just submit you to the bastinado."

Whether the situation was as sticky as it seemed—he was grinning, though cruelly—it was not allowed to develop further, owing to Zwingli's return at that moment. He too was grinning, and an unattractive sight it was: perhaps he had drunk red wine during his absence in the hallway.

Knox now plodded away in what looked like furious disgruntlement.

"He owed me a favor," said my putative friend. "Are you lucky!"

"Look at thisheer." The swarthy sleuth displayed the *pâté* to Zwingli. For some reason of his own he assumed a darky accent when talking to his colleagues. "He don't live on Hamburger Helper. Not this motherfucker." Uttering a series of *yaks*, he shuffled away.

Zwingli whispered confidentially: "God, that spade gets under my skin. . . . Look, I went way out on a limb for you. Now you owe *me* something. Give me the stuff, and we'll drop the rest of it." He shrugged. "Simple as that."

"What stuff?"

He sighed. "All right, I'll play along with your professional interest in vocabulary. What do you want me to call it? 'Smack' or 'horse' or 'H' or 'shit'?" He put a dirty finger on my chest. "Though I should advise you that nobody in the real world uses those terms. I've never heard a pro call it anything but heroin." The subject seemed to exercise him. "As with the word 'piece' for a gun. Nobody ever says that."

"Knox just did."

"Oh, maybe for a joke," said Zwingli, jerking his messy little face.

Now I was struck by the essential force of his previous speech. "Heroin!"

He seized my arm. "Shh. Keep it down." He peered around at Knox and Calvin, who stared at us. He waved a rejection at them.

To me he said: "This is just between you and yours truly."

"I have never *seen* so much as a pinch of heroin my life long," I whined. "I wouldn't know where to get any, and I wouldn't know what to do with it if I had some. I realize it bulks large in our popular culture, if one goes by television, motion pictures, and every type of periodical journalism, but to me it is as theoretical as the gold for which the old alchemists searched, or as the unicorn or the drag—"

"How can you talk that rot," he asked desperately,

"when you can see I'm dying for a fix—I mean, an injection?"

"You?"

"Alas," he confessed in a tragical tone, "if you continue to break eggs to make omelets, some slime will get onto your hands. It starts by finding a quantity of white powder in the possession of a suspected user. You test it on the tip of your tongue to determine whether it might be mere talcum powder or sugar. You do this long enough and you get enough of the real stuff to acquire a certain taste for it. Then you go further: you shoot up. You like the subsequent release from care." He jabbed me in the ribs. "Are you following this? You begin to suspect that the nirvana for which we all search, that sleep that all life is rounded with is—well, as Hopkins tells us, 'All life death doth end and each day dies with sleep'—"

"Are you saying that *you* are a heroin addict?"

My voice had been too loud once more, and again he cautioned me. Then he whispered indignantly: "I trust you're not getting moralistic. You know as well as I that the great big man was Giaccomo Cozzo, alias Jake the Wop, Big Jake, Big Jack, Big Dick, however you knew him. He was a major dealer, and he was here for more than a golden shower from some hooker."

Zwingli's trick of turning without warning from the cultivated speech he prided himself on to some base jargon again took me by surprise.

"I have already told you that I'm involved in these dreadful matters only by accident. I *don't* know Cozzo, who called himself Bakewell when he burst into my office this morning and struck me in the frontal bone. I *don't* keep a brothel, et cetera, et cetera, and if a prostitute has been using my apartment to urinate on customers, or to refuse to, I haven't been aware of it. I'm not a junkie, either, and still less a dealer. I have occasionally taken a

drag on a joint, I mean a draught from a marijuana cigarette, when with a girl who smoked it, but far from
disordering my apprehension of reality, it has had little
effect except to make me cough, because of the profound
inhalations one is exhorted to take, probably for ritualistic
motives in support of the communal mystique."

I stopped now to inhale air, and also, I confess, to see
whether Zwingli might make some expression of regard
for my felicitous phrasings. He did not. I went on: "But
what strikes me here, even more than these abominable
accusations, is your moral position as a police officer. How
do you justify the pursuit of narcotics dealers when you
are yourself an addict?"

"Superior force," he answered flatly, drawing from under
his plaid shirt an enormous automatic pistol. But then,
in the tone of supreme regret, he added: "I truly hoped
I would not have to use it on you."

7

Staring into the muzzle of Zwingli's blunderbuss, as if in
a dream I heard my name called in a strident female
voice. I did not grasp the fact of Peggy Tumulty's arrival
until she had rushed across the room, boldly thrust the
scrawny detective and his big gun out of the way, and
clasped me to her splendid bosom.

"You lay off him!" she ordered. "I'm from a long line

of municipal employees, and the accident rate among sanitation workers is a lot higher than with you bums, and yet you fight parity, and you're all on the take anyway, so go out and steal apples from a fruit stand."

Zwingli said, "Yes, ma'am," and put away his gun.

"Peggy!" I cried, belatedly but with enthusiasm.

Zwingli asked shyly: "This is the lady in question?"

Of the mixed emotions of the moment, I chose mirth. "He thinks," said I, "hahaha, he thinks you are a hook—" I claimed control: "Tell him what you are to me."

She extended her chest towards Zwingli, causing him to recoil in more fear, I think, than lustful awe, junkies having a notoriously feeble sex drive. "I happen to be Mr. Wren's associate in business."

"No," I pointed out, "that's still ambiguous in this context, Peg. . . . Miss Tumulty is my secretary."

"O.K., so I'm getting uppity," Peggy cried. "I'm entitled."

"She can confirm my story," I told Zwingli.

He rolled his bloodshot eyes. "What *is* your story?" To Peggy he said: "You see, miss, I'm not asking much."

Peggy drew back and squinted suspiciously at me. "Are you being weird again, Russ? Just tell him the facts. Nobody's asking for Shakespeare."

So I repeated the account I had given Knox in vain, and Peggy did support me on every detail, though she had not been a witness to any event but the initial appearance of the man who called himself Bakewell and the interview with Washburn. As to the latter, I soon had reason to wish she had not been conversant with the particulars of that visit.

"Washburn Two," she told Zwingli at the conclusion of my narrative, "exposed himself. Then he gave Russ a retainer of three hundred dollars."

The scrawny detective nodded his psoriatic nose. "Well, Miss Tumulty, I want to commend you for coming forward. Were there more citizens like you, the serpent of crime would not hold this city in its loathsome coils."

As he said this, I felt a touch at my sleeve on the side towards him, not a grasping so much as the tentative maneuvers of a squid to find a point at which to fasten a tentacle full of suckers. I saw it was rather Zwingli's small claw.

He asked Peggy: "I wonder whether I might have a private word with your associate?" He gave her his grotesque smile.

I might have known she would by now be enchanted with his deference. She even bobbed her body slightly in what I took to be the parody of a curtsy, and said, predictably: "Be my guest." Then she turned and spotted Knox, who was fondling the lingerie from the suitcase. She marched across the room, snatched a black bra from his fingers, threw it in the valise, and closed that container. Rubicund shame suffused Knox's beefy face, and he slunk away.

"Looks like a hot piece of poontang," said Zwingli, smirking horribly. "I suspect you are living the legend of the private eye, which I confess I had always believed mythical. You'll be happy to know that I'll accept the alibi provided by your so-called secretary, but I'm afraid I'll be obliged to impound that retainer given you by this man named Washburn Tew."

"What?"

"It's evidence, you see." He threw up his hands. "Oh, I'll certainly give you a receipt." He searched in his jeans for a moment and then brought out a filthy, crumpled piece of yellow paper. He found a fragment of pencil in his lumberman's shirt. "Turn your back, please." He put the paper between my shoulder blades and scratched upon it. I happen to be ticklish in that odd place, and I did a little inadvertent dance.

"Now the money, please."

"It's all I have in the world!" I protested. "How can I do the job for which it was paid me?"

Zwingli winced compassionately. "Were the rules of the NYPD my own, I should alter them instanter, you know that. Alas, we are all pawns on the chessboard of ineluctable reality." His fingers were extended and twitching.

I surrendered the two hundred-dollar bills. "Peggy has the third," I said vengefully. "Go get it out of her."

He shrugged. "I'm in no condition for that."

Which reminded me to ask: "Are you really a heroin addict?"

"Fortunately for you, I'm the new breed of officer," said he, frowning. "Knox would punish you severely for asking such an insensitive question."

"Was that just a ruse? And what about Big Jake the Wop?"

"No, Jake the Wop *or* Big Jake. To combine them is superfetation."

Damn him. I had never heard that word in speech, and never read it but in the text of T. S. Eliot.

"*Was* he a dealer in narcotics—or was that too merely part of your *shtick*? —Show-business jargon, derived from the Yiddish."

He sneered: "I know that! . . . As to the burden of your question, that's a police affair." He added curtly: "You'll be informed if we have further use for you."

"But I must stay in town?"

"If you don't have the fare to go elsewhere," the little detective told me. "Good God, man, I'm not obliged to give you a guide to life." He turned and made a kissing noise towards the other officers, and with a hooked finger conducted them out the door.

My apartment lay in ruins; the contents of every drawer were strewn on the floor and the pillows slit and emptied.

Fortunately the latter had been stuffed not with goose down but with solid slabs of foam rubber. I lifted the end of the bed and hurled it through the crazy-angled process by which it became a sofa. I threw the naked foam cushions in place, for they too had been flayed of their nubby fabric. Then I dropped myself onto them. I was suffering from what by my count was the third beating of the morning.

I remembered Peggy and looked for her just at the moment she emerged from the bathroom. For an insane instant I couldn't recall whether I had myself ever got to use the toilet.

"Peggy! You saved my skin, coming in just when you did."

She was habitually modest about her actual accomplishments. "Forget it, Russ. You'd do the same for me."

"I hope I would, Peg."

She was about to sit down in the suede chair when I warned her of the oil spot. I felt more bitter about that than even my three beatings: it could never be used again; oil does not evaporate, and the blotterlike hide would hold it in suspension forever.

Rather than share my couch, Peggy went to the kitchenette and got the high wooden stool I kept there and from which I ate my mean repasts—Fritos, cottage cheese, and raisins—off the counter. She clattered. The police had even emptied the compartmented plastic container in which I maintained my cutlery, and hurled my Melamine dishes and cups to the floor as well.

She brought her stool before the couch and climbed onto it. She was unaware that with her shoes on the top rung, I could see the underside of her substantial thighs.

"The first thing," she said, "is to explain how I happened to turn up here, uh, you know, unchaperoned and all."

"That's right. That's pretty fresh, Peggy." I winked raffishly.

"I shadowed you." Her smirk was vain. "Yes I did, Russ, all the way. Soon's I got across Twenty-third, I turned right around and came back and followed you, maintaining a distance of half a block. When you stopped to look in the pet-store window, I stepped into the line waiting at the bus stop. Whenever I saw a girl with a nice figure coming toward you, I got ready to hide behind a pole or in a doorway, because I *knew* you'd turn and watch her hips when she had passed."

I felt myself blush, though why I should be embarrassed by that, I do not know. It was normal. It was harmless. But nobody likes to be observed in secret.

"You obviously had a purpose in this, Peg. I mean, surely you didn't follow merely to catch me in some degrading and/or humiliating situation." Knowing I could do so with impunity, I made a joke: "I might have been on my way to a golden shower."

"I don't care what brand of soap you take baths with, sir!" she said indignantly, making, as she often did, a commercial interpretation of a term alien to her. "*I* got to thinking: a strange and sinister series of events has been taking place, Russ, and you are somehow involved, without your own volition, like the hub of a wheel which is forced to turn around and around yet doesn't travel anywhere itself, even if the car reaches California."

"What poetic understatement," said I. Yet I was not unimpressed by the image; as long ago as when I taught freshman composition I had become aware that no sensibility is so banal as never to have eloquent instants, though only to a Keats are they routine.

"I thought maybe if I kept an eye on you—without you knowing it, so you would act natural—I might be able to get some clue. Maybe"—she put out her hand—"now don't get mad, maybe there was something peculiar that you were doing that attracted freaks to you like jam attracts flies. Maybe—and you'll get ever madder at this, probably—maybe you did misinterpret some perfectly ordinary things. Because, you know, Russ, I never did really see with my own eyes anything out of the ordinary but a few drops of blood in the elevator, and they could have come from a cut finger. Remember that time I cut my finger and you got me a Band-Aid? You can be real nice when you want to be."

She wore the kind of expression that people assume when they want to look sweet; most children and all dogs can do this; it has no reference to *feeling* sweet, and in fact hoodwinks nobody. But suddenly I was struck by the thought that perhaps it was not intended to dupe or gull —that what one was supposed knowingly to accept was the gesture as gesture, *ars gratia artis,* and as such it had a certain gallantry.

Often enough I fashion such elaborations, arriving at an original and profound insight, only to experience a sequel in which I am proved wrong, the simply and obvious motive having been the operative one: self-aggrandizement. Peggy wanted something.

"I discovered I have a natural gift for investigative work, Russ. You must admit you never suspected I was tailing you."

"True, Peg. But let me point—"

"As you are the first to say, I've never been much of a typist. And shorthand, forget it." Here Peggy spoke with utter justice. I really did not need a secretary. I had kept her on for sentimental reasons, as one keeps an old pair of sneakers.

"And the advantage for you in a full partnership," Peggy continued, "is that you won't have to worry about coming up with my salary any more. After expenses have been met, we'll split what's left right down the middle."

I was gingerly going over my face with ten finger tips. I didn't yet have the nerve to look in a mirror. The ache in my right kidney was quiescent at the moment, but the left one, which had not been struck, throbbed in pain.

"I'll tell you, Peggy. In view of your having got me out of a sticky mess, and considering your implied threat to tell the police that you, on second thought, not having actually witnessed many of the salient events of my morning, cannot confirm my account of them, I'll—well, I'll definitely think about your suggestion. I'm not saying no, mind you. But I had almost reached the conclusion that unless business improved drastically, I'd have to go it alone, sans even a secretary."

I breathed regret. "Now that that detective has impounded the remainder of Washburn's retainer, I'm down to my original seven dollars—and this receipt, which looks far from official."

I examined the yellow rectangle of paper. On the obverse was printed the name of a business (characteristic of cacophonous New York: Nedick's, Gristede's, Bohack); "Krachlich Hardware" and its Third Avenue address. On one of the horizontal lines below was scrawled, in ball point blue, *Bug & Tar remover*, a price of ninety-nine cents, a tax of eight, and yet a total of $1.59.

Reversing it, I read what Zwingli had written with his stub of pencil: "Rec'd of T. Villanova, one cargo of slaves." It was signed, "A. Lincoln."

"That little swine!" I cried, balling the slip and hurling it across the room. "I suppose it's typical: the police have got even more corrupt since the Knapp Commission."

"You're sure right about that," said Peggy. "But these guys weren't the police, as it happens."

"What?" I howled: "Don't tell me—no, it's not possible

again. No, Peg, no. There were too many of them this time. Also, there were two black ambulance orderlies, also in uniform. And they had a stretcher with an authentic zippered body-bag."

She narrowed her eyes. "I'll tell you, Russ. I'm not saying no, mind you. I'm thinking about it."

"Oh, come on. This isn't the time for satire. You know something."

"Well, how would I know the explanation if I'm just a secretary, and only good enough to take your phone calls and type your letters, while you're the big macho, because you were raised from childhood with the idea you would become one of the people who ran things, who are always men, whereas I was given toys that kept me in my place, little muffin tins and bassinets, and do you know what I got one Christmas? A tiny sink, which came with a stain already in it and a little can of Comet and a miniature cellulose sponge, also a bottle of more stain so when you scrubbed out the original you could put more on."

The women's-lib frenzy had crested a couple of years before for everybody else in the urban areas of the nation, but Peggy lived in a pocket that caught and retained cultural runoffs. For her not only "hippie" but "beatnik" were currently usable words.

At this point I decided to try a piece of cunning. I realized that her aggressive address was based on something firmer than, say, the premenstrual unease which she might believe it fashionable to blame on the testicled sex. She could well be in possession of the key that would release me from the fell imprisonment of ignorance, which remained my worst problem.

"You've got your deal, Peggy. For that hundred-dollar bill in your purse I'll sell you a half interest in the agency, a full partnership."

She chewed her lip. "You're some sheeny, you know that?" She brightened. "O.K., so that's the sum total of the assets on hand. I'm a full partner, so half is mine. Wait a minute, half the profits *after expenses* goes to each one of us. The main outstanding debt at this time is three hundred and seventy-five dollars in delinquent wages. So I keep the hundred, and am owed, from future remittances, another two seventy-five."

"No, no, no," I cried. "If you're going to figure that way, then we split the debt, you see, and your share is half of three seventy-five." Amazingly enough, I worked this out in my head. "So you give me the hundred, and you owe an additional eighty-seven dollars and fifty cents." I made a gesture. "But, look, I want to be fair. You collect the two hundred impounded by Zwingli; I'll take my half, and you can have yours."

Peggy gave no evidence of following this argument, having begun to root in her purse when I started to speak. Now she raised her head and spoke earnestly.

"The hundred is gone. I must have lost it in the street."

I put my face in my lap.

"Aw, the heck with it, Russ. I'll tell you for free. The movies."

"Pardon?"

"They're filming a movie. They got a great big truck outside. You must of seen it when you came in, now that I think about it. Come on, Russ, you've been putting me on all day."

"No, Peggy," I said slowly, pounding one of the naked-foam cushions.

"It's called *The Reformers*. It's about this pair of detectives, one little and one heavy, you know, like Laurel 'n' Hardy, only they're not supposed to be funny, I don't think."

"Something's rotten in the state of Däne—I mean Denmark! Don't tell me Bakewell, or Jake the Wop, Big Jake, *et al.*, was some actor, playing dead?" I hurled myself erect, in a burst of pain. "That was real money that Zwingli took from me, and Knox really beat me savagely. Don't tell me *cinéma-vérité* goes that far."

Peggy was disgusted—with me. "For crying out loud, Russ, I only know what they told me when they pulled up in that movie truck. I was on my stakeout of your building, see."

"You didn't happen to spot a dog outside? A great big dog, a great Dane, in fact?"

"Never," said Peg.

"He, or rather she—it's a bitch, I gather—"

Peggy screamed.

"That's the standard English designation for a female bowwow, for heaven's sake. Ophelia—"

Peggy scrambled off the stool and raised her fists. "You try feeling me and you'll get a knuckle sandwich." She showed her teeth. "I don't have to kowtow to you any more, buster. We're partners, remember?"

"Peggy, I'm trying to bring a train of thought into a station," I said loftily. "This female canine may be a clue, the only reliable clue if so—in the sense that she cannot speak for herself and thus weave a tissue of lies, like all the other principals in this case." I took out my billfold. "Forget the movie, and take a look at this." I handed her the dog license issued by the ASPCA. "They've gone to a lot of trouble—that came from a computer, if you observe." With difficulty, owing to my bruises, contusions, and aches, I bent and picked up the volume of Ruskin and showed her the flyleaf. "The name is in at least one other book as well."

"That Villanova sure gets around," Peggy said in her lightest voice, tossing her locks.

"It's no joke, Peggy. We're dealing with professionals for whom the slightest detail is important. Take that underwear in the bathroom—"

Her nostrils arched. But I couldn't worry about her prudery at this point. "I'll wager that the labels have been carefully removed. Also from the clothes in the closet and those in the suitcase." Pursuing my theory, I went, or rather limped, to the valise, opened it, and found the black brassiere that Knox had fondled. It was a skimpy garment, made of lace netting, and at the point of each cup was a large aperture that would permit the nipple and aureole to project nakedly. I was wrong about the label. It was there: *Pierre's of Broadway.*

"Ha!" I exclaimed. "Hooker indeed. Prostitutes *never* wear this type of garb or gear."

Behind me Peggy said: "You should know."

"There'd be no point, you see. This is the food of fantasy, Peg. Frustrated housewives, unfledged maidens, even female impersonators . . ."

But Peggy did not stay in position to be scandalized. She had almost reached the bathroom in her mad dash, when I threw down the piece of erotic raiment and called her back.

"I'm afraid I have been the victim of an underworld gang again," I went on to say. "It's yet too early to determine whether they are in league with the earlier lot. If they can furnish hordes of fake policemen, they must be a formidable mob. But what do they want? Drugs? They took this place to pieces and didn't find anything. They would hardly go to all that trouble to shake me down for two hundred dollars. But maybe the cloud has lifted with this latest incursion. They must realize now that I don't have anything they want. But why do they keep putting that corpse on my premises and hauling it away?"

Suddenly Peggy's own story seemed suspect.

I asked: "If you thought they were making a movie, then why did you come in and save me from Zwingli?"

"Because I lost my head when I saw him with that gun!" Peggy cried. Then she colored and looked at the floor.

"You really *care*, don't you?" I said softly, betraying too much vanity.

"I'd do it for a dog," she replied, back in self-possession.

"Yes," I barked, back in harness myself, "that canine. I'm going down to look for him. And I'm also going to tackle that damned doorman."

"Let me do that, partner," Peggy said. "You get on the Washburn job. That's our sole hope of getting some ready cash. If you don't find anything to impress him with, make up something that will keep him on the hook for a while so we can ask another retainer. And when you get it, remember half is mine."

I did not recall having agreed to the partnership except on receipt of the hundred dollars, but I couldn't take another argument at this point, especially one involving numbers. Anyway, she was my only ally, and I needed no more adversaries.

I resisted making a show of undue affection, however, and instead went to the bathroom and, at long last, attended to my needs as quietly as I could: the door was embarrassingly thin.

When I emerged, Peggy had a finger tip between her front teeth.

"Now that I think of it, the truck maybe had *Movers* written on it, not *Movies*. Still, one of those actors in a cop's uniform outside did tell me this thing about *The Reformers*—"

"God," I said, distracting myself from thoughts of the outrageous imposture, "look at this place! I guess I'll continue to live at the office. Anyway, I don't have the money now to buy the super's good will."

"*Will* you get going?" Peggy commanded.

The next time I got my hands on any cash at all, I intended to declare our "agreement" null and void, because obtained under duress.

The doorman was not in evidence as I passed through the lobby, though the tomato sauce from his hero sandwich, along with one meatball, squashed, on which he had apparently sat, was still glazing the last cushion on the couch. I was really only too happy to turn that phase of the investigation over to Peggy, and the matter of the dog as well.

On Third Avenue I caught a cab and had to endure the abuse of the driver when I confessed that I hadn't yet thought of where I was going. He was an embittered middle-aged man with obviously dyed hair and a pair of glasses one lens of which was pulverized, yet stayed opaquely in place.

"I'll tell you this," he assured me splenetically, "I'm putting the meter on while you decide." And did so, using his wrist as if it were a wrench. And, as always with New York cabbies, took off as though in competition at Monza, en route to oblivion.

"Ah, yes," I said. "Sutton Place."

"Which is exactly where?"

I had been through this many times before, even when asking for Grand Central Station or Times Square. When I first arrived in Gotham, I assumed such questions were disingenuous. I soon learned better. To many veteran drivers Manhattan has remained a mysterious terrain throughout their careers; they orient themselves only by counting the numbered streets.

"No, strike that." I got out my poor billfold, full of the Villanova documents, but managed to find the Altman's envelope on which I had jotted down Washburn's wife's schedule. If I could read my Sanskrit, she should soon be at her yoga class, at the studio of one Chai Wallah, which Washburn had said, loosely, was in the Village. He had not however provided the precise address.

I dreaded asking the surly driver to stop at a phone booth so that I might look Wallah up in the directory, and therefore instructed him merely to deposit me on Eighth Street.

I should have known this would result only in his assailing me vocally for not furnishing a particular number. Somehow when the moment is at hand I can never realize my long-held intention to tell a New York taxi driver of the abysmal contempt in which I hold him.

"All right, all right," I said. "Let me out at the next light."

"Nothing doing," he said. "I ain't letting you dodge the issue. Whoduhyuhwannasee? I probly know the address cold."

He had gone too far in his arrogance. I decided to humble him. "It happens to be a little-known studio at which an obscure Hindu gives lessons in Yoga, a Far Eastern discipline of mind and body. *You* never even heard of Sutton Place."

His insufferably knowing eye appeared in the rear-vision mirror. "Mumser, you just lost duh bet."

He made a high-speed turn onto Fourteenth Street and roared west for several blocks without stopping once, though at best the lights were orange, then turned south and soon got involved in those Village streets which run on the bias, breaking the regular gridiron pattern of the rest of the island.

I was immediately disoriented. But the driver seemed in his element, swooping, twisting, tacking as if under sail, but sometimes merely ramming his passage through the congestion, human and vehicular, in the narrow by-ways. At last he drew up before a façade bearing the name YOGHURT CITY.

"So I rubbed your nose in it, yeah, wise guy?" he jeered. I forgot to say earlier that the metal frame was all that remained of the divider between front and back seats; the Plexiglas was gone. I could easily have leaned forward and throttled him with a mugger's forearm across the Adam's apple.

However, I instead stoically paid the fare, the rates on which it was calculated having seemingly risen another twenty percent since yesterday, and even added a lavish tip, for which I got no thanks, and in fact the door was ripped from my hands by his quick getaway. I was almost projected into the gutter. Within thirty yards he braked sharply and the door slammed shut of its own inertia.

Yoghurt City was a health-food emporium. One window was stacked with bottled vitamins, the other with bags of horse fodder, hanks of slimy kelp, and a pile of blanched nuts like tiny skulls.

Averting my eyes, I slunk to the corner, where one of the new public-phone arrangements stood: two instruments hanging on a panel exposed to the weather. Involved in a conversation, you might have your pockets picked—or, in certain areas (and this might well be one, many deviates being diet cranks as well), be quickly, deftly sodomized while making an apology for dialing a wrong number. Paranoid fantasies, perhaps, but New York is a bad place in which to offer the unguarded spine.

In the old phone booths, which were invariably carpeted with urine and vomit, the directory was always either defaced to illegibility or gone altogether. With the new type of apparatus, no book was offered. I had no combination of coins to make ten cents with which to call Information. I was not yet so desperate as to waste a quarter. Nor did I wish to ask change from either person just then adjacent on the sidewalk: an extremely obese young woman with a sweaty face and green-streaked blonde hair, and a comely, almost beautiful young boy in the beanie and blazer of a private school; because she was talking violently to herself, and he might have assumed I was but another of the pederasts no doubt familiar to him on his homeward route.

The store at the corner, an ex-tobacco shop by the fading letters on its window, was now a lair of gypsies. A mustached woman in a filthy saffron dressing gown, show-ing a pneumatic cleavage, leaned forward on her camp chair behind the glass and beckoned to me in what she believed was a lascivious gesture (a pistoned index finger plunging into a cylinder of fist).

With the next step, I saw, for the first time, the dingy doorway between the health-food shop and the gypsy den. It seemed to have been inserted there as if in a dream— I could have sworn. . . . A cardboard sign appeared behind its panel of glass: YOGA WALLAH.

I pushed in. I ascended the flight of stairs that rose directly behind the door. Winded when I reached the second floor, I was disappointed to see at the end of the hall a twin of the downstairs sign, with the difference that a red arrow was appended to this one, pointing upwards. The signs proved eventually to be quadruplets, the last one, on the fourth level, sans arrow: it was afflxed to a solid door.

I was gasping, and my bruises ached. I knocked at the door and then opened it. I looked into one large room that occupied most of the fourth story of the small build-ing. The floor had been lately refinished, varnished, and waxed. The impeccably whitewashed integrity of the walls was broken only by windows here and there: there were no decorations. Neither was any furniture in evidence. It seemed a place that had lately been made ready for a new occupant, who had not as yet moved in.

It was, I think, just as I stepped across the threshold that I was sapped. Had I not been in motion in a direction away from the source of the powerful blow, my skull might well have been sundered.

8

When I came to, another face was very close to mine: its skin was polished brown; its lips were thin yet flabby. It wore a white turban. Its breath smelled of a mélange of spices, which I was in no state to identify severally and name, though no doubt cumin, coriander, and turmeric would have been among them.

A high-tenor voice had apparently been speaking for some moments before I regained full consciousness. Its tone must be called morally hectoring.

". . . leading to wiolence, madness, and strife, and concupiscence with vimmin, you see?"

It took me a moment to understand that the pressure on my chest, which thoroughly inhibited my breathing, was due to the kneeling of this man thereupon. It was far from easy to dislodge him: he had some Oriental mastery of balance, such as is used with advantage in jujitsu, and his sharp little kneecaps were seemingly prehensile at, or in, my rib cage.

But, at last, by first feinting left with my shoulders alone, and so evoking his compensatory movement in the opposite direction—though effortlessly, and he was still lecturing me—I proceeded actually to twist my trunk leftwards rather than to the right, tricking his anticipation of equilibrium, and he was thrown.

He was not however helplessly toppled. He used the momentum to such practical effect that when his narrow buttocks met the floor they were transformed into two brown points intersected by a tense white *cache-sexe*, and his heels were joined behind his neck.

Within this singular frame his face assumed a smile that glittered in one gold tooth and a pair of jet eyes.

He continued to speak: "Pain does not exist of itself. It is but the absence of vell-being. And den one goes farther: vellbeing has no reality, because it cannot be defined except as the absence of pain. Reality, therefore, finally has no existence. The man who stands upon a bridge over a river and reaches the first level of awareness by understanding that the vater is still and that the bridge is moving, goes on to the next: the realization that there is neither bridge nor water, because there is no self."

My skull was roaring with the brutal blow it had received. I was in no condition to toy with metaphysical concepts, not even such farcical ones as I have always considered those emanating from Asiatic sources, at any rate, when they reach the West, far from the Ganges, leprosy, untouchables, chutney, etc., which give them perhaps greater substance on their own terrain.

I clasped my head and determined that at the first recession of the pounding surf between my ears I should rise and place-kick that little turbaned swine through a window. Meanwhile, I had only strength enough to promise him this treatment in a roar that was perhaps incomprehensible, for it did not seem to jar him.

At length he unraveled himself and stood up. He was a tiny person, utterly hairless, with no visible muscles or sinews; his diaper, small legs, and positively minuscule feet gave him an infantile cut of jib.

"Good heavens," said he. "Vot a naughty man you are." His grin became more intense. "But dis is the study of a lifetime, and you can have been but one hour at it. Instant serenity cannot be expected. Traveling the path of truth is to tread the edge of the razor. Before the next lesson, you must, incidentally, read the well-known volume by W. Somerset Maw-gum."

The tide flowed in behind my eyes, obscuring them for a moment, and when I looked next he had vanished, without benefit of the legendary rope. I was actually relieved to see him again, when he emerged from a door at the rear of the room, which I had not previously noticed.

He carried a book, a sheet of paper, and a ball-point pen. I had not yet managed to get to my feet. Sitting on the floor, I was as high as his navel, "that tortuosity or complicated nodosity," in the definition of Sir Thomas Browne.

The wallah handed me all three items, directing me to sign and return the paper and keep both pen and book. I examined the trio: the volume of course was a used copy of Maugham's *Razor's Edge*. The barrel of the pen was imprinted with some advertisement. The document was a contract by which I agreed not only to advance one thousand dollars for a preliminary course of instruction in the Nonreality of Existence, but also to pay $2.98 for the novel and 79¢ for the pen.

Infuriated by this swindle, I found the strength to rise.

However, I was frustrated in my intent to hurl the book at him, owing to a sporadic multiplicity of vision and also a constant sense of bonelessness in my limbs. I was able only to threaten him with a suit for assault.

"Your state of unhealthiness is much worse than one first assumed," said the little Hindu. "Indeed, it was one who found you upon the floor and brought you round. One perceived that you were in a pseudoreligious trance, but one has no respect for such rubbish. It is merely the spurious response to accumulated rage."

"It wasn't you who sapped me?" But on the instant I had begun to think that unlikely: he could scarcely fleece me of $1,003.77 if I were dead or thoroughly disabled—and believe me, that blow was intended to be lethal. "Then who did? I suppose you claim you saw nobody." Though exonerating him, I still had reason to be peevish about his manifest lack of sympathy.

"Betveen appointments one meditates in private," said he, indicating the rear door with a backward push of his little brown heel, succeeding which he exhibitionistically sank on one leg until his knee was perhaps an inch above the floor, the other ankle folded up against the small of his back. He stared at nothing interminably, and then sprang erect as if impelled by an expanding spring. I realized that no man who could do that sort of thing could be called simply a charlatan.

I told him who I was and why I had come there, adding: "I'm afraid that I'm not in the market for your course, though I must say your acrobatics are impressive to a man who has himself always been extremely inept in that area. As a boy, for example, I was never even able to perform a backward somersault."

"You are not then Mr. Frederick A. Vashburn?"

As if I needed a further confusion! It took some time to clear up this matter, for he was incapable of remaining immobile for half a minute, unless delivering one of his own lectures, and it is disconcerting to interrogate a man who incessantly transforms himself into inhuman figures— which suggests to me that the mythical Proteus may well have been an actual yogi.

But eventually I determined that, at least according to his statement, a male voice had telephoned him the afternoon before and made an appointment for the hour at which I subsequently arrived. The name given was Washburn. Hearing "Frederick A." rather than "Frederika" was understandable, given his alien ear.

"But I thought she was a regular student long since?" I asked, when each of us had got through his own account.

"Never," said he, and as if mocking my confessed boyhood inability, performed not only a backward somersault, but his began and ended in a standing position. When he landed he squinted suspiciously at me.

"Though despising all that is vordly, one is not to be considered gullible. One should like to examine your documents of identification, you see."

I groaned. "I'm afraid this will take a further explanation, Mr. Chai. My own were mysteriously replaced by those bearing another name, a name that has repeatedly appeared elsewhere in my affairs, beginning only with this morning, as it happens. Indeed, it is a sinister matter."

I withdrew my billfold and took from it my sheaf of licenses. I handed them to him wholesale, before he could twist himself into another guise.

His vision was apparently the faculty in which his physical fitness was lagging. He took one document and held it so near that it seemed impaled on his nose. At last he lowered it and said: "But dis driving permit is surely in order?" He returned it to me.

My own name had returned as magically as it had

left. The driver's license had been issued to Russel Wren. The same was true of all the other credit cards and permits. The famous dog license was not to be found at all.

In one sense I had gained an advantage: the motive for my recent bludgeoning was now obvious. But I was no nearer an understanding of why my identification had been switched with Villanova's in the first place.

The Hindu was annoyed when I voiced Frederika Washburn's name again and requested him once again to certify that she was not his regular student.

"Hell's bells," he said in a fluty liquid lisp, "it is mosth irritating! Though time does not exist, you must not persist in vasting mine."

I was still holding the contract, Maugham's novel, and the pen, which I had not been able to put down, because of the absence of furniture, nor to return to him owing to his going into a new gymnastic performance whenever I tried. It now occurred to me that I had no implement on my person with which to jot down the notes I should have begun to take long since; the details in this case were getting too profuse to commit to memory.

"I'll tell you what I'll do: I might buy your pen, but seventy-nine cents is highway robbery. It's a giveaway item, from the look of it." I read the silver legend on the blue barrel, which I had not hitherto examined that carefully: REAL ESTATE WALLAH, with an address in Yonkers. "Unless I miss my guess, it's in fact an advertising souvenir for another enterprise of your own."

Something else, in tiny printing, caught my eye: *New House or Old, It Must Be Sold.* Mere banal doggerel of the trade, or was it still another pugmark of the stealthy tiger of whom I knew so little I could not yet identify him as either hunter or prey?

I barked at the Hindu: "Teddy Villanova! What does that name mean to you?"

His response was unexpected, as I suppose that any, unless in the negative range, would have been at this point.

"A very bad man, sahib." The yogi's visage took on the appearance of a dried apricot.

"Good God! You do know him?"

As his grimace grew even more violent he lost the trappings of the cosmic sage. He virtually spat: "A damned bloody bugger."

I tend in moments of excitement to take terms literally. "A practicing sodomite?" This would tie him in with The Ganymede—but no, for an instant I had forgotten that firm was clean as the incisor of an Irish setter: except, perhaps, for the presence of that .25-caliber slug I found in the brownie.

"A scoundrel," said the yoga wallah, impatient with my question. "Blahst him. He was a bloody police constable in Goa."

My blood ebbed. "That's a world away, I'm afraid. I don't believe it likely he would have followed you to New York, unless the charge was murder. More likely it was mere smuggling."

By chance I had hit a nerve.

"You bloody sod," said the Hindu, advancing on me as if he were soon to discard his nonviolent principles. True, he was tiny. But in the hierarchy of living things the deadly cobra is a midget. I could not chance more punishment. In a word, I immediately took the leave that for some reason is called French—except in France.

So the visit to the wallah had not been fruitful except in its revelation that Donald Washburn II, like all the other principals in the case, was not to be trusted. Why had he told me that his wife was a long-time student of yoga?

Of course, it was still possible that the Hindu was pre-

I pushed myself erect. He held *The Razor's Edge* at the level of my chin and slowly opened it about halfway through its text. It was more box than book; a hollow had been cut through the depth of pages and extended to within an inch of the margins. In this depression was embedded a glassine bag full of white powder.

The detective grinned at me. "Villanova, this is the end of the line." He handcuffed me, then doffed his hat, burlesquing a congratulatory gesture. Another few strokes of a comb and he would be totally glabrous of crown. "Some chase, huh? Well, you had a good run. Know what led to your downfall? Huh?" He poked me in the ribs. "Pussy. Huh? You kept it in your pants, you might of been a free man still. Huh? Not you. Gotta keep the old sword oiled, right? You know who blew the whistle onya in the end? Huh? None of the dark meat, boy. It was the little mick from the old home town, what's her name, huh, Tumulty, one with the big jugs?"

I couldn't come up with anything better than: "It's not *my* home town."

He himself was obviously a native. "It's some shithole," he said with satisfaction. The crowd that had gathered to watch my shaming continued to increase in size.

"What's next?" I asked. "I'm not going through my story again until I'm safely inside a police station. Do we take the cab?"

He seemed to find pleasure in standing there chatting on the sidewalk with a manacled suspect, enjoying a bit of notoriety with the public before returning to the necessary obscurity of his profession. In fact, like a Catskill comedian in his first Broadway play, he soon began to perform directly to the audience without regard for the other members of the cast. He hooked his gold badge into the moire of his hatband, and opened his topcoat and, with one fist to his hip, draped it back so that the gun he carried there could collect interest.

He said loudly: "Yeah, it's a real interesting job sometimes. It's not for everybody, that's for sure. Takes somebody with a whole lot of guts, but like I say, you get the satisfaction of knowing you got what it takes."

While making this unsolicited statement he cast beseeching glances at the assembled civilians, who I now noticed were all men, all husky young men in fact, wearing knitted short-sleeved shirts and blue jeans. They were a very fit-looking crew and suggested a team of athletes in mufti; to be precise, a mufti that was uniform.

As the detective started to list his Ten Most Interesting Cases, answering a question he had asked himself, I was in the ridiculous situation of having to plead to be hauled off to jail.

Several of the athletes, really remarkably robust chaps with the pronounced musculature of weight lifters, now came up to us. This approach caused the detective to blush and stare demurely at his feet, as if he were a wallflower about to be asked to dance with a series of popular lettermen.

One of them nodded kindly to me and said: "We're here, Brother."

The largest, a fair-haired youth with a porcine face that bore several cleat-scars, addressed the detective: "Let this man go."

The officer displayed wonderment. "Come again?"

"We constitute GAT, the Gay Assault Team," said the large blond. "We won't tolerate police harassment." The little detective disappeared from my view as a ring of these worthies closed around him.

When the circle of men opened a moment later, the large chap who had spoken to me emerged with a key and unlocked my handcuffs. "Get going, Brother, and good luck."

I was in an embarrassing situation. I didn't want to hurt anybody's feelings, on the one hand; but though I have nothing against those professing to the persuasion of Marcel Proust, André Gide, and perhaps even the great Will himself, I am not myself an invert, having, when it comes to intimacies, an absolute addiction to the *other* and not the *same*.

"Thanks," said I, "but I'm afraid I'm not gay, and in fact I'm not being charged with that."

"Oh, that's quite O.K.," he said. "We protect *any* man from the police. Men have always been the niggers of society, but we will no longer accept that state of affairs." He showed me a clenched fist, large as a rib roast. His biceps were stout as my thighs.

The other joined him. One had the detective's gun, from which he emptied the cartridges plinkingly on the pavement. Another, his knitted shirt straining across the massive pectorals, had taken away the officer's leather-covered blackjack, a cruel-looking implement with a looped strap.

"A thing in a thong," said he, evoking a smile or two from the others: no doubt it was some coterie term.

I was suddenly frightened to be dwarfed by these powerful men. "Uh," I asked my particular benefactor, "I don't have to *do* anything in return . . .? I mean, no offense, but . . ."

The question caused a general guffaw.

"No offense," said this ruddy-faced husky, "but we don't find you personally very attractive. You're simply another victim of injustice, guilty of no crime but being born male."

Strangely enough, I *was* somewhat offended, such is the nature of human vanity, while being relieved as well;

and also my lifelong attitude towards athletes having been one of mixed contempt and envy, of which for their part they returned only the former, I now had a new reason to question my virility.

So I accepted their gift of liberty. Before I left the area, however, I made my little speech to the detective, who sat stunned on the hood of the cab, to which he had been lifted, like a doll, by the members of GAT, though going otherwise unharmed by them.

"I'm not Teddy Villanova, and I'm no heroin smuggler, and I'm not going to let myself be framed. If you are so inept or so corrupt as to arrest me, you can't be trusted to prove my innocence, so I'm going to do it myself. When I've got the proof, I'll let you know. What's your name?"

"Hus," he answered dully.

Wishing me Godspeed, the stalwarts of the Gay Assault Team gave assurance they would maintain their guard for ten minutes, before returning Hus's weapons. Projected, as it were, on the clenched fists of their en masse salute, I went hastily away. I rounded several corners and passed through a number of short streets and long alleys. I had got lost every time I came to the Village to seek a restaurant, though having beforehand plotted my route on a map of Manhattan. Now, having no sense of where it was that I had begun my flight, I feared I might, Vico-like, be on a course of mere recirculation. Though utterly innocent, I was a wanted criminal and "at large"— never before had I appreciated the force of that term. Claimed by agoraphobia, I slowed my pace and peered longingly into crepuscular cellarways and the cozy crannies amidst bales of rubbish awaiting the Sanitation Department, service in which was the hereditary career in the Tumulty family: a garbage can was handed down through the generations like a coronet.

Nor, at that point, would I have said Peggy had a

kind heart. That bitch. I could not even reach her by phone: mine, at the apartment, had been disconnected, if you recall. At length I found myself on a residential street of brownstones and ginkgo trees, the kind of handsome block still to be encountered in Manhattan but only by accident, and always polluted somewhere by an abandoned car, stripped to the axles, or a mountain of trash. This one was no exception: a third of the way in from the corner the sidewalk was clogged, from wrought-iron fence to gutter, with enough furniture to outfit an apartment of some magnitude.

In another culture this would have constituted the trappings of some poor devil dispossessed of his home, he himself perhaps languishing in debtors' prison, like Dickens' father in Marshalsea, but here it probably indicated no more than the discard of spring house cleaning: the slip covers were slightly soiled.

I considered hiring a U-Haul and fetching these furnishings back to my own abode, my suede chair having been ruined forever; and also, I don't know whether you have noticed that once the covers have been removed from foam cushions they can never be restored precisely to their original state: the seams are always a bit awry; and if adjusted here, they go off slightly there. It is a maddening pursuit. Wearied by this reflection, I sank into one of the discarded overstuffed chairs on the sidewalk. It proved to be a Barca-Lounger, and when I put pressure against the back it moved towards the horizontal, the base rising to support my calves.

Now that I had stopped running, my head began to remember its hurts. I closed my eyes. . . .

When I returned to consciousness the sun had fallen beyond even the low roofs of that part of the city. I looked for the time on my wrist, but it seemed that someone had snaked away my watch while I slept. . . . No, I had twisted into such a position that in the confusion of awakening I took my right arm for my left. My watch still encircled the latter. So, as a panicky search established, was everything else in place. It was almost six o'clock.

My mouth tasted as if I had licked the verdigris off a half-dozen pennies. For two hours I must have been the helpless cynosure of passersby, yet I had gone utterly unmolested, in a city in which persons were regularly mugged in the well-policed high-rent *quartiers* and held captive in the lobbies of grand-luxe hotels while bandits blew open the safe-deposit boxes. The truth I drew from this was that effrontery provided its own protection.

I eased my brittle limbs from the chair, erected myself, and walked towards the corner, which seemed much farther away than before I had fallen asleep. Whoever had passed me when I was dormant, I saw not a soul now. I suspected that the entire block, chosen because it was handsome, had been condemned for demolition and cleared of tenants, but that the ill wind of the recession had blown some good by chilling the architectural sadists and freezing their project.

Despite my resolve, just prior to falling asleep, to work from now on according to plan, when I arrived at the corner and was forced, by the traffic light there, to halt and thus to consider whether to cross the street or turn and proceed in the direction permitted by law for the next half minute, unless a turning car intervened, I was absolutely devoid of volition.

However, there was a nearby public phone, again in one of those chest-high alcoves, and having stared at it in lieu of thinking about a possible destination, I suddenly remembered that ten years ago, which was to say last evening, I had made a dinner date with a girl—for seven P.M. this day. Now I have mentioned often enough that I had possessed but seven dollars at the outset. I had spent almost three in taxiing to Yoghurt City. I had little hope of getting more by the hour for dining.

Having fed me a sequence of meals from her own kitchen, the young lady could with some justice expect me eventually to pick up a check. Rather vulgarly, I had used that very term, to which she replied: "You've already done that!"

"Huh?"

"Picked up a Czech!" Her name was Natalie Novotny.

It is a mistake to believe that every stewardess is but a superannuated cheerleader—for that matter, it may be wrong as well to assume that all cheerleaders are happy cretins, or that all cretins are blissful, life being as various as it is. Natalie was actually a person of some complexity, and contrary to the impression that might have been given by this first example of her dialogue, seldom stopped her sentences with a point of exclamation. Indeed she was inclined to melancholia, especially on her immediate return from a flight to Rome and back, which she characterized as a shuttle between the two most degenerate cities in the world. I took this judgment seriously until I subsequently heard her make the same on flights to and from any European metropolis, and came to suspect that she simply disliked every large center of Western civilization.

Despite her pun, it was really *she* who had picked *me* up, darting in front of me on upper Second Avenue to seize a cab for which I had waited twenty minutes in the rain at clamorous rush hour. Having done that, however, she invited me to share it, which I did with an odd mixture of emotions, which soon however coalesced into the positive when she said she would of course pay the entire fare. She was also very blonde.

Well, here it was, only an hour before I was to collect Natalie at her apartment in the far East Seventies, and not only was I yet without funds, I had also put in the worst day of my life.

This being an emergency, I put a quarter in the telephone and dialed Natalie's number. She answered quickly and in a bright voice that did not necessarily reflect her mood, which might well be Dostoevskian if the caller proved an intimate, whereas in the case of a wrong number she might chat merrily for some minutes.

"Natalie, I find myself in an uncomfortable situation—"

"Russel? You're alive, thank God." Her tone suggested she was not joking. Yet she had had no means of knowing about the horrors of my day. I kept Peggy in innocence of the names and local habitations of my female friends, requesting them, if they phoned my office and got her, to give a pseudonym, and describing her as an advanced case of emotional imbalance, with homicidal tendencies. I never found one who would not play along; not, I think, from fright but rather from the natural attraction my girls invariably had for conspiracy: I suspect they thought Peggy and I were lovers, if not man and wife.

"I don't know about that," I said, with a snigger of self-pity. "I've been put through the paces today. I don't know that I'm in a condition to go to dinner." I corrected that: "To go *out* to dinner."

Natalie was breathing with a noise that came over the instrument like applause from a stadium. "Russel!" she screamed. "I can hardly hear you!"

Natalie Novotny was not given to inordinate displays of emotion. I imagine her placidity was all to the good with the potential hysterics on any aircraft, if it left something wanting at intimate junctures in her private life. It may be ungallant of me to reveal that when making love she often seemed asleep.

Therefore I was struck now by her manifest anxiety. "Just a moment," I shouted. "Let me check this equipment." Surely enough, the mouthpiece of the telephone was masked with a squashed blob of pink bubble gum, no doubt the prank of one of New York's unlovable urchins. Fortunately, this had dried sufficiently so that it could be prized off with a fingernail.

I resumed: "Now then—"

"I might have gone off to Hamburg with the conviction that you were lying dead in some alley or floating face down and bloated in the East River."

"I don't understand these fears," said I. "It's true I had several close calls today, but only one, really, that could have had the kind of issue you refer to. And you couldn't possibly have known of that, unless you are a student of the yoga wallah, which is unlikely in view of your oft-stated distaste for anything to do with Asia, including the Indonesian *rijsttafel* that is a specialty of restaurants in Amsterdam, one of the many cities you dislike."

"What was I to think?" asked Natalie. "You have been missing all night."

"Just a moment. The night is not yet upon us. It's just after six o'clock."

"In the morning," said she.

"The sun is falling through the western sky."

"The sun is climbing through the eastern sky!"

"It is the twelfth," said I, raising my Timex and looking at the little calendar window. "It definitely is . . . *the thirteenth*."

"Yes it is," cried Natalie. "And unless this is a joke, which if so reveals a new facet of your character, and unless something terrible has happened to you, which you haven't specified, your sense of time is deranged, probably as the result of narcotics. Don't expect a lecture, Russel. I simply never want to hear from you again."

Good gravy, it wasn't possible that I had slept in the discarded Barca-Lounger, on the sidewalk, for fourteen hours, I told myself at this point in the usual instant it takes for such reflections which when written, as here, exceed a dozen words—one basic reason why literature should never be confused with life. I was also simultaneously eying the street, on which I was alone and had been since arising, and trying to reorient myself with the new understanding that my internal compass had been reversed since I awakened. And in fact, just behind me was indeed the gypsy den and, a little farther along, Yoghurt City, with the wallah's windows above, everything internal of course quite dark now.

In addition I was struggling against an impulse to swoon. However, all this consumed nothing in elapsed time, and I was able to forestall Natalie's obviously imminent withdrawal of her electronic presence, but only just.

"I have an explanation for all this, believe me," I cried. "That is, an explanation for my failure to appear last night, not an explanation for—"

"Oh, Russel, why bother? Obviously you are playing a devious game. When you were two hours late I called your home phone and got a female who said it was the number for a Teddy Villanova."

At that instant I felt a hard, muzzlelike object press against my spine and heard a rough clearing of throat behind me.

9

My immediate reaction was not one of thought. I dropped my right elbow and whirled about, violently thrusting the weapon aside, indeed dashing it to the sidewalk, where it smashed with a crash of glash—I mean glass, for it had been a bottle. My assailant was a purple-faced wino, as usual of indeterminate age.

He grinned through teeth like grains of parti-colored Indian corn and said: "It was empty. Buy me a refill, else I'll abuse you in a stentorian voice, embarrassing you in front of your fellow man, and you'll have no recourse, because I fear nothing. That's my weapon, and it's no secret."

"You have, in other words, opted out of the social contract," said I.

"Shamelessness is the answer," said this contemporary Diogenes. "All the ills of the world can be traced to the foolish desire to look well in the eyes of others."

"Very clever, but *circumspice*: there are no others present at this moment. Haha!"

"Hoho!" said he. "There's *me*. I'm audience enough."

He was a psychologist of keen penetration, and I told him as much.

"But praise is as useless to me as punishment!" he replied with asperity.

"And death is the same as life. Therefore, why don't you die?"

"*Because it's the same!*" He had topped me again and, furthermore, plagiaristically, one of the pre-Socratics having said that a good 2500 years before, which I should have remembered.

I gave him all my change, some quarters and pennies, and decided against mentioning that the liquor stores were not yet open, because I dreaded another expression of his scorn, which I realized, in our relative positions, would be evoked by any utterance of mine.

I lifted the telephone, which I had dropped, and expected to hear that Natalie had hung up. But she was still there. In fact, she was speaking and, I suspected, had been doing so throughout, in ignorance of my absence from the line.

"Excuse me," I said. "My story is too complicated to give here in toto. The woman you talked with was my secretary, no doubt. We are looking for a man, something of a scoundrel I should say, whose name is Villanova, who would seem at the center of my problem. No doubt she was employing a ruse, by saying he was I, hoping to smoke him out, if the telephone call was bogus, as so many things have been lately—"

During the last several words Natalie had been talking under my as usual carefully constructed clauses, and now, with a burst of volume, claimed the wire: ". . . tell you, I *know* Teddy Villanova!"

At this the phone went lifeless. No doubt the recorded warning that my time was waning had come while I talked with the derelict-philosopher. I looked around for him now, because he had got all my change. He had vanished.

I searched for a cab but saw none on the deserted streets. I began to walk, with my now corrected sense of direction, towards the northeast. Eventually, after quite a hike, I reached Union Square. I had still not seen a taxi. I was about to descend into the Avernus of subways under that complex crossroads, but halted for a moment to look at a gaudy car that glided to a stop at one of the nearby traffic lights. It was a Cadillac and painted in mother-of-pearl. The black man behind the wheel wore a white sombrero, a red jacket, and a tiger-striped tie. I could have sworn he was Calvin, the Negro who, dressed as a drab detective, had been at my apartment that afternoon in the company of Zwingli & Knox. On the passenger's side sat a girl so blonde as to make Natalie Novotny swarthy by contrast. She seemed in fact an albino.

My attention thus focused on the Cadillac, I was not aware that a panel truck had pulled noiselessly up to the curb, and I failed to notice, until they were upon me, the two men who had deboarded.

"Whadduhyuh gonna do with a fag who won't get outa town when he's tole tuh?" asked one of them, to the other, though both stared fixedly into my face. I recognized them, terribly, as the first team of fake cops, those who had savaged me in my office. They now wore green deliveryman's uniforms.

"You listen here," I said, backing away but extending my finger in reproach. "You didn't tell me anything of the kind. You beat me up, looked for the gun, snarled, 'Fuck this,' and carried out the body."

The one with the mustache said, with sinister geniality: "Yeah, that does sound like us. You got some memory, you know that?" He pushed his low forehead at the other. "A fag never forgets, like uh nelephant."

"Dammit, I'm not queer!"

"Who's talking about queers?" said the clean-lipped but hairy-nostriled thug. "He meant you was stoopid, a real fag."

This usage was a new one on me. "Oh, I beg your pardon. Well, look, is it necessary to brutalize me again? I don't have anything you could possibly want. Also, I am just on my way at last to discover the identity of

Teddy Villanova—" I bit my tongue, remembering too late my previous belief that they were Teddy's own boys.

"Who's he?" asked Mustache. "Some other stoopid fag?"

"You don't know the name?"

The other said in disgust: "Don't try and kiss our ass by mentioning all the guineas you know."

I found their apparent ignorance as incredible as the recognition of the name by every other principal, though none of the latter thus far had known the owner of it by sight. If Natalie did, I must talk with her without delay.

"If Villanova's not your friend, then he's your enemy," I said. "Believe me, he's in this up to his ears. You fellows help me find out his identity, and you can have the heroin or whatever it is you are after, no questions asked. He's undoubtedly the guy who killed, or had killed, your pal Bakewell or Big Jake—if he was your pal, that is. Anyway, you carried out his body. Of course, you did refer to it as garbage."

I had not forgotten that Hus took the heroin from me; I was playing for time. "And while we're on the subject of who's who, is that black man over there with you or against you?"

The pimpmobile, sitting patiently all this while at the red light, which as usual was interminable when so little traffic occupied the streets, had only just begun to move. Neither Calvin (if it was he) nor the blonde was looking in our direction. They were eating something from a shared bag.

Clean-lip squinted briefly over his shoulder. "I never could tell one eight ball from another."

Mustache did not bother to look. He said: "We never noo that stiff. We was just supposed to get rid of it."

"Mind telling me why you were dressed as policemen?"

"Guards at the club."

Ah, the Wyandotte Club. A lot of money must have

gone across their gambling tables. And indeed nowadays most supermarkets, even delicatessens, employed private guards, who wore blue uniforms, very coplike to the glance, for their deterrent effect—on respectable customers; shoplifters brazenly ignored them.

Clean-lip said: "We was supposed to tell you to get outa town. Maybe we forgot. We wanted to get the stiff outathere, see. Gives a bad name. Mr. DiGennaro don't like that, around a building where you got a nice club where judges and councilmen can come and relax, ya know, and union officials, ya know. Somebody cawls on the phome, says some schmuck got blown away on the third fla, so Mr. DiGennaro says, 'I don't like that, in a building where you got a nice club and all, Tony and Pete you go up and get ridduh the garbage, roll it in that old rug in the closet, ya know, and take it to the dump, becawss we don't want to have it around, ya know?'"

Beyond him the meretricious Cadillac had made a left turn from Fourth Avenue onto Fourteenth Street and was crawling very slowly in our direction, the occupants seemingly absorbed in what they ate from the bag.

Mustache took up the explanation: "He says to get the piece too, and trow it away, becawss we don't want no firearms inna building where you got a nice club, and anyway Mr. D.'s on a committee for gun control with senators and all."

"Then," I cried, "you Wyandotte folks had nothing to do with the murder?"

"That's a laugh," said Clean-lip. "*You* did it, din't you? That's what Mr. D. says, 'Tell that fag to get the fuck outa the building and outa the town, if he ain't got no more sense than blow away somebody for some personal matter right inna building for Jesus' sake.'"

Mustache said: "See, you want somebody blown away,

you *cawl* somebody. You don't do it yourself for Christ almighty sake. You don't wanna shit where you eat."

They had turned so earnest and, I thought, sympathetic, that I began rather to like them. Still Zwingli had said my "Bakewell" was actually Big Jake Cozzo, a dealer in heroin.

"Cozzo!" I said, intending to follow it with, "Does that name mean anything to you?"

But Clean-lip roared, "Who you calling a prick?" and buried his fist into my poor belly. Alas, I was not fluent in Neapolitan obscenities. I folded onto the pavement.

However, in the sequel this was one blow I did not regret taking, for at that moment the pimpmobile had come collateral with us, at the end of a slow diagonal roll to the wrong side of the street, and, from my writhe on the concrete, I saw Calvin, for it was surely he, put out the window a brown hand, holding a white paper bag, the bottom of which was translucent with grease, and call: "You motherfuckers want some ribs?"

Then, cackling, he dropped the bag into the street, ducked from sight, and the girl leaned across him with flour-blanched face and platinum hair and a double-barreled shotgun, and in quick series, thunder and lightning, blew my companions out of their shoes, across the sidewalk, and through the show window of a discount lingerie shop, the shattered glass from which sprayed me like the exhaust from a snow blower.

Calvin's white hat and brown face came back into view, and the car accelerated through the left turn into Broadway and vanished.

I can report that, at least for me, being a witness to violent death has a stupefying effect. I rose in an orderly manner, the stomach pain having been, as it were, expunged by the shots; adjusted my clothing, even buttoning the corduroy jacket which had swung free since the day I bought it; and strolled across the empty street on an angle that brought me to the boarded-up façade of the former S. Klein department store, on which were pasted the usual advertising posters such a surface collects: karate lessons, rock concerts, and pornographic entertainments.

This montage is my only memory of the several-miled walk to East Seventy-third Street near York Avenue, where I entered the lobby of Natalie's high-rise apartment building and asked the seated doorman, over his copy of *El Diario*, to announce my arrival to her on the intercom.

He sighed, crackled his paper, and asked: "You nang?"

"Villanova," said I, with the same utter lack of mental volition that had characterized my long comatose hike from downtown.

He was a plump young fellow, wearing horn-rimmed glasses, and his temples looked as though he might be bald before his time: Spanish genes still ran in his veins after centuries. Making this observation, I was conscious of emerging from my coma.

"Excuse me. I meant Wren."

"Chess," said he, rising with a grin that all but reached his earlobes. "*My* nang is Villanova." With a thumb smudged from the newsprint he gestured at the little black Bakelite plate, with its white legend, over the breast pocket of his beige uniform.

I read it aloud, using the Spanish pronunciation: "T. Villanueve."

"Chess," said the doorman.

"The *T*. means what?

"Tomás."

"Well," said I, "as long as I'm here anyway, I might as well go up." As I went towards the elevators I heard him say "Meester Ran" into the mouthpiece on his panel full of buttons.

Natalie took forever to answer my buzz at her door, and when she appeared she was transformed into another person, a stocky little soul in a floor-length housecoat of lime green. It was in fact her roommate, the girl hitherto referred to as often having been ejected by her unpredictable boy friend in the wee hours, from whose abode she returned home, thereby displacing me in the lone bedroom on East Seventy-third.

This girl's name was Alice Ellish. She had the kind of snub-nose rubber-ball face that could be called cute by those with a taste for such physiognomy. Having met her on several occasions in the course of three weeks (having luckily missed her on many more), I had not yet succeeded in evoking from her any sign of recognition at any outset, though Natalie was ever wont to say hastily, with significant emphasis: "You remember *Russel Wren.*"

I was in no mood now to aspire to the stars. I gave my name to her obviously newly risen face—before she applied make-up it was difficult to see that she had any eyes at all, though with liner and shadow and mascara in place, one saw little else, and with a certain forward brush and frizz of hair she could resemble a lemur. Of course, with my taste for tall blondes I am admittedly a bigot towards a person of Alice's breed.

Alice's coiffure was covered now with an off-white bandanna. My name, which she had also heard from Tomás Villanueve, meant as little to her as my person.

I added: "Natalie's friend?" But I knew of old that she was impenetrable on any subject but her love-hate relationship with him to whom she habitually referred as "my guy," a term that in my always questing ear I heard as the title of a Chinese dish, all the more when it was conjoined with the diminutive of his Christian name, Douglas, and delivered, with her perhaps impedimented disregard for the purity of consonants, as *Mai gai Duck*.

"Natalie?" said she, pursing her lips quizzically as if she had no better memory of her long-time roommate.

Suddenly I was overcome by a sense of the absurdity of my standing there begging for an acknowledgment of my peculiar existence from this little person, I who had but lately witnessed a double murder of the most extravagant kind, in fact a legendary mobster-slaying that might well take its place in the annals of gangster Grand Guignol with the St. Valentine's Day Massacre and the rubbing out of Crazy Joe Gallo in Umberto's Clam House; all it needed to be cherished by posterity was a memorable name.

"Out of my way," I said, and without waiting for Alice to comply, I proceeded through the door Bakewell-style, which is to say, with the intent of forcing her retreat with the threat of my superior bulk. She did not back up, however, and she was a sturdy little thing, plump but firm. Her breasts and belly felt, to the instantly sensitized façade of my own thorax and loins, as if they were nude under the housecoat. And immediately I thought better of her than I had thus far in our remote acquaintanceship.

I took one discreet step backward; however, this did not seem to alter our relative positions; she was quite as fleshly evident as before.

Nor was Alice repulsive of countenance, for that matter. I realized at this point that I had never looked carefully at her in the expectation of being pleased, owing to her habit of appearing at inconvenient times.

So much for that. I still expected, as I looked down, to see an expression of her negative regard for me.

Instead she was grinning, and she said: "Hi."

It was I who separated us—because, if you must know, I was made uneasy by the sense that my briefs had begun to throttle my left thigh, being no Leopold Bloom, who, if I remember correctly, was atypical in dressing right.

I cleared my throat of the obstruction that had simultaneously formed there, and said, apologetically: "I really must see Natalie on a matter of grave import."

Alice marched into the living room directly beyond the door, a long, narrow, rectangular enclosure fitted out like a travel agent's foyer, with very low furniture in neutral colors, hairy throw rugs tanned from the hide of the imaginary animal called the shag, and framed posters. These last, however, though routine in the peripheral vision, were unorthodox when studied closely, showing Red Square during a review of earth-to-air missiles, an obese harlot leering from a window in the red-light district of Copenhagen, and a dog voiding his water on the Left Bank while, across the Seine, Notre Dame serenely flew its ancient buttresses.

Alice's hands found her hips in the undifferentiated tube of loose housecoat, and she whirled about on tiny bare feet, displaying flashes of dirty soles.

"Whee!" she exhaled. "Peace again. Nat's gone to Hamburg."

I suppose it didn't make much difference, Natalie's Teddy Villanova having turned out to be his own Tomás Villanueve, and her absence did free me from having to explain where I had spent the night, the absolutely true account of which would, to a rational ear, necessarily sound cock-and-bull.

Alice flounced away, made a right turn at the windows, and entered the kitchen.

I asked: "You wouldn't have a cup of coffee?" And followed.

The girls had a pitiful garden in the corner: a moribund wandering Jew in a hanging basket, a fern gone to burnt umber, and a sterile avocado supported on four toothpicks above a tumbler full of lacteal water.

As I entered the kitchen Alice Ellish seemed in the act of swallowing a whole lemon. But when she removed it from her mouth I saw it was but a half.

"Without this," she said, screwing up her face in answer to the astringency, "I could sit on the can an hour without results." Then she stared as if seeing me for the first time. "You're a new one, aren't you?" She threw the lemon half in the sink and gave me a handshake moist with citrus and saliva. "I'm Alice Ellish, Natalie's roommate, but don't jump to conclusions. It's due to the high rents in this part of town. I always feel I have to say that nowadays, or some people would think you were going down on one another just because you share a place to live."

She made a high-pitched sound, almost a whinny, backing away from me in a partial crouch until her bottom met the refrigerator, at which contact she said: "Oh?" and turned in wonder as if goosed by someone who had stolen up silently.

I lifted the teakettle from the stove and sloshed its contents: an inch of water and, from the sound, also several particles of loosened corrosion and sediment— which is why I don't like those whistlers, with their strait spouts.

"O.K.?" I asked, already turning the faucet at the sink nearby and, first, rinsing my sticky hand. I ran enough for six cups, but having done so, upended the kettle and let the water gloop out between instants of gasping aspiration. When it was all gone, the particles still rasped within on the shaking of the vessel.

Despite my bizarre experiences of late, I was still capable of attending to such minutiae, the recognition of which was somehow comforting. The petty features of my character survived unchanged. I wondered whether the same was true of the bedrock into which my moral pilings were sunk, for when I put the kettle on the stove and ignited a burner, Alice raised the skirt of her housecoat and examined its interior surface in the area of her rump, her trunk twisting as she looked back and down; in front, her pelvis was but scarcely covered, and again I was stimulated in my own.

"I think," she said, "I got some jam on my tussy."

One word is often enough to quench my ardor, even though I have proceeded a lot farther towards an expense of spirit in a waste of shame than I had now. I turned to the above-sink cabinet in which, if memory served, Natalie kept her bag of Bokar. I found the coffee makings, including the six-cup Melitta and an envelope of No. 4 filters.

With still-torsioned torso, bare buttock against the stainless-steel lip of the sink, Alice blackened the green of her gathered housecoat-skirt with running water, then blanched it with a two-fisted squeeze so violent as to roll the front hem of the garment above her navel. She was not altogether nude below the waist; she wore the ultimate in minimalist underwear: a pale-green vee whose scope was restricted to the mons veneris, on her so hearty a hillock as to pass muster in a locker room that would have permitted the wearing of pastel jockstraps. From the superior points of this triangular convexity, strings climbed the steep of her belly and, cutting their own grooves through the soft investments of her hips, vanished over those summits. The entire device seemed under the extreme tension of an aimed slingshot.

I decided to await the water whistle elsewhere and left the kitchen, again passing the wretched little garden in the corner just outside its door, where a coleus displayed, with a stalk like the neck of a plucked starling, its last leaf of desiccated purple patent leather. I drifted along to a waist-high bookcase and bent to peruse the spines of the volumes therein, though I knew them of old. As I have said, Natalie's was not the feeble spirit a bigot might expect to find beneath a stewardess' cap (or, with her airline, a cloche). I imagine she was the rare bird who had persisted throughout one entire year in purchasing at the checkout counter of a supermarket the weekly pamphlets which, assembled in a stout three-ring binder, constituted the one-volume *Cyclopaedia of Universal Knowledge.*

She also possessed, as surely a family heirloom, ten small uniform volumes, bound in red, comprising the *World's Hundred Best Short Stories* (neither 99 nor 101), with contributions by such eminent scribblers as Count Leo Tolstoy, Honoré de Balzac, and Octavus Roy Cohen. She owned *An Essay on the Military Police and Institutions of the British Empire,* on the flyleaf of which some wag had written "Miss Jane Austen"; a novel entitled *How Grete Was Plagued by Her Husband Hans*; a cookbook—

Alice, who had padded up silently on unshod feet, said: "Reading about eating a steak is nothing like eating a steak: it's just words."

"Have you ever had to eat your words?" I asked. "In the beginning was the Word, and man is what man eats." This was one way to fill the time till the water boiled. "In German, that's a pun: *man isst was man ist.*"

"Are you trying to tell me something?" asked Alice

Ellish, bumping me with her hip. "I never fool around with Nat's guys. You should be aware of that. I ought to warn you, so you don't get your hopes up."

"What have I done to deserve that admonition?"

Alice turned away and said to the floor: "I don't want to embarrass you, but you were staring at my crotch." She brought back a pout with her face and, furthermore, pigeoned her feet.

"What do you expect if you pull up your housecoat?"

"I wasn't even thinking about that. Sex means little to me."

"I didn't *stare*. I glanced. You would do the same, I'm sure, if I suddenly lowered my trousers."

"Don't try it!" said Alice, making a chimpanzee-face to bite her upper lip. "Nothing turns me off more than the bulging pouch of a pair of Jockey shorts, which might be quite yellowed by the look of the rest of you."

Defensively I rubbed the stubble on my face. She had me on the run. "Look, I've had an unfortunate day, an unconscious night, and an unprecedented morning. I'll drink a cup of coffee and be on my way." I started for the kitchen, but halted, turned, and said: "I don't wear Jockey shorts."

"I hope you wear something," said Alice. "But don't tell me what, please. Let's drop the subject. You're obsessed with crotches in an infantile way. Everybody's got one, for God's sake. Grow up! When I was a kid, the boy next door always wanted to see my underpants, and once he stole a dirty pair and—"

A piercing sound came from the kitchen. "Be that as it may," I said, "the whistle's blowing."

"Don't expect me to," Alice disagreeably replied. "And believe me, Nat's going to hear about the way you've behaved behind her back. This is not the first time, either. I wonder if there's something about me—?" Her wince was speculative. "I always seem to drive her guys off the deep end, when all I do is pass the time of day."

The steam was protesting ever more maniacally against its constraint. Dashing to relieve it, I seemed nevertheless to be in frozen motion: forever wilt thou run and it whistle. I had time in this interegnum to wonder whether Natalie's "guys" were invisible concomitants of mine or had been but my predecessors.

Eventually I reached the stove, extinguished the source of the kettle's agony, applied the filter to the Melitta's funnel, poured coffee from the bag by estimate of eye, then inundated it with steaming water.

There was Alice again, at my elbow, or rather, as Spenser might say, "with child of" my elbow; the joint of my forearm seemed captive of a soft envelopment. I did not investigate this, being occupied principally with the matter of why I had neglected to grind the beans before submitting them to an infusion, which was, in their state of integrity, futile: clear water dripped through the paper cone into the underlying Pyrex vessel.

Wryly raising my hands to my hips, in the well-known gesture of dismay, I inadvertently did something to Alice with my right arm. Though hardly what she claimed.

She threw herself back against the refrigerator, as if hurled there, perhaps no more than two paces in the narrow kitchen, and said: "You struck me!"

I looked around with no great concern, seeing which deficient reaction she slowly slid down the face of the appliance, with knees that could not have parted company to such an angle had she not raised the skirt of the housecoat to accommodate them, and her strained green groin was once again on display.

As if this were not enough, she sounded a loud *click*, obviously made with her tongue behind her teeth, and outrageously proceeded, eyes closing, chin falling towards sternum, to pretend her neck had been broken.

Though this act would have rendered me hysterical if it had been performed at any time preceding the Union Square Slaughter, I was unmoved by it now, and turned back to my soaked but whole coffee beans and wondered whether they might be ground though wet.

It took no lengthy period for Alice to rise from the dead behind my back and brazenly make another effort to discomfit me.

"I don't want to hurt your feelings," she said, "but there's a bottle of Scope in the bathroom."

Her *ad hominem* approach was again effective. Though facing the stove and three feet from her, I spoke through my hand. "I told you I had a bad day and night. If you'll please let me just drink a cup of coffee, I'll leave."

"I've got it, at last!" Alice cried. "Wow, am I dense. Sorry. I thought you were one of the straights."

I spun to see her leave the kitchen. I abandoned the stove and caught up to her at the turn into the short hall that led to bedroom and bath.

"I'm not gay!"

She shrugged. "Why should I care? The day is gone in which it was considered a psychological disorder."

"I am aware of that. I simply didn't want you to get an erroneous idea. I have too frequently been the victim of misidentifications lately. Anyway, on several occasions during the last few weeks, I've had to leave the bedroom when you came home in the middle of the night from seeing your guy Doug. Don't you remember that?"

"*Duck*, not Doug."

"Oh."

"A nickname I gave him," said Alice Ellish. "His real name's Al Orange. Get it?"

She looked severe for a moment and then her little front teeth chattered in a violent giggle. She was a childish sort, and ordinarily I should not have found that character attractive, but suddenly I was conscious of being alone in a narrow passage with a ripe young woman who was virtually naked under one layer of cloth—and I also remembered my bad breath. I did not uncontrollably desire her, yet neither did I wish, in my current crisis of identity, to be recognized as but a case of morning mouth —for she evidently did not recall me from those wee-hour crossings of paths.

I said, turning my face to the wall, in fact addressing a novelty bullfight poster on which the name of Domin-guín's opponent had been replaced by ALICE ELLISH, "I don't think I'll bother about the coffee. I'll just run along. I need a shower more, and a shave, and . . ." My voice dwindled to a murmur, reflecting my gradual but utter loss of any purpose but not to breathe upon her.

"You know," she said, putting her protuberant delta against my right thigh and a cupped hand on the high inside surface of the left, "you're real shy. I like that. You're even blushing. Gosh."

When I tried to return the favor, however, she managed by twists and writhings to elude any embrace that could be called firm, and she seemed at least as strong as I, at least in my current disadvantage.

Still clutching me, she however protested: "You're Nat's guy. I told you I don't fool around."

"Then what are you doing?" I complained. "And are we in the right place?"

She released me at once and strutted huffily into the living room, where she plumped down onto one of the sofa units. Her little mouth, made smaller by defiance, suddenly yawned and produced a wail: "You come right over here!"

"If you have further use for me," I replied, *de haut en bas*, "it must take place in the bedroom."

I took the two paces to the entrance to the bath and the one more that brought me to an open doorway through which I should have stepped had not it been filled with the large naked figure of a man in the process of exiting.

"Wren! Good gravy." This was pronounced with a certain startled pleasure, but no embarrassment whatever.

"Donald Washburn the Second!" I cried. For it was indeed my client.

10

Behind me Alice Ellish came running and howling. "I tried everything I could think of!"

Ignoring her, Washburn lightly observed: "You're quite the Javert, old boy. I must say I'm impressed."

Alice grumbled: "I don't know what else I could have done," and plodded with slapping footfalls into the bathroom behind me.

I decided not to reduce my stock with Washburn by admitting I had found him by chance. Again, my reaction might seem odd: there he was, having emerged in the nude from my girl friend's bedroom—but she had flown off to Hamburg and anyway she shared that chamber with Alice Ellish.

The really important concern was that Washburn represented my only source of income in weeks—and his advance had been confiscated before I could use a penny of it. Washburn was also my only hope of getting more funds: I had been a fugitive from justice, remember, following my liberation from Hus.

"No," I assured him gravely, "I'm no turncoat." I went on: "In fact, being involved in other phases of the investigation, I haven't yet laid eyes on Mrs. Washburn herself."

His voice now betrayed a faint tone of impatience. "But *she* is the investigation, old chum."

I made a long blink for effect. "It might interest you to hear that the yoga wallah denies any acquaintance with her name, that furthermore he is a dealer in narcotics."

Washburn threw up his hands. "Oh, come off it, Wren. Who doesn't sniff a little coke these days? I mean, we're all under the pressure of a sense of futility. No wars worth fighting, no causes that are not obviously farcical."

"I'm speaking about heroin."

"Oh," sighed Washburn again, wrinkling his tan brow. "Surely you have got your geography wrong? I believe that comes from Marseilles, like *Allons enfants de la patrie*, and not, like duck, from Bombay."

I decided his purpose in speaking so exotically was to be incomprehensible to Alice, if she were listening from the bathroom. Therefore I said in an undertone, with the knowledge that "Bombay duck" was not fowl but rather a piscine dish: "This whole affair is quite fishy. I've hit a few snags while trolling the gong-tormented sea. Do you suppose you might chum the water again?"

"You're being obscure, Wren. Is that deliberate?" Washburn wore a thin, insinuating smile.

I thrust my thumb towards the entrance to the bathroom, to which Alice had not closed the door; neither

, as his head went into the garment. A mummy-
ss of his face appeared in sharp relief and then
d as it ascended behind the fabric. Only after the
it of his blond thatch had emerged from the neck-
lid he endeavor to find an accommodation for his
m in the wad of stuff bunched between shoulder cap
eck. For a moment the gun in his right hand, re-
ing the bill of a Canada goose, pointed at his own
ally emerging skull.

looked very like that weapon of mine, which I
dropped down the dumbwaiter shaft.

s eyes emerged, the whites slightly pinked from
ordeal. He spoke through the fabric, which gave
minor lisp.

ake this piztol, Wren. You're reinztated. You could
jumped me then." His mouth was at last free. "Sorry
bted you, but probity is rare these days."

lid as he asked. It seemed even more like my own
matic when I held it: the clip was missing. He had
tened me with an unloaded gun.

Did you know this was empty?" I asked.

wouldn't carry any other kind," said he, at last
thly white-swathed from clavicles to navel. "Else
e'd be corpses all over town. My dander is easily
sed, I'm afraid. Only yesterday I put my shoe through
screen. I could not endure the haircut of the popin-
n the six o'clock news."

Getting back to Natalie Novotny," said I.

e chose next to find and put on his shirt. In a like
lition I should first have clothed my groin. Whether
was an exhibitionist or merely an opportunist in prac-
matters—the shirt being at the top of the heap—
uld not decide. Of course he *had* appeared at my
e with an open fly.

Which seems," he said, "to be another of those names

was she making a sound inside, though she seemed the
kind who would be brazenly noisy about private matters.
Reassuming my *sotto voce*, I said: "I'm afraid I was
robbed of your retainer."

Washburn's smile turned definitely chilly. "Suddenly,"
said he, "I see something very chicane in your manner.
Blackmail, is that it? All right, Wren, I'll pay it." He
started into the bedroom, halted, glared over his shoulder,
and raised one finger. "But my respect for you has taken
a precipitous plunge."

"Just a minute—" But I was talking to the unresponsive
groove between the muscle masses of his back, which
swooped to a narrow waist below which his naked hams
were in the tense movement of departure.

I tried again. "You misinterpret me, Mr. Washburn."

He had squatted to go, like a savage grubbing for
roots, through a heap of clothing on the floor beside
one of the single beds. On the bed itself, that nearer the
doorway, Natalie's, was a varicolored taffy-twist of inter-
mixed spread, blanket, and sheet. Whereas Alice's place
of repose, under the window, was made up tight as a
trampoline. The Venetian louvers were shut, but a
bright sun against their translucent plastic furnished adequate light for these observations. No, the tangled bed-
clothes were not of sufficient mass to conceal a person,
as for an instant I found myself suspecting. Natalie was
indeed gone, whatever she had done before leaving.

"You are a thoroughgoing scoundrel," said Washburn,
defining his jacket from the bundle.

It might be wondered why my efforts to disabuse him
were so feeble. If he believed me a blackmailer, he
would hardly continue to employ me as investigator. But
he would undoubtedly pay me more for the new role
than he had for the old, and I might do worse at this
juncture than accept money for refraining from what I

anyway had no intention of doing. However, if he had used that bed while it was also occupied by Natalie, taking payment from him would, I suppose, be tantamount to declaring myself, at least to myself, as a pimp and thus confirming the accusation, erroneous at the time made, of Knox.

The foregoing deliberations were rendered nugatory by Washburn's coming up from his naked squat with a fistful of gun, not money.

"You won't get a sou from me, you contemptible cur." Despite his arch terminology, he appeared authentically grim; and though I was genuinely frightened, I replied in kind, subtly trying to curry his favor by emulation of idiom.

"I'm not the knave you take me for, sir. The day is not more pure than the depth of my heart!"

But he was not mollified by the famous line, and it is a general pity that Racine, like Goethe, is notoriously banal when Englished. He proceeded to put the gun's muzzle so close to my own that I could smell the fluid with which its riflings had been sluiced and, judging from the strength of the sweet reek, recently.

I had to do better. I called out for Alice. In response I heard the sudden torrent of the shower.

"Once she has toweled," I assured Washburn, "she can vouch for me."

"For all I know," said he, "you and these tarts may be in cahoots. How *did* you track me here, Wren?" He lowered the pistol to my breastbone, permitting me a clear view of his complete grisly grin. "I didn't accept your story for a moment. Naked and unarmed, I was only playing for time."

"Are you speaking literally or simply in pique?" I asked, wondering whether to be seriously dumfounded. "*Prostitutes?*"

"You squalid little coxcomb,"
ing hands with the gun and off

"Please," I cried, recoiling. "I'r
I'm here on purpose, but have
dent. May I possibly ask you t
assure you I am unarmed. I did
tually—I admit this freely—I h
do much about the assignment f
I have been blocked at every
road."

"You're whimpering incoherent
man for this dangerous game."

"No, I'm not, Mr. Washburn,'
enunciate more precisely. "I am
realize that. I'm no more blackm
well, pander."

He stared at me for a long mon
you, Wren," he said at last. "My
trust my fellow man."

"So, in spite of all, is mine," I ave

He grimaced. "How's that? . . .
might take the liberty, your style
to inspire faith. It tends to sugge
not downright humdrum appearan
ample, at the moment you look as
in a doss house. Yet you often spr
Thomas Babington Macaulay."

He should talk. But the balance
that I could rebuke him.

"A moment ago," I said, "you
Having been acquainted with the
weeks, at least with Miss Novotny—'

He bent and swooshed up a T-s
clothing. He continued to clutch tl
hand, aiming it, in turn, at floor

you ask me to identify, none of which I have ever heard before. Don't tell me you have intercepted another letter purportedly written by me?" He sat down on the edge of the bed, groped on the floor, and came up with a sock. He determined that it was inside out and plunged his fist within. "I've given the first one some thought. It's undoubtedly the work of Freddie. She's a sinister woman."

"But the chronology is wrong, I'm afraid. I received that letter *before* you appeared at my office, which visit you anyway kept secret from her—am I right? Surely you would not have told her you were hiring me?"

"Surely," said Washburn, reversing his sock. "But she may have acquired certain telepathic powers under the tutelage of that depraved little Hindu, whom you so negligently dismiss as an influence. He seems to have gulled you."

I was still holding the gun. Whether or not it was my own, I might have use for it if things continued to go as they had for almost twenty-four hours.

"Do you mind if I borrow this?"

Washburn squinted as if he had forgotten the weapon. "Oh . . . well, it will leave me at a hideous disadvantage. . . . I don't know whether," he went on, swooping the sock up his calf, "I have made it evident that I am passionately in love with Freddie. My consorting with a prostitute is precisely an expression of that love."

He finally put on his second sock. He took his trousers from the floor and rose to step into them. I now saw why he had not begun to dress, as I should have, by donning drawers: he wore none.

"Bear with me," said he. "I do have a point. To put it starkly, I suspect I have a social disease." He zippered gravely, as it were making an event of the passage of each tiny metal tooth through the fastener. Still shoeless, he fetched up his jacket and entered it. He took from a pocket a tangle of necktie, which was of such fine thread that when he had hurled it around his throat and mixed its elements in a fat knot, soon slimmed by half, its silken skin was sleek. Neither had his shirt and trousers suffered from their low exile.

"I have reason to believe," he went on, "that I contracted this disease, if such it be, from my wife. The inconvenient thing is that we have a doctor in common, and he is a family friend as well. I don't dare consult him, you see. I don't suppose you know some obscure sawbones to whom I could go anonymously or failing that, under a *nom de guerre*? The sort of practitioner who, until the change of law, one slunk for the abortion of an underage girl, gaining admittance to his sordid abattoir by password, paying in cash of course."

"I could take you to my Aesculapius, old Doc Humphries, curved pipe under a walrus mustache, dusty rubber plants in his waiting room and historic copies of *The American Mercury* and other extinct periodicals." The physician named was but a product of my fancy. My purpose was to exceed Washburn in clichéd imagery; a bit of baseness, no doubt, but his narcissism had begun to smart.

"Uh-huh," Washburn muttered indifferently, scanning the floor, surely for his shoes; he was otherwise completely outfitted—in the same ensemble in which he had appeared at my office. I wondered whether it would be politic to ask if he had been home at all; he seemed the sort who would necessarily practice a diurnal change of attire. "Now where in the world?"

At length he descended to his knees and lowered his head to the floor. In this situation, peering beneath the bed, he resumed the subject of his possible distemper. "The symptoms are these: my teeth feel furry even after a brisk brushing; the Achilles' tendon in my left ankle aches; a tic comes and goes in my left eye; and I have a visible pulse in my forearm. I put it to you whether these details, inconsequential enough when isolated each from each, in sum don't give the classic picture of syphilis."

"If so, an ancient case," said I, strolling between the beds in support of his search. "The kind that in the days of primitive medical practice brought down Oscar Wilde, among others. Quite rare now, I should say, in this era when one is exhorted everywhere to have his annual physical checkup: I even saw it the other day in skywriting over New Jersey. I remember thinking: why should *they* care? And furthermore, who are *they* so intimately to address ten million strangers?"

I came upon a windfall: Washburn's shoes. They were neatly aligned under the edge of Alice Ellish's bed, which furthermore, I only then recognized, was, though blanketed neatly, without a spread. I picked up the footgear, a hand inserted to the wrist in each upper, and jocularly "walked" them in the air before me as I went back to a position above his crouch. It was quite possible for him inordinately to have hurled his garments across Natalie's bed before plunging to extinguish his lust in her roommate. It was indeed probable—which accounted for my lightening of spirits—though shameless of course, if Natalie were coincidentally recumbent.

Meanwhile, he had reclaimed the arm with which he had penetrated the under-bed space, bringing back a sleeve coated with hairy dust to the shoulder and a fist from which he had subtracted all but two fingers as he elevated it in demonstration: these pinched, at the crotch-piece, an undergarment that would seemingly be, from its size and immateriality of substance, feminine. Why this discovery should necessarily have served as petard to hoist to kingdom come my lovely theory, only just completed to the last jot and tittle, is perhaps a matter for the psychopathologist. For they could easily have been Alice's rather than Natalie's. Not having a panty fetish (though I might well acquire one if underwear continued to appear inexplicably in this case), I could not anyway have associated them with any particular owner after close inspection—unless, which was improbable, they were vulgarly embroidered with initials or nickname, like those available among the multitude of offerings in the catalogue of Pierre's of Broadway, which nevertheless operated out of a box number in Los Angeles.

At any rate, I did not make an attempt to examine the wispy briefs depending from Washburn's forefinger and thumb. Losing utterly the self-possession which until that moment surely deserved to be called heroic, I dropped the shoes and struck him on the jaw just as that prominence of bone was, in his ascent to the floor, level with my abdomen. He was hurled first to a seat of heels; then he toppled forward, putting brow to ground, like a Muslim at sunset.

He stayed in that situation for a moment, offering me his nape, and then slowly raised his head.

"I seem to have irked you," said he. "Believe me, it was not by design. I'll try to be more careful in future, but my difficulty is the basic one of having no idea of what will trip your hair trigger. Why retrieving my athletic supporter from the floor has earned me a punch, I have no clue. Or was it a retroactive response to my having doubted your good faith a moment ago? I thought I had apologized for that?"

His lack of anything resembling resentment evoked my contrition.

"These sudden accesses of paranoia frighten me," I said, fingering my temples and sinking to a seat on the end of the bed.

"Poor devil," Washburn said with compassion. He

erected himself and probed his front teeth with his thumb. "No damage," he announced cheerfully.

"Let me explain something," said I, "now that I have broken the ice but not, fortunately, your teeth. I believe you disregarded my early attempts to say that a girl, an airline stewardess named Natalie Novotny, has, at least for the the last three weeks, lived in this apartment and occupied this bed. She is slender. She is very blonde. I have never had reason to believe she was a prostitute. I have on several occasions accompanied her to the curb outside, she in uniform, and seen her picked up by the limousine sent around by the airline to collect their crews."

Washburn worked his lower jaw while the remainder of his face stayed static, as one does when secretly tonguing, say, a poppy seed lodged between one's teeth.

"This inquiry seems frivolous," he said suddenly and left the room, in stockinged feet: his shoes were where I had dropped them. I plucked them up, thumb against the inner wall of one upper, third and fourth fingers in the other, index over the junction. Try this; and if the shoes are as heavy as those I so carried, an excruciating cramp will soon claim your wrist. I seemed to chase Washburn down the hall though to catch him was not my especial motive.

During the short dash to the living room I realized, as I should have done when lifting them for the first time, even though their weight was then distributed by both hands, that Washburn had never worn these shoes unless in some jolly masquerade as a clown, his own modest hoof being obviously no better than a size larger than my own nine and a half, if that; while these brogans must have run, or tramped, to a good fourteen. They were also of a rugged, even brutal, model unlikely to have been favored by my chic client, being higher-topped than the fashionable jodhpur boot; and from the beginning of their vertical rise onwards, the lace holes gave way to stout hooks as broad as the nail of my little finger. They were gravel-grained and, I suspected from their weight, metal-toed. They suggested the professional footgear of an outsized construction worker.

As I debouched precipitately from the hallway, I saw that Washburn stood before the modular sofa, addressing someone seated thereupon, someone so large that my client, between him and my eye and much nearer me, failed to obscure him in any degree.

This someone was Bakewell, or—but I haven't the patience here to go through that roster of aliases again. There he was, breathing cavernously, a huge hand twitching on the enormous kneecap that terminated a gigantic thigh.

His massive feet wore only white socks. Obviously it was his shoes I carried: that actually occurred to me, such are the vagaries of consciousness, before I received the shock of finding him alive after having thrice discovered him apparently dead. When I did feel that tremor, I dropped the heavy shoes. A short moment later, the tenant underneath replied with a series of enraged blows on his ceiling that suggested he kept ready a bludgeon for that exclusive purpose.

"See," disgustedly growled Bakewell to Washburn. "We should of scratched that little punk in the first place."

Though particularly cryptic, as had been virtually everything I had yet heard in this case, like all else its general significance seemed not to my advantage.

▐▐

"See," Bakewell further growled, "you deal with this type dumbness, you're always getting problems you never noo you had, so you can't work out no plans to deal with them before they hap-*per*—" He hooked a huge thumb into his upper gums.

It was the first time I had heard him speak since he had burst into my office and begun the case, and once again his dentures had slipped. This detail assured my faculties that they were not working for a man in a dream.

"I hope you won't think this an impertinent question," I said, "but why aren't you dead?"

Bakewell merely sneered in response, but Washburn said to him: "We've nothing to lose now by clueing him in."

"I don't like to tell nothing to a schmuck," replied the great big man.

Washburn shrugged, and heel-and-toed a soft circle in his socks on the shag rug, a wool-to-wool effect that for some reason caused the rims of my ears to tingle as if with a charge of static electricity.

After two such revolutions he stopped to face me. "You may not find this flattering. But then I shouldn't suppose you suffer anyway from an undue burden of *amour-propre*, given your seedy calling."

"Just a moment," I cried. "True, my own practice may at the moment be down-at-heel in a commercial or venal sense. But my profession *qua* vocation is good as any. I believe your own is criminal, for example. You are at least a skein in a complex web of crime, involving addictive drugs, such as that consignment presented me by Mr. Chai, who is neither a wallah of tea, which for your information is what his pseudonym means in Urdu, nor of yoga, nor for that matter"—I touched the ball-point pen in my pocket—"of real estate in Yonkers of all places. . . . Not to mention mass murder, if the term can be applied to the simultaneous slaughter of two gangsters on Union Square at about a quarter after six this morning." I breathed. "In fact, I'll go so far as to say that you, yourself, are Teddy Villanova."

Bakewell slapped both knees and threw his oxhead forward, uttering a bellow that caused the travel posters to vibrate on the wall above, and across the room, the wandering Jew to swing violently in its basket.

Washburn joined him in mirth. "Wren," said he, "I suppose we can lose nothing now by revealing that there is no such person as Villanova. He does not exist. He was pure invention."

I dropped myself into a nearby chair that was constructed in the form of half an egg and mounted on a wire crisscross that looked too frail to bear a body, and more or less was, quaking when one moved. I had avoided it in the past; I should have done so now.

"Oh, no you don't," I said. "Hus, the real detective, confirmed the reality of Teddy Villanova."

"Hus is *our* man," said Washburn.

"A corrupt cop?"

"Merely a counterfeit."

"Wait a moment." I sandpapered my hands on my beard of twenty-odd hours. "The two Italians, who incidentally were guards at the Wyandotte Club, the Italo-American association in my office building, and were, I gather from what turned out to be, in effect, a deathbed statement, named Pete and Tony, did not actually pose as policemen, but merely wore the navy-blue coplike uniforms of their private calling."

I now rubbed my hands together and felt the sand they had carried from my cheeks—no, that couldn't be right: I examined its sparkle and saw it was rather glass dust, from the pulverized show window through which Pete and Tony had been scatter-gunned.

"Zwingli and Knox were the fakes!" I nevertheless said with ardor, brushing my hands on my legs. "Hus had a gold badge."

"Well of course he had a badge!" Washburn assured me. "What kind of imposture goes without the furniture of disguise? And you have got it precisely reversed, Hus being the fraud, whereas Zwingli and Knox are authentic detectives. They have in fact gained widespread notoriety as a crack team of the Narcotics Squad and recently contracted with Ziggy Zimmerman, the well-known producer-director, to make a film of their exploits."

"Do you mean to tell me—just a moment: but what does that make the black—no, first you must admit that those names are impossible."

"I shall do nothing of the kind," Washburn said self-righteously. "They are precise, they are genuine. Hence the projected title, *The Reformers*, for their picture."

"Are you a detective, as well?"

His risibilities were once again provoked. "My dear fellow, I'm an avid filmgoer, and keenly follow the gossip columns."

I persisted: "I'm sure it was the black officer, Calvin— you must admit that that name, in conjunction with—"

"Harry Zwingli and Carl Knox. 'Calvin,' however is a first name. Calvin Peachtree. Coincidences are rife, Wren. I don't know why you jib at them, good gravy."

"Forget the names for a moment," I cried. "I'm sure it

was Calvin whom I saw on Union Square, in a Cadillac, both meretriciously adorned, the car in mother-of-pearl, he in white sombrero and scarlet jacket, accompanied by a murderous female albino, who thereupon discharged a double-barreled shotgun into Pete and Tony, projecting them through a show window behind which, displayed in various attitudes, were a number of half-mannequins— that is, literally topless, their figures terminating at the waist—clad in either panty hose or panties alone, or a combination of those garments."

Washburn pointed a derisive nose at me. "Wren, are you a deviate of some sort? I catch a whiff of underwear addiction—then I remember too your recent inordinate demonstration on my recovering my own supporter from under the bed."

"Frankly," said I, stung, "I don't know why you'd wear that in the first place, nor even less, in the second, why it was where you found it."

"It is my regular practice," said he, "to do my yoga every morning." That was the extent of his explanation in this regard; it far from sufficed, but he was correct in his implication that there were matters of higher import at hand.

"Calvin Peachtree," he went on to say, "if it was indeed he you saw, and not some mere hallucination conjured up by bigotry, may be a rogue cop."

"You will at any rate admit that the assignment for which you hired me was totally spurious. There is no Frederika Washburn, and she has no illicit lover; in fact, you are unmarried. You are involved in the heroin traffic, your confederates being the so-called Chai Wallah, the large gentleman seated on the modular sofa, and the bogus detective named Hus. But Zwingli, Knox, and Calvin are real Protestants; I mean, policemen, whatever rascal-ity the black man moonlights at, and for that matter

Zwingli admitted to me he was himself a heroin user; Knox alone seems clean, perhaps even standard, being the routine sadist of law enforcement. . . .

"That leaves, let me see, the Wyandotte group, who are your rivals and enemies, and the Gay Assault Team, or was their timely appearance a mere coincidence? And what of the gesturing gypsy and the Diogenes of muscatel—can they pass muster?"

Washburn touched his temples. "Please, Wren, please! Never have I encountered such a mélange of truths, whole, half, quarter, and misapprehensions in the same variety and profusion.'

"I gather, then," I said, "that you intend to disabuse me without delay."

"I don't know that I should," said Washburn. He seized an egg chair for himself; his was colored lapis lazuli, mine being pomegranate. "To remove the sense of wonder is often tantamount to emasculation. However, if you insist . . ." He deposited his hams with the usual insouciant grace. "I was a sickly child, braces on my teeth, lenses on my nose, undersized yet ungainly, never nimble. My mother was overprotective and my father austere—"

"Is your early history germane to this affair?" I asked. "I don't mean to be unsympathetic in regard to your deprived boyhood, but for two days I've been incessantly savaged, mocked, and swindled spiritually and, in Zwingli's case, financially. I'm wanted by the police—no, that's not right if Hus was the *fake* cop. But why, if he wanted the heroin, did he not simply go to the yoga wallah himself, Mr. Chai being one of your mob, or is he? Oh, yes, I see: he had to use me as intermediary, should he, Hus, be under surveillance by the real detectives, Zwingli and Knox."

On the printed page this is an interruption of Washburn's *apologia pro vita sua*; in life it was not: he had continued in a solipsist fashion to bring himself, in narrative, to the age of puberty or at any rate the age when it claimed *him*, rather later than for what the English call the Man on the Clapham Omnibus, being coincident with his leaving preparatory school at eighteen, on which birthday he assertedly discovered for the first time a sparse growth of hair in his armpits and on his privy parts.

"Washburn, desist!" I cried.

From the sofa Bakewell said to me: "If you don't shut up, I'm gonna peel your skull like a peanut and I'm gonna grind your brains into peanut butter and put a gob onna window sill for the birds to peck."

To Washburn, who had in fact not halted his narration, he said, with a geniality of which I should not have believed him capable, "Just go on, Donnie. I heard this a hundred times and I could hear it a hundred more. You got a way with words."

I knew a certain jealousy, Zwingli having made me the same praise—I hoped, in spite of all, not altogether in a disingenuous effort to gain my confidence.

But in view of Bakewell's threat, I had no option but to listen. However, because Washburn had continued to speak relentlessly throughout, when next I heard him he had, *grâce à Dieu*, gained his early twenties in reminiscence, leaving me only with an obligation to suffer another decade, judging from his apparent age currently, which give or take a year must resemble my own.

". . . than in the observance," he was saying, smiling cavalierly at an imaginary auditor in the middle distance, i.e., neither Bakewell nor I, "and I'm afraid that for a decade thereafter the only scents I detected were those of a succession of red herrings. Nevertheless, in my obsession I followed where they led: Chittagong, Chiswick, Churubusco, and Churchill County in Nevada; Pa-

dua, Pittsburg, and Piltdown, in East Sussex, which in
itself suggests the fraudulent, the remains of the Lower
Pleistocene humanoid found there having been identified
—just as I arrived in the area in 1952—as the skull of a
much later man superimposed on the jaw of a modern
ape. Incidentally, the perpetrator of that hoax has never
been uncovered."

"Forgive me," I begged Bakewell, and to Washburn I
said: "In nineteen fifty-two I was nine years old."

He had stopped to ponder, staring into the palm of
his hand—a term not redundant here, owing to the
presence, in the miserable window-garden, of a stunted
miniature palm tree, and in fact it was towards this
arboreal entity that he peered next.

However, he addressed me: "Well then, you could have
served no purpose at the time. There was, however, a
child who came into play at one point, or perhaps a
midget."

"My implication was that surely you, as well, are at the
most in your early thirties."

His eyebrows sought his crown. "How flattering. Good
gravy. Fifty-odd summers have I seen."

"You can't mean that."

"I assure you I do." He saluted; for some reason, like
a Household Guard, finger tips at an imaginary bearskin.
"But now if you'll permit me to continue my account
of the quest for the Sforza figurine."

I was giddy. "The which?"

"I refer of course to Ludovico Sforza."

"He's the leader of the Wyandotte mob?"

Washburn leered at Bakewell, who guffawed, then
growled: "He ain't just a little punk: he's a dumb little
puh—" As usual his teeth slipped on the approach to the
voiceless velar.

I tried to recover: "Certainly I am aware of the Renais-

sance prince of the same name, but what would a
fifteenth-century Milanese have to do with heroin traffic
in New York in nineteen seventy-six?"

"*Rien du tout*," said Washburn. "Ludovico, surnamed
Il Moro owing to his swarthy complexion, usurped the
rule of Milan from his nephew Giangaleazzo *circa* fourteen
eighty. In fourteen ninety-nine, after he had broken an
alliance with the French, he lost the duchy to them, was
taken prisoner, and as such died in France. He was married to Beatrice d'Este, et cetera, et cetera. While all
this is of interest to the historian, it is not to the point
here. What *is* germane is his patronage of Leonardo da
Vinci." Washburn halted here to insult me: "No doubt
you have dined on his scallopine, in Thompson Street."

I rose above that, yet spoke levelly: "The Sforza figurine
is a work of art? . . . A product of the hand of Leonardo.
Priceless. Unknown to the catalogues, yet the subject of
the rumors of three hundred years. Glimpsed, or alleged
to have been, throughout the centuries; yet never verified
by witnesses whose reliability went unquestioned."

"You're gaining ground," said Washburn. "True, it has
been considered legendary. But in fact I have seen it. I
have held it. *I have owned it.* IT IS REAL."

His intensity, I thought, partook of the synthetic, but
I played along. "The representation of a wood nymph. A
naiad, or perhaps a Muse."

"Not so," said he. "No, it is actually a group, two
figures in conjunction: one a man of some years, hirsute of
head and face; the other a hairless stripling. . . . We're men
of the world: the former is performing an aberrant act
on the latter. I expect it is a representation of Zeus and
Ganymede."

At this point Bakewell gave vent to a hurricane of
laughter that by contrast made zephyrs of his former

sounds of amusement. "Them old guineas was real fruits!" he thundered.

"No," Washburn told him, "I doubt that Ludovico il Moro was gay, Gus, though there is reason to believe that the same could not be said of Leonardo. Moreover, in classical times, where these myths find their origins, the sexual sensibility was very different from ours—"

"Ganymede Press," I said. "Could it be, despite that sucrose story—which may be another hoax, ruse, or feint —they do after all have more up their sleeves than pots and pans?"

"Is working one's way through that mixed metaphor worth while?" groaned Washburn. "But aren't you referring to those pornographic publishers in your office building?"

"*Gott sei dank!*" I said. "You have just confirmed an assumption of mine, which has been ridiculed by everyone else. . . . They pretend to be distributors of housewares."

"Naturally, with my interest in the figurine, I was struck by the name on the lobby directory-board." He made a peevish smile. "But, to correct your sense of the situation, very few people know of the statuette. We have left many a false spoor. . . . Gus and I have been a team since he served as my batman in the Second German War."

The reference pleased Bakewell, who felt his upper plate and then lowered his thumb to point at his hogshead chest. "Thirty-year man. Went in in sixteen to ride through Chihuahua with Black Jack. Heinies later gassed me in the Argonne. I never breathed right since. I also picked up a dose from the Madamazel from Armenteers." He fell into a smiling reverie.

"We both," said Washburn, "left the colors in nineteen forty-six."

I looked now at Bakewell with a new eye. If he had gone into the army in 1916, stayed thirty years, and spent the next three decades as Washburn's partner in crime, he must currently be almost eighty years of age. To the naïve eye he would appear rather to be in the early fifties that were instead Washburn's own situation. They were an extraordinarily well-preserved team.

"We remained in Europe," said Washburn, "where for some years we were occupied in commercial ventures having to do with the disposal of war matériel."

"A euphemism for black-marketing, I suspect. But I trust you will soon tell me how I happen to find myself embroiled in the Villanova Affair, which now, according to you, turns out to be misnamed as well."

"It is not oxymoronic to say that your role has been massively petty," Washburn asseverated, "yet essential, because the same could be said of a shoelace. As it happened, as I have already suggested by choosing Chiswick and particularizing Piltdown as among my ports of call—unlike you, I do not resort to idle wordplay—the British Isles figured prominently in a certain phase of my quest. There was reason to suspect that the Sforza figurine, during most of the decade of the nineteen sixties, was in the possession of a depraved duke." This memory was obviously bitter; Washburn glared and spat on the fricatives. "A rheumy-eyed old party, who wore lip rouge and hennaed his hair, reeked of sandalwood. An extremely distasteful encounter when we finally tracked him to earth on his estate in Hertfordshire. He possessed what was surely one of the world's most extensive collections of indecent literature and pictorial art, all of the sodomist persuasion, I might add. I expect he was almost ninety at the time, yet had his daily birching at the hands of the husky young local rustics, who like all peasants were

mercenarily complaisant yet spiritually uninvolved. . . .
Are you following this, Wren?"

"Breathlessly."

"He was of course immune to public shaming, *le vice
anglais* being considered only one of the more modest
eccentricities in its native land. And as to violence, though
Gus was too old to make it peculiarly attractive to him,
his erotic pleasure was to be its recipient. However, all
speculation on how we might have got the statuette
away from him, this side of dynamiting the vault in
which he kept the gems of his collection, are irrelevant:
he did not then have, nor did he ever, the Sforza figurine."

"But why—"

"In fact, in an access of deviate lust, noble greed, and
English commercial cunning, he offered, should we come
upon it elsewhere, to buy it from us for a hundred thousand
pounds." Washburn sneered. "Its value, of course, would
be rather in the millions, if at all calculable. The very
materials from which it is molded, gold, with sapphire
eyes for the boy and ruby for the bearded ancient, nates
of chalcedony, diamond member—"

I said: "How vulgar. One would think Leonardo had
more subtle taste."

Washburn spoke solemnly. "The fantasies of geniuses
are no less inordinate than those of *l'homme moyen
sensuel.*"

"I am willing," I said, with a glance at Bakewell, who,
despite his earlier statement that he enjoyed hearing this
to him old yarn, seemed now to have fallen asleep, "I am
willing to wait for my place in the sequence. But perhaps you could tell me first why you so yearn to own the
figurine." With the large man dormant, I even took the
initiative to ask: "Do you, yourself, share the erotic orientation of the queer peer?"

"It was ours!" cried Washburn in answer to the second question. "It was stolen from us by the Turk, that circumcisèd dog."

I asked derisively: "Malignant and turbann'd?"

"Mustached and fezzed," said Washburn. "A vicious fellow." He soon shrugged, however, and cleared his fine brow. "He is no longer extant. Gus held him under water in the Sea of Marmara until the bubbles failed to rise. Alas, though, he had previously disposed of the figurine, and vengeance was our unique profit."

I shuddered. Until this moment I had not quite been able to rise above a suspicion that the entire affair, behind the screen of painted gauze, was the elaborate japery by which a pampered parasite, and his enormous retainer, sought to allay quotidian ennui.

"You mean," I asked in horror, "you murdered a human being, for no better motive than a lust for this *objet d'art*, which furthermore depicts a myth of no credit to the culture in which our own took its source? No Sisyphus, struggling, as we all must in the wretched human race, endlessly to push the boulder of our aspirations up the slope of grudging actuality; no thirsty Tantalus whose lips the water forever eludes—these are symbolically comforting. But Zeus, having his beastly pleasure with a boy—"

"Wren, like most sinners you are peculiarly offensive when you wax moralistic. For one, I have never come upon a suggestion that Ganymede found such sports in any way obnoxious."

"Getting back to the fezzed Ottomite," I said, "is not Turkey a major supplier of heroin to the West?"

"Forget about drugs," said Washburn. "We are not performing some vulgar thriller for the silver screen."

"Yet your assertion is that Zwingli and Knox *were* when they burst into my apartment, mocked and brutalized me, reduced the place to ruins, and carried out the supposedly dead body of your mountainous confederate—now, I am happy to see, sleeping on the sofa?"

Washburn replied blandly. "Gus sometimes picks up a shilling or two in bit parts."

"Just a moment. . . . Then his earlier imposture as corpse, in my office, was also in the performance of a role for *The Reformers?*"

Washburn frowned. "No, not at all." He flipped his chin as if to dispose of the need for elucidation. "I now regret having begun to explain anything. You have unwittingly completed the job for which you were chosen precisely because you were witless. A strain of sentimentality caused me to go as far as I have, with the maudlin thought that you deserved at least to know how it was that you came to destroy yourself." Washburn cleared his throat behind a genteel hand. "You do not."

He removed his hand from his lips, I thought routinely, but was soon to discover the gesture served rather as signal to someone behind me, someone who had stolen there silently and put the end of a cold, unresistant object at the juncture of my nape and cranium. I had forgotten about Alice Ellish.

"His pistol's in his pocket," said Washburn, his eyes focused above my head. "Empty. Put the clip into it. Put a cartridge into the chamber. Put the weapon in his right hand, his finger on the trigger. Put the muzzle into his ear. Squeeze his hand."

Despite my thrill of terror, I was able to say: "And you think I will suffer this passively?"

"My dear chap," Washburn said, "you'll die in any case. What's the difference to you, whether from the gun against your medulla oblongata or from the little Browning in your clothes? The difference to *us*, however, is that with the latter we can give your death the appearance of suicide. Since you cannot help yourself, why not do us a favor?"

I was so enraged by this arrogance as to reject my fright altogether. I leaped from the egg chair, crying: "Why should I do *you* a favor, you damnable, insolent, murdering swine!"

My cry awakened Bakewell, who squinted at me and then returned to sleep.

I turned to put much the same question to Alice, who, cretin that she was, had surely been gulled into service as another of Washburn's cats'-paws, under God knew what duress or what promise of reward: no one who had looked into her blank eyes could believe her consciously evil.

. . . Whether that was an accurate assessment was not to be here put to the test, for it was not Alice Ellish who held the Luger towards my abdomen, but rather Natalie Novotny.

12

Natalie was attired in a one-piece suit of high-gloss leather that closed with straps and buckles under her chin and at her ankles plunged within boots of the same material. Had I been in another state of mind, I might well have admired the ensemble of this gear with her alabaster face and golden hair.

Instead, I pursued an intent anyway, before I died, to

clear up at least one of the many mysteries subsidiary to the main.

"You were concealed in the bathroom? Quite a crowd, with Bakewell and Alice as well."

"How like you," wryly said Natalie, "to dwell on such a detail even while under a muzzle. In fact, Gus and I came in while you were with Donald in the bedroom. I've been in the kitchen, puzzling over someone's attempt to brew coffee from the whole beans."

"Ah," said I. "It's Gus and Donald, is it?"

"Isn't that appropriate if we're confederates?"

"Then you haven't been duped or gulled?"

Natalie swept a strand of fair hair from her neck, and its weight soon returned it to the position from which it had been flung: a common effect with the straight-locked, but she had used the Luger barrel, and not her finger, to work it. She was as casual with a firearm as her ally Washburn had been when dressing, with the difference that his automatic (actually mine) had been empty. I wondered whether hers was in a lethal condition; considered jumping her, whatever, having nothing to lose in view of Washburn's instructions; made an affirmative decision; advanced—and soon retired with two hands uselessly cupped at my groin, for the damage had already been done: obviously she had received training in the martial arts of the Orient, for her crotch kick was accurate and disabling.

Uniquely, however, I did not fall. I bent, I hunched, and I groaned.

"Sorry," said Natalie, "but the alternative would have been to shoot you." She seemed genuinely contrite.

Of course my voice was strained. "You . . . treacherous baggage. . . . A pox on you!"

"You're in real trouble, Russel. I don't think eighteenth-century billingsgate will answer your needs."

Washburn rose on the balls of his feet. He spoke to me in his usual tone of exclusive self-concern. "I'll take any measure to avoid witnessing bloodshed. It upsets me unduly, even when I care nothing for the victim, I suppose because I too am mortal and have a similar red fluid in my own veins. Therefore, we're leaving now."

"You"—my speech still came between gasps—"contemptible . . . jackal."

Indifferent to the epithet, he summoned Bakewell to consciousness, and easily the large man erected himself from the low modular sofa. Both left the apartment forthwith.

I was trying to snarl again at Natalie when she shushed me, the Luger against her lips.

She whispered: "They'll be back. They forgot their shoes."

The detail infuriated me further. "Why . . . are they in . . . stocking feet?"

"So they can't be—"

Bakewell flung the door open and entered with a baleful glance for me, then one of discovery for his enormous brogans, which lay where I had dropped them. Washburn came in behind the giant, went into a clothes closet next to the door, emerged with his jodhpur boots in the caliper of one hand and flicking a nasty-looking quirt in the other. Each man shod himself in silence, Bakewell being very deft, despite his sausage fingers, with the laces at the clips of his high-tops. Both departed once more, Washburn with a peevish slash of his lash at the doorjamb.

By this time I had begun to recover from the impact of Natalie's boot against my testes; it had not been the worst blow sustained in my many episodes of damage. I was more resentful of her general treachery.

"I suppose," I said, "that having lied to me for three

weeks, you will have no compunction about shooting me in cold blood. But I assure you, I shall die with a curse on my lips."

She tiptoed to the door, listened with her blondeness against the cover of the spyhole, and then returned to where I only now felt it feasible to stand fully upright.

"Don't be so melodramatic, Russel. I have no intention of shooting you."

"Will you then kindly put away your weapon?"

"Oh." She threw the Luger into the lapis-lazuli-colored chair.

I felt like a bathtub being drained. "Excuse me," I said when I could. "I seem to be struck more forcefully by salvation than I was by the menace, like a country liberated by American troops." I groped for the pomegranate egg-chair and lowered myself. "Or is this but a temporary reprieve? Judging from the feathers of the rest of your flock, you are yourself of criminal plumage."

"I am," said Natalie, "a Treasury agent. Those men who only just went out the door are members of a counter-feiting ring."

I pounded the rim of the chair with one knuckle and put another in my mouth. At length I removed both and arranged my hands as if in prayer. "No, they are inter-national art-thieves. They stole the Sforza figurine from the legendary Vatican collection of pornography; it was in turn purloined from them by the Turk. But the fezzed Ottomite had previously sold the indecent statuette to the queer peer, who however bamboozled Washburn when the latter applied to him at his stately home on Pillicock Hill—"

"That entire tale," said Natalie, "was made out of the whole cloth. There is no Sforza figurine."

"Very well," said I, groping for a purchase on the

plastic rotundity of the egg half beneath me and allowing my eyelids to fall of their own leadenness. "Let's begin again. Have you ever worked for an airline?"

"That was my cover."

"In the interests of which you actually served those toy dinners on transatlantic flights, cajoled distraught children, skillfully evaded the importunities of traveling lechers but stoically submitted to those of the flight crew when benighted in a foreign capital—"

"More or less," said Natalie. "Though I don't know whether anybody could live up to your appetite for the legendary, Russel, which applies in all areas of experience. Which is why so many people have found it possible to dupe you so easily."

"No doubt," I admitted. I rose. "I must say your leather gear, with its new suggestion of the bizarre, becomes you, Natalie. I can hardly control my urge to peel off that swarthy hide and uncover the creamy velvet of your own pelt—"

Natalie backpedaled her boots. "None of that! I have a job to do. Think of this garb as a professional uniform, Russel, and not as erotic advertisement."

"The livery of the Treasury Department?" I asked sardonically, extending a hand with the intention of plucking at the horse brass that joined the ends of her belt over her navel.

But her resistance was not capricious. She even feinted for the discarded Luger. "I'm not being coy, I warn you."

I recoiled dramatically. "I never force my attentions on anyone to whom they are obnoxious." I had some memory of having said, or thought, the same in regard to Alice Ellish. "I suppose your roommate is another undercover operative?"

Natalie shook her head. She stepped to my side, made

her hand into a parenthesis, and applied it to my ear. "She knows nothing."

"Can that be?"

In a voice of some volume she addressed the hallway: "Hey, Al. I'm back."

From the bath and cavernously, owing no doubt to her situation near the tub—the shower had ceased to sound some time earlier—came Alice's return: "Gee, what a quick flight."

I whispered to Natalie: "I can't accept that. No stewardess is so torpid towards air times."

"She's no stew. She's a physiotherapist."

I frowned. "I think you owe me an elucidation, Natalie. You've used me ruthlessly. I suspect that my involvement in these matters—which until a moment ago I knew in the aggregate as the Villanova Affair—"

"There is no Teddy Villanova."

"—is due entirely to your machinations. Did you or did you not put Bakewell onto me, and then Donald Washburn II?"

She struck a noble attitude. "We do not what we wish but what we must, Russel. Counterfeiting debases the currency. A country whose money is not stable inevitably falls victim to mob rule. Rapine and pillage became the order of the day; the family collapses and is replaced by the wolf pack; children become chattels, women are sold at auction, and—"

"That takes a while, doesn't it? I'm not denigrating the fine jobs done by you chaps, but surely you can't mean that a few fake hundred-dollar bills immediately usher in the Thirty Years' War."

"I'm talking of billions," said Natalie, stamping her boot heels in series. "There is reason to believe that all the currencies of both hemispheres, *eye ee*, the world, now in circulation are counterfeit." She peered. "Feeling faint?"

"Is that all?"

"Great God, man, either you are a monster of cynicism or you are mad."

"Let me say this, Natalie, with all respect. I think you tend to confuse your particular area of interest with reality at large. I have noticed that effect in many professional persons: the lawyer with his eye always on that which might be adjudicated, the fireman on the flammable, the ophthalmologist on the squint, et cetera, et cetera. But in point of mundane fact, most human beings have no vocation worth the name, no deity, ideology, or discipline. They breathe, eat, defecate, sleep, and die—to name the only essential activities. As to their aims, I believe it was the Stagirite who put it succinctly: men pursue pleasure and avoid pain."

Natalie looked solemn. "I wasn't wrong in my assessment of you, Russel. In short, you are expendable. I have no apology for using you as pawn."

Spitefully, I struck back. "I can only now reveal that I wasn't gulled for a moment. I was onto your game from the first: no one in New York, having unfairly beaten another to a cab in a rainy rush hour, be the loser even a helpless cripple, offers to share it with him except from an ulterior motive. True, I first assumed yours had to do with prostitution, and I was astonished that you allowed me into your bed without demanding a fee."

My barrage proved absolutely ineffectual. Natalie was smiling derisively. "Do you suppose that vanity plays so large a role in my mystique?"

"Certainly pride does not: I found Washburn naked in your bed. I refuse to believe that serving as his doxy is required by your department." This was sheer bravado; in fact, nothing was more likely, nor more useful in gaining a confidence.

"As it happens, that was not my bed. Pretending it was was part of the hoax, I'm afraid."

"Never have I been such a butt," I wailed. "Why, Natalie, why?"

"I urge you for once to rise above the merely personal, Russel. Your well-being was not considered; neither was your pain. War abhors the individual, and this is war. I for example have had to eradicate the last vestiges of my own self. I have neither id nor ego."

"That explains much." By which I suppose I meant her lassitude in bed. "But what a fool I've been! I don't mind saying it will take a time for my bile to ebb. I trust that despite your fanatical dedication to a cause greater than both of us, you retain enough humanity to understand that." I made a latticework of fingers across my eyes and peered through the interstices. "Ratiocination will help. Here's my theory: Washburn and Bake—"

"Will have fled the country," Natalie said in sudden haste, turning on her boots and starting towards the bedroom. "Help me change. These zippers and snaps are complicated."

Pursuing her along the hall, I asked, "Why are you anyway wearing that leather?"

"New stew uniform." She turned into the bedroom, dampening her voice. "Nostalgia. Nineteen thirties aviatrix."

I crossed the threshold. She threw her hips on the bed and projected her boots at me. They were closed with laces high as the knee. "Helmet and isinglass goggles go with it. Grotesque when you put on the apron to serve meals on dinner flights."

While unlacing the boots as rapidly as I could, I tried again to fashion my hypothesis: "Washburn and Bakewell use this apartment for their hideout. They walk in stocking

feet so as not to arouse suspicion in the tenant underneath. Alice is unwitting. You pay half the rent, and she
is notoriously indifferent to your friends. You are in and
out, which spasmodic activity is explained by your job as
stewardess, which in fact you actually perform. There is
no Sforza figurine; that was another red herring with
which Washburn, being unarmed except for my unloaded
pistol, distracted me until you arrived with the Luger.
Bakewell of course could have overpowered me, but he
seemed exhausted this morning, perhaps owing to his
having played the false corpse too often." I removed the
left boot and began to work on the right. "Though some
of the lies I've been told were insultingly incredible. That
movie called *The Reformers*, for example."

Natalie had at last unfastened the several buckles at her
collar. "No, that was true enough. Gus from time to time
plays bit parts, nonspeaking always."

I had reached her ankle with the unlacing. "But why
did he give a prior performance, unpaid, in my office?"

"To compromise you."

I peeled off the remaining boot. "Excuse me?"

"To put you in bad odor with the management of the
Wyandotte Club." She pointed to the two snaps revealed
when the collar straps were drawn aside. "Get these. I'd
break a nail."

"Aha! Who would then send Pete and Tony to threaten
me and remove the putative corpse. I wonder what they
did with it—Bakewell's body? They were themselves
slain, genuinely, before I could ask."

"Wrapped it in an outsized rug, put it in the rear of
their panel truck. They started for the New Jersey
marshes, but at one traffic light he slipped out, the noise
of his escape covered by the deafening din of a Consoli-
dated Edison jackhammer nearby."

The snaps had small tolerance; I nicked my own nail.

"Isn't it odd that they never mentioned losing the body of the man I presumably murdered?"

"I imagine that's routine," said Natalie. "The Mafia isn't nearly as efficient as you might think. Remember that time all their leaders were captured en masse at a cookout?"

The successful opening of the snaps revealed the tab of a zipper. I had been kneeling between Natalie's leather thighs, not in this case an erotic posture. At the risk of being coarse, I might say I felt no urge to bury my snout in her horsehide loins. My brief access of lust, perhaps only a substitute for the anxiety relieved by her throwing down the Luger, had been long forgotten.

Deciding I had done enough as valet, I rose and drifted towards the window. "I suppose you would call it churlish if I asked you for identification."

"Undercover agents scarcely carry documents which would betray them were they stripped and searched," Natalie said behind me.

The concerns of modesty seemed irrevelant with a girl into whose flesh I had inserted my own repeatedly, and anyway I assumed, in a general sense of things and with a particular consideration for the chill leather, that she would be routinely underweared. But when I turned and saw her, standing, unpeeled to the calves, each of which had its peculiar zipper, I understood the error of my anticipation. She was altogether nude.

Having lately seen Washburn in the same condition, and in precisely the same place, I asked: "Then you insist that you and Donald the Second share only in the fellowship of crime—for your part, an imposture?"

Natalie laughed rhetorically, by which I mean not with sufficient energy to agitate her breasts, which anyway were firm cones and not of the pendulosity that is sensitive to reverberations. "If you mean sex again, I should tell

Yes, two underthings were found and perfunctorily donned. The dress was lifted and dropped over the fair head. The skirt when lowered did not fall beyond mid-thigh. From another drawer she had taken strips of stark white cotton; these when drawn over feet and up the calves to just below the patellae identified themselves as stockings, the sort that are appropriate only when rising from blunted-toe strap-shoes of patent leather—and Natalie produced a pair of these from a striped box, lined with pink tissue, discovered on the closet shelf.

Another box yielded a wig: flaxen, pigtailed, and when well seated over her scalp, her own locks tucked up within, gleamingly fringed to the lower extremity of her brow. So haired and shod in the Mary Janes, white-calved and short-skirted, she was, though taller than the mean but credibly suggesting the gangly, a schoolgirl of beginning adolescence—or at any rate the version thereof depicted in movies made three or four decades earlier: a period piece in this day of pneumatic puberty, massive mammaries and brewery-horse behinds being so often the burdens of twelve-year-old baggages.

She had neither rescued me from existing pain nor put me in more with a clarification of her own sexuality; but now, mincing as a gawky awkward fawn, with flip of skirt disclosing flash of lean high thigh, twists of trunk that peekabooed projections, imitations, of nascent bosoms, and a set of face that diminished those of her features that were obviously mature, she instead proceeded to characterize the erotic state of affairs that pertained to another personage altogether.

"Boris," she said, "is a pedophile."

She found in a drawer a pair of spectacles rimmed in very thin horn and with perfectly round lenses of a diameter so vast that when the glasses were astraddle her nose, the button of which she buffed to a gloss on a heel of hand, half her forehead and most of her bangs were visible through the perspicuous discs, surely nonprescription circles cut from a window.

That I was silent throughout the transformation of Natalie Hyde into Wendy Jekyll should not seem strange: from self-proclaimed Lesbian to child-molester's prey is a stupefying gamut.

But I found my tongue when I closed my mouth.

"Boris?"

"The Russian. But then, aren't they all?"

Pondering on that immoderate statement, I could come up with no more than what Viskovatov told Strakhov, who forwarded it by mail to Tolstoy: that Dostoyevsky, who "spent his entire life in a state of emotional upheaval and exasperation that would have made him appear ridiculous had he not been so malicious and so intelligent," had bragged of having had a little girl in a public bath.

"Which," I added, "might have been no more than the typical vile canard a great man's lackeys circulate about his principal rival."

Three-quarters of this speculation was to, and for, myself, Natalie having given her costume a final survey in the dressing-table mirror and then left the room, already so caught up in her role as to move with a childish gait, knees bumping, heels splayed. I followed her to the living room, entering which she skipped two paces, pigtails flying.

She retrieved the Luger from the chair. She extended its butt to me. "No place for this in my current garb," she said. "You carry it."

"To where and why?"

"Teterboro." She forced me to accept the weapon. Realizing that this episode might thrill a Nosy Parker peering through binoculars from an overlooking building (unshaven man pointing firearm at child), I put it hastily away, though she had not won me for the project.

"The New Jersey airport?" I asked. "Not bloody likely."

"I'm drafting you for government service," Natalie cried. "By the powers vested in me. I have a GS rating equivalent to a full colonelcy in the land forces and the comparable grade in the Navy."

"Sorry," I said. "The military is mercenary, and I am immune."

"After your release from Hus' custody by GAT, the NYPD put out an APB—"

"Hus is one of Washburn's henchmen. I won't be duped again."

"You are already," said Natalie. "That's his cover, you gull. You're wanted for heroin-pushing and the gypsy is prepared to charge you importuned a schoolboy for immoral purposes if need be."

"Whose need?" But I realized terribly that the Romany hag in her storefront was another undercover agent no doubt on stakeout to register the traffic at the yoga wallah's. "The gypsy is—"

"With a sister agency" said Natalie "but we scratch each other's backs."

Perhaps literally, in view of her self-admitted orientation (and add to that her current roll of eye); but what it meant to me was that I should be successfully extorted into what, if pistols were brandished, might be a lethal enterprise.

But between Natalie and me at the moment, I carried the only weapon: actually two: each side pocket of my corduroy jacket sagged with hardware, though my little Browning was sterile without its clip. I had been hoaxed once too often by my adversaries, criminal and otherwise, and at this point I could see no distinction: the demands of all were made at the cost of my unique and precious self.

Therefore I crafted a scheme, but would put it into action only after we had left this place. Too easy here to be cornered. Even Alice might yet prove an undercover agent for some constabulary thus far unrepresented or, failing that, an adept in another area of crime.

"Very well," I barked. "I will answer the call to the colors." I marched to the door and flung it open.

Natalie crossed the threshold in her giddy new stride. The hall was empty, but I decided to wait until clearing the building before I made my move. The elevator ride was quick and inconsequential.

Tomás Villanueve still served as genial Latin Cerberus at the street door.

"Gone to schoo'?" he asked Natalie, apparently not penetrating her disguise. "Learn to be reech, hahaha." The laugh seemed in no way uncivil, and I returned the amenity with a wish for his good morning.

"The say to joo, Meester Villanova!"

"Remarkable," I observed to Natalie when we had gained the sidewalk and circumnavigated the soft pyramid of dog stool that been mounted before the door during the last hour, "extraordinary how the name of a fanciful personage so persists! At a later date I want your explanation of this choice of appellation for an imaginary character, and for that matter, why you, or Washburn and Bakewell, found it necessary to invent 'Teddy Villanova' in the first place, and beyond that, I still have no idea of why I am involved in this complex caprice. But now"—I touched the outside of the pocket containing the Luger—" I must bid you good-bye. I have no intention of serving as nanny to your Alice in Wonderland—Lewis Carroll, by the way, was at least a latent if not a practicing pedophile, and so far as I know he had no Russian blood."

"You're a knave, Russel," Natalie hissed and assumed a posture, in her schoolgirl dress, virginal stockings, and patent-leather shoes, from which she could deliver one of her karate kicks, but there was some sidewalk traffic now, humorless pedestrians en route to melancholy work, and she was soon jostled violently by a man oblivious to the antics of the underaged at such an hour, and naturally I moved myself out of range as well.

Physically frustrated, Natalie resorted to a moral weapon. New York passers-by being notoriously stony to the appeal of even the freshly wounded, I sneered with impunity at her anguished screams. But my nerves went to pudding when I saw a police car swoop into the gutter and a blue-capped minion surlily emerge.

"This old man," wailed Natalie, "made me an indecent proposal!"

"Go wan, he woont meet ya price," the officer growled. "I thought we *tole* you hoors to stay off our beat." He was scarcely friendlier to me: "Take off, John."

I walked briskly towards the west. Halfway to First Avenue, I turned and saw that Natalie had been sufficiently intractable to require that the second cop leave the car to support the efforts of his partner. It looked as though she would inevitably be subdued and hauled off to incarceration.

I had never intended such an issue. Before she could get her undercover status confirmed by the Treasury Department, and believed by the New York police, Washburn & Bakewell, and perhaps also the Russian named Boris, would have fled by airplane from Teterboro.

Thus far I had been less than a hero, unless assessed by a negative gauge, and yet I had accepted a punishment that could be termed Herculean. But suddenly I was in an intrepid mood. I had not been touched by the albino's shotgun lightning that sent two other souls to Hades. Actually, none of the attacks I had sustained throughout was murderously launched, with the possible exception of the sapping on the Hindu's threshold, and my proprietary god had deflected that blow from the mortal to the merely painful.

What I am saying is that, for whatever motives, severally or in combination—greed, the summons of a swashbuckler's superego, perhaps even a jingoism concerning Western Civilization, which according to Natalie was threatened by the *faux-monnayeurs*, and two semesters on the Literary Masterpieces of which I had taught at State (from Sappho to *The Counterfeiters*, the latter by Gide, Zeus to many a Ganymede); and despite my short title for the course, used as classroom joke, seldom understood, "Great Movements in W.C."—I think I have demonstrated here that I am nothing but a loyal product of my cultural heritage. . . .

Whatever, when I reached First Avenue, in civilization's contemporary Western capital, depraved, debased, degraded, and declining though it be, and under constant Vandal siege, I stepped into a gutter full of filth and lifted my arm, not to wave an oriflamme but rather to hail a taxi.

If this quixotic appeal would be answered at demonic rush hour, I should instruct the driver to proceed with all haste to Teterboro Airport.

I was immediately run down by a homicide doggedly steering a van.

B

Or nearly.

Having failed, by the breadth of a cuticle, to murder me with a butt of the perpendicular complex of bumper-grille-windshield, the van now lurched to a brake-keening halt that defied the law of momentum, reversed its gears with the sound of Sam's baseball bat against the boiler, and came viciously back in the obvious intent to plaster me against its broad spine, on which was displayed the painted admonition: SCHOOLBUS—STOP WHEN I STOP!

I had of course regained the curb and could sneer at the brutal sortie, clutching the Luger within my pocket, should the driver emerge to try by foot what wheels could not achieve.

The vehicle stopped again when I was just opposite its middle, access to which could be gained by a large double door. It was in fact not a proper van but rather a minibus of many windows and, beneath them, a legend, painted in avocado against a mauve ground; STAVROGIN ACADEMY FOR YOUNG LADIES. A cargo appropriate to the sign stared through the oblongs of glass, producing many little discs of oral condensation and squashed dirty-pink palmar surfaces of paws. Here and there a tongue waggled.

The twin panels of door were forthwith hurled open, and I was summoned to enter by a score of small fore-arms bearing fistfuls of writhing fingers, visibly an invitation to penetrate a congress of adders, while the ear was smote with the shrieking cacophony in which bluejays couch their peeves.

Through the flock I could see glimpses of the driver at

his horizontal steering wheel. Owing to my fragmented perspective, he appeared initially as an outsized head of animal hair, and though a gorilla would not have been an incredible helmsman for this simian freighterful, I checked my impulse to find correspondences and at last identified him as but a man wearing a large fur hat—in fact, a kind of hussar's shako.

He leaned sidewise, angled, and swept three tots from our common route of vision with an arm of gold buttons from wrist to elbow. There were more buttons and embroidered frogs on his thorax, and a set of cartridge loops on his right shoulder, with no doubt, if symmetry were served, a twin on the other bosom yet invisible. I could see one shiny black knee-boot as well. Assessing him in ensemble, I judged that the man was costumed as a Cossack.

His heavy voice rumbled under the bird cries; his large gauntlet beckoned. Never immune to the lure of the bizarre, I put my head near the entrance, then recoiled slightly from the odor of bananas that the underaged seem to exude.

"To get in," called the Cossack. A walrus mustache matched the fur on his shako. Pouches of *Weltschmerz* hung below his eyes; his heavy mouth was lugubrious.

"Pardon?"

"Please to enter, my dear gentleman," said he.

The schoolgirls, who wore ribboned lavender pancake hats and striped blazers with silver crests over their nonexistent left breasts (*S* and *A* in Gothic letters, divided by a unicorn rampant), now tried to seize me like importunate harlots.

I withdrew. The Russian's large face, melancholy enough in its standard mien, seemed as if it might distintegrate in the despondent effort to produce a smile.

"You are Rissole Rain?" he cried. He pointed to his embroidered chest. "Is Boris!"

He provided neither a family name nor, conspicuous failure in one who stems from the steppes, a patronymic. Already this encounter had begun to give off the familiar stench of hoax.

I caressed my pocketed Luger. But I did not want to make an ass of myself by pointing a weapon, at rush hour, into a conveyance full of little girls. Besides, he was offering me no clear and present harm, and I needed a ride.

Therefore I stepped aboard, carefully threaded myself through the serpent cluster, though not without a painful sting or two, and reached the forward passenger's seat; inertia hurled me into it as Boris accelerated violently.

The volume of traffic was no deterrent to this willful Slav. He steered with whiplike wrists. His steed knew only the gallop and the precipitous halt, four feet together, following which came the rearing of forehoofs and the forward hurtle. In this fashion we rapidly devoured several blocks to the north, then turned east and charged towards the river.

I found my voice box, which had been disordered by the slamming of my head against the seat back, and said: "Teterboro is in the other direction." I was still enmired in my old resolve, and I assumed that Boris, as one of the conspirators, would naturally seek that airport. The schoolgirls had no doubt been hired, possibly kidnapped, to provide his cover.

His heavy eyebrow rose and fell; I also studied half a mustache and one coarse nasal lobe, pitted with pores.

"Are you really one of the gang," I asked, "or is this another ruse?"

"*Mais oui!*" he answered. "*Je suis russe. Je ne parle pas . . . l'anglais. Seulement . . . le français, n'est-ce pas?*"

I proceeded to put to him a question that would have earned me a beating from the late Pete & Tony, no doubt, with their quick ear for possible vile epithets.

"*Vous êtes cosaque vraiment?*"

Boris shook his shako. "*C'est un costume.*" We had now come to a feeder lane into the FDR Drive, and he wheeled riotously through it and into a mass of traffic that I should have said did not permit such ingress. "*Pour les petites filles,*" he added en route. A dreamy smile dissipated some of the gloom in his visage. "*Aimez-vous . . . les petites filles?*" His eye drifted up to the rear-view mirror.

From behind me came a chorus of chirping voices: "*Nous aimons Boreees!*"

I received the ugly confirmation that he lived up to the character Natalie had given him, and with some heat I replied: "*Absolument pas!*" I mentally groped my sketchy lexicon for a reinforcing phrase. "*Je ne suis pas un—un sale type!*"

Boris was unmoved by my negative ardor, with its condemnatory implication for him. "*Moi,*" he said, pointing at his gross nose, "*j'adore les petites filles!*" He smoothed his mustache. "*Parce que . . . parce que . . . elles sont si jeunes!*"

In disgust I cried: "What a swine you are!"

I suppose he did not understand this. My temple was abraded by the sharp rim of a schoolgirl's hat, and a high-pitched voice intoned into my neck: "*Alors, alors, alors . . .*" A tendril of arm insinuated itself into my peripheral vision on the left. Its fingers became a duck's bill and, cheered on by strident *quacks*, it assaulted my nose.

Boris took this as a drollery to which only uproarious guffawing was the proper response. He had the dental terrain of a boar. Another little hand came from behind, bearing in its grubby fingers a poison-green lollipop, already tongued to a loathsome lozenge the size of a lima bean, and sought to insert it into my mouth, in revulsion gone slack as an emptied satchel.

Whatever my happy fantasies of dealing with disorderly children (burlap sack, millpond), I do not offer violence to the undersized. Carefully, warily, I took my head away as far as my situation permitted, pressed it against the window, and tried, in my insecure French, to elicit our destination from Boris.

"Où roulons nous?"

"Au bac," said he.

Either I did not quite hear the word or I could not English it. As a diminutive for "tobacco," it was senseless.

"Comment?" A little tentacle was now snaking under my right shoulder, the cap of which was compressed against the window sill.

"Au bateau de passage pour Stah-teen Issland."

"The Staten Island ferry? *L'Academie, est-elle là-bas?"* No doubt such an institution had good need for isolated grounds. Perhaps the name Stavrogin was a code word to attract degenerates who shared Boris' persuasion and used the school as brothel, their subsidies thereof serving as legitimate deductions under the naïve or quite possibly disingenuously corrupt tax laws of New York, notorious for punishing the maladroit and rewarding the malfeasant.

"Merde!" cried Boris, in answer not to me but rather to the raised fist displayed by a taxi driver whose vehicle he had but narrowly missed defendering. Then, mouing into the rear-vision mirror: *"Je fais mes excuses, mes petites!"* For which he was celebrated with a flockmeal peal of silvery laughter and several iterations of the indecency, along with variations, in compounds, of which I had until then been ignorant.

Finally the Russian gave me the, or a kind of, answer: *"Non."*

"*Pourquoi allons-nous à* Staten Island?"

"*Pour voir,*" said Boris, "*la Statue de Liberté.*"

I had enough of his mockery. I clawed for my Luger, intending to thrust it at his mustache in support of my demand for a straight story, but my pocket was empty. The groping little hands had done their work.

I hurled myself about and looked into the rear of the vehicle. A carrot-haired moppet held the big black gun in the proper position to shoot me between the eyes, if such was her purpose. In my fear I forgot French practice and addressed a child in the formal third person.

"*Donnez-moi le joli pistolet, mademoiselle, s'il vous plaît!*"

"*Va te faire foutre!*" she obscenely replied, and Boris' stentorian mirth roared in competition with the engine.

"*Si charmante,*" he then crooned. "Ah, oh!" He made a forceful right turn that threw me towards the gearbox but failed significantly to alter the command with which the little girl kneeled on her seat, both hands on the raised gun.

Guile was needed here. I groped for my *mouchoir,* while saying, approximately, what I must translate as follows for those who have no French or, conversely, use it with the felicity of Flaubert.

"My little cabbage, you have need of a handkerchief with which to clean your visage. Your nose is not dry. Is it possible that mine serves such a purpose?" I removed mine from my pocket; it was balled and had a crackling core. "Ah, perhaps it is not clean. What a damage! *Zut alors!* Perhaps Boris lends you his."

I did not dare turn to consult the Russian directly on this matter: her cold little green eyes were diminishing in circumference as she prepared to squeeze the trigger. How grotesque to be shot by a *sang-froid* schoolgirl.

"*Non, non, mignonne! Défense de tirer!* Do not shoot the *gentil gentilhomme,* I pray of you. It is not droll. It is an affair very serious—"

She discharged the Luger point-blank at my forehead, and continued to pump out successive shots. The reports were feeble for such a formidable weapon and accompanied by but tiny wisps of smoke, from breech and not muzzle, and instead of hot brass shells, the ejecting mechanism produced a thin strip of chewed paper. I had been assassinated by cap gun.

I began to doubt whether Natalie was really an agent of the Treasury Department. I turned to Boris.

"*Ecoutez! Pas encore de perversion! Pour qui me prenez-vous?*"

"I take you for a committed human being, I hope," said he in limpid English, standardly accented. "Dedicated to the cause of civil decency, I trust."

"Good gravy," I blurted. "Then neither are you what you seem!"

"If you mean that for general application, then it is the mere parroting of an outmoded psychoanalytic platitude," Boris said, continuing to drive in his new role as inordinately as of old. We were already clearing the housing project on, if I knew the lay of land, East Twenty-third Street. The plan to view the Statue of Liberty from the Staten Island ferry had been doffed, I supposed, with his mask.

"But if," he went on, "your reference is made peculiarly to me as a discrete individual, then it is well made. Forgive me for putting you to the test, and my congratulations on passing it. You're no child molester, else you'd have lost control when brought into juxtaposition with this shipment."

I cannot say the judgment was a relief to me, not having been aware of the threat, and I was insulted by his implication that it was my status that required definition, not his.

"Who are *you?*" I asked in foul humor.

He smirked. His walrus mustache now looked so obviously bogus that I wondered why I had not penetrated its falsity at the outset. Nor did he appear to any degree Russian in any other point of visage or mien; the strong features, along with the melancholia, had vanished with the coarseness of palate. "We're safe in English," said he. "The girls don't understand it, of course. By the way, you speak French *comme une vache espagnole.*"

The well-known abusive phrase applied by the Gauls to any foreigner who essays their precious tongue evoked derisive giggles from the girls in back.

"Whoever you are, you're a rude sod," I said.

"I should think you might have understood why I used that idiom," Boris told me, raising a gauntleted index finger from the wheel. "To give *them* an explanation for our resorting to English. . . . I'm Boris, of the Vice Squad, NYPD." He plucked open one of the befrogged gold buttons on his tunic and found a little leather folder within. He passed it to me furtively. "Examine it inside your lapels, so they can't see over your shoulder. Chuckle, or titter and snort as though it's an indecent picture."

I shielded it with my jacket, but refused to perform further until I had confirmed his claim. . . . Indeed, badge and *carte d'identité* were in order, unless they too were counterfeit. He was Sergeant Conrad Garnett Boris.

"All right, Sergeant, I'll play along—"

He nodded at the rear-view mirror. "*Oui, monsieur, je suis sergent cosaquien!*"

"Very well. But despite your authentic-looking credentials I don't intend to cooperate unless I hear a reasonable statement of your game and its goal. Is it your contention that these small female persons are assisting in the pursuit of the counterfeiters? . . . Yes, I think I see it clearly now:

curb. "They are a depraved lot of hardened criminals, most of them recidivists, on whom compassion would be wasted. In the reformatory they'll make indecent pottery and finger paintings."

"You will arrest *them* and not the procurers?"

"Ah," said he, "though a citizen of New York you have much naïveté to expunge. Don't be bamboozled by their size: these individuals are wily degenerates. Their games are not the spillikins and conundrums that Jane Austen played with young relatives; they are rather the decadent Roman entertainments that followed Trimalchio's feast. And long investigation has revealed no panders but themselves."

God wot, this was an unhappy subject. I turned to another. "Like Detective Zwingli, a colleague of yours though in Narcotics—"

"Now a movie star," Boris said enviously.

"You seem a man of more liberal culture than the routine officer. I live just there, as for some reason you seem to know, and thank you for dropping me off! I wonder whether, after delivering these miscreants to the Tombs or wherever they will be deservedly incarcerated, you might like to come back for a glass of champagne, a bit of *pâté*—"

The sergeant gave me a withering look and a coarse question which demonstrated that, also like Zwingli, he was *au fond* a cop.

"You a dirty faggot?"

"Certainly not! I'm a dramatist. I thought you might like to look at a play of mine."

His face became radiant. "I do have a theatrical bent, it's true. And vice-squadders have been unjustly ignored, while the limelight plays on the narcos."

"Very good, then!" I offered a handshake. "*A tout à l'heure!*"

"Oh," said he, "we're going into the same building. What a coincidence."

"We?" I asked. "And whatever, why?"

"The girls and I," Boris said. "To apartment five-K, to arrange an entrapment for a slippery customer who has long eluded law-enforcement bodies the world over."

"That's my own number!"

"Surely you are in error. It is the current hide-out of one Teddy Villanova."

"There is no such person," I said quickly, hoping thereby to treat what felt very like the onset of a severe pulmonary malfunction. Recovered so suddenly from obsolescence, the name asserted all its old power over me.

"Would that that were so!" Boris sighed so dramatically that the ends of his mustache pointed briefly towards the roof. "He is the personification of evil. I hope only that these little trulls are young enough to meet the requirements of his appetite. Also, he may soon see through the hoax; his pleasure is to corrupt the innocent, and these minxes are anything but naïve. Still, we must work with what we have, no?"

"Just a moment," I said, arresting with my urgency his hand upon the lever of the door. "I gather that you know Natalie Novotny, who poses as girl Treasury agent, for she knows you, in fact assumes you are of the sexual persuasion which you here ascribe to Teddy Villanova—"

"The rivalry between local and Federal law-enforcement services is notorious," Boris said sadly.

"Natalie has confirmed Donald Washburn's statement to the effect that Teddy V. is a creation of the whole cloth."

"I'm delighted to hear that," said Boris. "That means that the ruse worked. She will follow the red herring to Teterboro Airport, and meanwhile I shall singlehandedly capture Villanova, garnering all kudos and plaudits."

"She doesn't give a fig for Teddy," said I. "Her prey are Washburn and Bakewell."

Boris smiled. "That little hussy will get her comeuppance if so. Washburn is Special Branch, Scotland Yard; Bakewell, French Sûreté."

Going through the dramatis personae of the past day I could now find only the Hindu as yet unassigned to some constabulary. I used him in the recovery of a shred of pride.

"The yoga wallah is of course some Indian policeman."

"Certainly," said Boris. "Villanova's operations are world-wide. It would be no exaggeration to lay at his door most of the criminal phenomena of the past two decades: the efflorescence of the youth cult, obviously; the corruption of most modern languages; the pseudo revolution, actually a retrogressive movement, in sex; the journalistic enshrining of mediocrity, the publicizing of the banal, the investigation of the inconsequential—while he himself has realized the Renaissance ideal, the prince-poet-satyr, autocrat, gastronome, dandy, and I should be tempted to add 'sage,' were it not for Baudelaire's formidable statement that 'the Sage fears laughter, as he fears worldly spectacles and concupiscence.' Whereas these are precisely Villanova's delights."

Boris flung open his door. "Were it up to me," he concluded, "I should sit here all day toying with abstractions, but meanwhile Teddy lurks monstrously in apartment five-K. It has taken years to run him to ground. The kill is at hand."

Something clattered as he lowered himself to the street. For the first time I saw his left side and the saber scabbarded there.

"I trust," I cried, "you have more modern weapons."

"*Mon Dieu!*" gasped Boris, caressing his trunk like an autoerotic. "I left my thirty-eight in my locker. It made an unsightly lump in the sleek fit of this tunic. I felt it would give the show away—" He looked as if he might sob.

"Just a moment," said I, fetching forth my little Browning. "This is unloaded, but 'twill serve, perhaps, unless Teddy calls your hand."

"Which he will," wailed Boris. "By all reports, he is vicious as fer-de-lance."

"The Luger, though a cap pistol, is a credible imitation of the real thing, fooling me, an old adept at weaponry."

He leaned in, appealing across the seat. "I believe you have your own score to settle with Teddy—or should have, considering the way you've been used."

"Or rather with the various policemen," said I. "I still don't understand the part I've played, but I assure you, I'm nursing a massive grudge against someone."

"If five K is your own apartment, and if all other measures fail, you might bring trespassing charges against him." Boris was begging now.

"You have arranged some sort of assignation with the fiend?"

"To furnish him six girls below the age of ten," Boris explained, "at precisely six minutes before ten o'clock. He has the pervert's taste for symmetry. That may be a weakness. But, alas, I cannot arrest him until he does something sufficiently indecent to violate an ordinance, and before he does that, he may well produce a weapon of his own, and I am underarmed. Also, this is entrapment, and no court would sustain an arrest so made. Wren, unless you act, this beast will go free."

I had momentarily forgotten about the actual girls, and Boris, occupied with his plans for me, was also oblivious to them. I looked insolently into the rear of the bus now, in dramatic support of some cynical comment I was crafting —and saw the last of the half-dozen, or rather her strap shoe and knee sock, as she left the vehicle by the double side-door, which had been spirited open during our confused colloquy. The others were already scampering up the walk beneath the torn canopy of my building.

I had only the sergeant's word that they were strumpets; juveniles they were certainly. I had learned that a policeman would do anything to serve his purposes. That these little flowers, if already darkened at the corollae, would be further polluted by a devil, was insupportable to my moral mystique. Also, the swine *was* trespassing in my sanctum, had perhaps found my play and wiped his porcine posteriors on it, for its fine tolerances between necessity and virtue would be hateful to his Mephistophelean rationale.

I groped my passage between the ranked seats and leaped through the exit to the sidewalk. Boris presumably followed me, whether yet with drawn saber I did not turn to know. Pelting feet propelled me into the lobby. Five girls were already enclosed in an ascending elevator, a little blinking mobile light told me. But the redhead lingered, with the doorman under the muzzle of her Luger, which, judging from his blench, he believed potent.

She seemed to be relieving him of his money: the rascal had more greenbacks than I had seen in an eon. He had been no friend to me, and I saw no need to rescue him from what was a nonlethal menace.

Therefore, cool to his predicament, I passed him in hot pursuit of the schoolgirls. Atypically, the other lift was free, with yawning door. I pressed the button for 5. Before the sliding portal had horizontally guillotined my view of the lobby, a saber came on board, and then Boris.

"Careful with that blade!" I warned.

"It's a stage property, blunt as a fence paling," he said, but lowered it, resting point on boot toe, from which it rose like a large leisurely parenthesis to the pommel on which his knuckles were tensed to white bone.

I produced my empty Browning .25. "Perhaps surprise will compensate for lack of firepower," I said, brandishing the minuscule weapon, and triggering it for emphasis, luckily towards the ceiling panel, for it discharged, making in that compartment a thunder to which it could not have aspired outdoors.

"O most unruly man!" cried Boris, wheezing at the acrid odor of cordite.

I admit I was myself shaken. "Must have been a cartridge in the chamber. . . . Well, the die is now cast. We are definitely sans shells. There's an advantage in that: no one will be shot accidentally."

A tiny hole had been pierced through the ceiling of the car. We reached the fifth floor without further event, deboarded with dispatch, rounded the corners to my remote door, and though I felt justified in using my trio of keys, I deferred to Boris' wish, in the interests of his imposture, to ring discreetly.

When at length the door opened sufficiently to reveal the most depraved countenance I have ever seen on humankind, I fisted my automatic into the position to deliver to those obscene features a savage pistol-whipping.

14

Luckily my hand did not descend, for it was Peggy Tumulty, not Teddy Villanova, who flinched, retreated, and wailed: "I can explain this, Russ!"

Her condition was not such as to cause a revision in my statement on manifest depravity. For one, her normally swart hair, usually lank, had turned to red-gold ringlets; then her lips were gore-red as the wound of clichéd metaphor and her eyes kohled like a houri's.

Even so, her face was soon obscured by the meretriciousness of her figure, or rather the raiment in which it was scarcely restrained: she wore a net brassiere, the mammaries clutched in black satin hands, and a companion nether garment the breadth of which at its widest expanse did not exceed half that of Alice Ellish's slingshot at its narrowest. Conjoin these with a garter belt designed from the mingled fantasies of an *Obersturmbannführer-SS* (portions were of leather and what seemed corroded bronze) and an underwear fetishist of the Edwardian era (tatwork, satin rosebuds); black-lace operetta hose and spike-heeled, stiletto-toed shoes; and you had an ensemble the wearer of which deserved the pistol-whipping planned for Teddy Villanova, whose pedophilia now might seem a harmless caprice.

However, I eventually lowered the gun. "A likely story, Peggy," I said, "but I pray you can sustain it. Meanwhile" —I pushed past her—"where is that venomous toad?"

The champagne bottle, corkless, in fact empty, stood on the kitchen counter, the little glass saucer, its late caviar remembered only by a single bird-shot pellet and a streak of green-yellow oil, nearby. The *pâté*'s tunnel-tin was merely a tunnel of tin, a fat-flecked void where the loaf had dwelt.

The little girls were sporting clamorously on the sofa; no adult male was visible. Before I could act on my assumption, saber and Boris arrived at my side and then cleared it, plunged into the bathroom, and, if my hearing served, slashed my shower curtains to tatters, then reappeared, sword drooping and officer shrugging in dismay.

"Teddy est disparu," said he, and added, I thought in impertinent coyness: *"Comme Albertine."*

I considered Peggy Tumulty's apparent transformation into a gaudy bawd, endeavoring to conceal from her, until it could be instituted, my decision to call 911 for a brace of husky Bedlam-keepers and a strait waistcoat. Obviously, this case that had so unremittingly threatened my sanity had already claimed hers. I dared not look at her too closely. She displayed even more flesh than I had supposed she carried beneath her quotidian attire, yet in a form of more luxurious definition: the famous breasts, for example, were of a stately thrust to which the spidery black fingers of Pierre's bra could contribute but feebly; her thighs I should call columnar rather than the firkin-fat cylinders I had foreseen; and though harness would move me more to mirth than an expense of spirit, the sateen rosettes on her garters had a loadstone attraction for my mettle.

Therefore, in speaking to her I physically addressed Boris, causing his mustache soon to flutter with his eyebrows, for, given the Cossack uniform, my demand could, by an extravagant sensibility, be taken to apply to him.

"Remove that outlandish attire!"

"I thought you said you weren't a fag," he noted, but shrugged and began to grope for the closing of his breeches. Dedicated vice-cop that he was, no doubt he yearned to make some kind of arrest.

"I'm not," I frostily replied. "I'm speaking to Miss Tumulty. She's under a strain. She's not at all well. She's actually a genteel young lady of a fine old family of Queens."

He chortled coarsely. "Queans, jades, wenches!"

I found it was necessary to look at Peggy. Her right forearm guarded her bosom; the left hand, flattened with fingers aligned, was her rigid fig leaf. She was furious.

"You bums have blown it now! You jerks, you saps, you creeps! I *had* him, and you had to blow it!"

I identified this outburst as more evidence that she could be ultimately dealt with only by means of a radical lobotomy, poor thing, with bleak future as vegetable, taken out to air daily in the sooty ozone of Ozone Park, otherwise kept in an indoor corner with instructions to watch the nice geranium grow.

But Boris, denied his anticipated sodomy-arrest, was keen to her plaint and soon misidentified her point.

"You *had* Teddy Villanova?"

"*Would of* had him," she wailed, "but you bums bust in and blow the whole shebang, and what's these kids for? You look like a dirty old wino, Russ, and who's this guy in the lodge uniform?" She was raving, but I no longer thought her mad.

"Aha," I said, "I begin to see some light. You had an appointment—in view of your costume, a rendezvous of some sort, an entrapment of your own, with and for the notorious Teddy. Instead you swing back the door for an invasion of schoolgirls, a bogus Cossack, and your disheveled employer. Teddy, you suspect, has been scared off." I turned accusingly to Boris. "This person, a disguised vice-squadder, professed to have his own appointment with the archcriminal."

"I insist," Boris said, "that I spoke on the telephone to a man calling himself Teddy Villanova. He had dialed the Stavrogin Academy, on whose switchboard we maintain a constant tap, he said, in search of six little girls to take to view the Statue of Liberty in this the bicentennial year. American maidens, said he, should be made aware of the source of the national mystique, which happens to be both colossal and feminine. Small wonder, he added, that male homosexuals abound: the thought of that massive copper pudendum beneath that great skirt of green patina must be terrifying to a certain type of juvenile constitution—male, that is; a female's must find it exhilarating."

"Aha," I exclaimed at low volume, "for his own purposes, whatever they are, he is willing to pose as fellow traveler of the feminist movement, while—"

"He phoned this number and ordered me to put on what I'm wearing," said Peggy. "He said he would come here at ten o'clock and flog me with a bull's pizzle, whatever that is."

"—while at other times he will play the brutal male tyrant," I continued. "A protean character, a veritable prism of—"

"Ten o'clock!" cried Boris, and resorted to French either in sheer excitement or mere taste for euphony: "*Montrez votre montre!*"

I displayed my electric Timex. "Two minutes to the hour, unless the battery, eleven months old, is reneging on its promised year."

"Precision is his hallmark," said Boris. "Another trait of the pervert. We have one hundred twenty seconds—make that one-ten, after your lengthy commentary—to arrange an ambuscade."

"A hundred, allowing for your own," I riposted. "Where will we stow these tots?" Who, throughout the foregoing colloquy, had been occupied with a magpie congress of their own on the sofa.

"The bathroom," shouted Boris, polishing his saber blade on his back-of-knee. "Lure them within by offering to expose yourself."

I suppose his sense of their corruption had been gained by experience, but I still had no stomach for it, and ordered Peggy, as superannuated female child, to deal with her own breed. I drew my empty Browning, which I had put away, and posted myself beside the door.

"Hey, kids," Peggy said ingenuously, "what say we float

some rubber animals in the tub?" She took her hands from her body to gesticulate.

A little blonde chirped: "*Vous avez des grands tétons!*"

I didn't want Peggy upset at this moment; she might, in her anticriminal zeal, be willing to dress as harlot to capture Teddy V., but I feared she might swoon at such talk from a little maid.

"She means the national park," I said. "Contiguous with Yellowstone, visited last summer in the family camper. Silly Daddy was pawed by a bear."

Perhaps Peg had a semester of French at St. Dottie's. "Yeah, so what, you little snotnose," said she, and proceeded to burn my ears: "*You* don't have any tits at all. You all uh yuh get your little cans in the can." She pointed and began to count cadence; the girls rose in unison and marched into the bathroom.

My admiration was arrested by the sound of the doorbell. Boris had taken pains, I saw, to be behind the door when it opened, though he had the only effective weapon. I hefted my tiny automatic, which seemed to wither in the degree to which its use was needed.

Boris turned the knob and with great energy swung the door back to conceal himself absolutely. Strain caused my gun arm to perform as though waving to a minuscule figure on a remote horizon.

In actuality I proved to be greeting almost as small a creature in the foreground. It was the red-haired schoolgirl who had stopped to rob the doorman: she had discarded the cap pistol, but clutched the roll of bills with the command of a street-corner crapshooter.

She entered in the mode of a Casbah cooch-dancer, tinkling imaginary finger-cymbals. I injected my head into the hall: the corridor was yet empty.

I pulled the door to, exposing Boris, who, not yet seeing who had entered, quailed. Identifying the girl, he displayed *l'esprit d'escalier*, snickersnacking the air with his blade, like the character in Marlowe, "whisked his sword about, / And with the wind thereof the king fell down." If I tripped briefly, it was to avoid impalement.

"*Dieu*," he phewed. "I might have cut her to ribbons!"

Further saucy performance by the dwarf redhead was frustrated by Peggy's conducting her forthrightly to the bathroom. Boris and I reassumed our old positions. Tension falsely relieved returns with triple strength. When Peggy's piercing cry came, I felt the thrill of brittle coherence known to a goblet about to be shattered.

"There! Outside!"

Over the jagged socket of the half-demolished building, onto which my principal windows gave, hovered a helicopter. The clatter of its arrival I had heard previously, I realized, as the laboring of my own organs, ventricular, intestinal.

Our faces were soon monkeyed in trio and compressed against the glass. The pilot sat alone in his pellucid plastic bubble beneath the whirling parasol that produced the *pocketty-pock* of a great percolator. Helmeted, and goggled like the caricature of an owl, he offered no discernible feature—except perhaps the cruel mouth, though that feature invariably seems sinister if it alone can be clearly seen, as may be proved on your next encounter with a child garbed as astronaut.

"Can that," I heard myself breathe in obsequious awe, "be, at last, the legendary Teddy Villanova?"

And vice-squad Boris, sophisticated as he must have been in figures and arrangements that the naïve would call mythical, struck the same note.

"Such style!" he moaned. "In a more noble time the man would have been a prince. If we ever nab him, we will thereby have taken all the color from the world."

Peggy alone sounded the dull gong of disenchantment.

"Well, he's not Our Lady of Fatima. He's just a lousy crook in an egg beater, and if I could get ahold of him I'd cool his gravy all right." She shook her fist at Teddy, who thus far rode his Pegasus inscrutably. "Damn his dirty hide." She hurled herself off the sill. "I'm gonna look for something to throw at him."

"One moment," I said. "There have been enough mis-identifications." I went to my desk. My apartment, incidentally, had been put in order during my overnight absence, presumably by Peggy; all drawers had been closed, after having been seemingly refilled, for their contents were no longer on the floor; all pillows re-covered; all books reshelved, though doubtless not in my fastidious arrangement. It was not unjust that she had rewarded herself for the labor by consuming the champagne, caviar, and *pâté*, which had anyway not been of my purchase.

The manuscript of my play, manhandled by Knox, had been reassembled and put into its nest. I could find no fresh paper in my haste; therefore I seized a sheet of dialogue and the laundry marker I use for revisions, rushed to the window, and in dumbshow told Teddy, if it was he, still hovering and surely with his clatter attracting an audience above and below us, that I should scrawl a note and display it to him.

He returned no signal, but neither did he soar away. On the reverse of my scene I hastily inscribed the following in capitals of great magnitude:

ARE YOU TEDDY VILLANOVA?

And held it to the glass.

His change of controls was imperceptible, but the machine moved closer to the building, so near indeed that the windows would seem in imminent danger from the extravagant vibration. He pressed his goggles against the Lucite wall of the bubble, a wall-eyed pike in an aquarium.

Finally he drew his helmet away and nodded deliberately.

"It is he!" I gasped.

And Boris, after flinching from my immediate side with a grimace, which I suppose meant Alice's animadversion on my breath had had cause, confirmed in like wonder: "He bestrides the narrow world like a colossus."

"Get that damn window open!" shouted Peggy. She swung the empty champagne bottle by its neck.

But now that Teddy hung there before me, he who had been fabulous as the griffin, I did not wish him ill. Also, an unprovoked attack on him who has offered you no harm is illegal in any society however barbarous. No doubt it was in violation of some ordinance to operate an aircraft so close to a multiple dwelling, but to be brought down by a makeshift missile, in the unlikely event that Peggy could launch it accurately, was grave punishment for what as yet was more lark than crime—and as if so to characterize it, Teddy decompressed his lips and smiled, true, in a fashion that might be seen as saturnine, though one must always remember the effect of the grim jet helmet.

"Come on," Peggy cried. "I'm gonna nail that bird." She shoved between Boris and me and assaulted the window. I supposed that I must help her. Despite his rococo style, Villanova was no doubt, as she had said, but a brute—and in fact it was surely he who had sapped me, with intent to kill, on the Hindu's threshold. Assailing him now would be mere self-defense, if anachronous.

"There's a trick to that," I said, clearing Peg and Boris from the window. It required a punch-and-lift effect eluding description and achieved gracefully only by my bimonthly ham-handed window washer. With some battering and more agitation, I had worked the sash up an inch or two when suddenly it ceased to resist and shot to the top of its travel in the immemorial mockery of the mortal by the material.

Peggy inserted herself across the sill, bottle, both arms, and, necessarily, breasts. With more than half her corporal mass beyond the exterior face of the building wall, and warming up her arm with great revolutions of the vessel that had lately held the Widow Clicquot's froth (no doubt emptied down Peg's hatch; she looked, now that I thought of it, drunk as a tar), she began to pedal her spike heels, and the angle between her calves and thighs rapidly alternated between the obtuse and the acute—as she proceeded to kick herself farther through the open window.

She did not bring this venture to the sorry issue for which it would have been destined: I seized one limb and Boris the other, though his hand, so far along her thigh as to be more wanton than supportive, was of such small help in retrieving her that I was sole creditor of her debt for life.

Peggy displayed no gratitude. Indeed, she resisted the effort to withdraw her, hooking her elbows over the outside sill. What Teddy thought of this grappling match could not be known. Perhaps by the cruel gauge he might routinely apply to all phenomena, he assessed it as rather our attempt to defenestrate an exhausted tart, quite a standard disposal in his degenerate world.

Meanwhile Boris went too far in applying Father Hopkins to a helicoptered hoodlum, shouting: "Daylight's dauphin, dapple-dawn-drawn Falcon . . ." as his hand was also too inordinate in tracing an imaginary line on Peggy's upper inside thigh.

I dropped her ankle and seized his wrist, exhuming his buried hand with the old schoolboy probe of nerve-amidst-sinews.

"Ouch! Damn your eyes," said he.

"This wench is my ward," I told him. "Toy with her

fine foot if you like, but eschew her quivering thigh and the demesnes that there adjacent lie."

"I assure you," he replied, "that I was distracted by Teddy's purchase on plain air, to what purpose I cannot say."

Peggy yet swung her bottle and, presumably, sounded fishwife expletives, given the yaw of her back-of-head, this clamor unheard over that of Teddy's whirligig. Boris and I had spoken in yells.

I might have commented on the NYPD's assigning the vicious to Vice, as with Zwingli it had employed the addict in Narcotics—a Dantesque practice of condemning the sinner to a surfeit of same, as life's gluttons are literal pigs in Inferno—did not Teddy Villanova at that point produce an alteration not in his attitude but rather in the furnishings thereof: a Jacob's ladder began to unreel from the basement of his portable heaven.

His hover was so firm that this hempen device, metal-runged, scarcely swung or swayed.

At the same moment Peggy hurled the Veuve's dead green soldier, and as foreseen by anybody not in thrall to megalomania, the shot was far short, the heavy bottle scarcely climbing before it obeyed gravity's command to plunge. If Teddy's demonstration had collected a crowd, one of them might soon be brained.

The lowest aluminum rung of the ladder was soon near enough to tantalize my secretary, but never quite within her reach if my restraint of her ankle was maintained; and it was. In fact, I seized the other calf as well and, catching her by surprise, wheelbarrowed her from the window altogether now, her hands accepting the fall to the floor.

I took myself to the sill. My belief that the ladder hung near enough to be grasped had been based on an illusion of my former perspective. Though in length its dangle reached my level, the breadth of intervening air was some dozen feet, and not to be crossed by any unfeathered creature.

Boris shouted: "He'll go now, if he can't have her, and God knows when we'll look on him again, or on his like."

"It occurs to me," said I, "as it should have to you, that the police have helicopters, have they not, and if they had been called when we first sighted his whirl, he might now have been chased to the landing pad he must necessarily maintain somewhere in the metropolitan area."

"Alas," said Boris, "I don't know the drill for getting hold of our sky arm. In Vice we seldom need air support, you see, the typical pimpmobile being so burdened with accessories, with a consequent reduction of its horsepower, that the unmarked cars we favor, rusty old high-finned models that suggest the Puerto Rican family chariot, can easily overtake them in hot pursuit."

With asperity I yelled: "Though some of you have attained to a level of civilization undreamt of by the low-brow copper of yore, you have acquired a concomitant fecklessness. . . . Speaking of panders, do you by chance know a Calvin Peachtree, who may be a policeman as well?"

"A Moor?"

"Yes, and his Desdemona is a murderous albino."

"Black gangs compete with white for control of the rackets," said Boris. "Owing to his hue, Peachtree goes easily under cover in that milieu—as he could not, say, on the Olympic ski team."

"Meanwhile, Signor Villanova continues to hover." And, as I looked up now, was gesturing at us with a hooked finger. "What can that mean?"

"From all we know," Boris shouted, "he may well be a polymorphous pervert, as ready to sodomize a man as flog a strumpet or molest a child of either sex."

"A veritable fiend," I agreed. I had waxed and waned

towards Teddy throughout, though the charges against him, while growing more immoderate, had stayed unproven.

"I think he has now taken a fancy to *you*," said Boris. "Exploiting which, you might nab him."

Before I could respond to this insolent suggestion, Villanova swung the craft so that the end of the rope ladder whipped, more smartly than could have been anticipated from its lazy look, almost into the window, and luckily so, for at the same moment Boris defenestrated me with one great shove, and willy-nilly, seizing the aluminum tube of the terminal rung, I embarked on my career as Flying Wren, death-defying aerialist.

Perhaps you have never hung from a helicopter: the lack of a palpable surround is uncanny. Add to this the shock of being untimely ripped from the womb of one's home, from which Boris' bawdy cries of encouragement and Peggy's keening soon became inaudible as Teddy simultaneously soared the machine and winched me towards its abdominal trap door.

We topped Manhattan's towers in that district; a gust spun me briefly to see my apparent fellows in altitude to the north, Empire and Chrysler; and on the backswing, the World Trade Chang & Eng, to whom at that distance I seemed superior. The last phase of my ingestion into the helicopter's maw seemed endless; the winch grew reluctant when my forehead reached the level of the cabin floor; the blur-blown focus of my eyes stayed for an eternity on the struts of undercarriage; my body felt as though stripped by the wanton wind.

Finally, helped less by grudging gears than by fingers, forearms, and elbows, I scrambled within, crawled two paces forward, and, swallowing to reseat my gorge, stared gingerly ahead at what I could discern of Teddy Villanova over the back of seat, which was: mere hemisphere of black helmet.

The guest accommodation in this craft was filed behind, not ranked with, the pilot. I knee-walked to it and sat on, then withdrew and buckled, a safety belt. Trying to address Teddy by voice, under the din of engine and blades, would have been useless. But after a moment's study of glossy Fiberglas pate, I reached over the seat top and tapped his shoulder.

I don't remember what message I meant him to read into this.

His response, without turning, was to raise his left hand, gloved continuously with the black leather of his flying costume, and with index finger and thumb form the familiar *O* of the deaf-and-dumb alphabet, the *K* signified by the three digits erected erratically in diminishing perspective beyond.

I added this impudence to the account I would draw up against him and present for payment when we landed. I felt my pockets for my Browning, loosened the constraint of the seat belt, and felt again: it was gone, had long since plummeted, no doubt, through skylight or skull. Whatever Teddy's crimes, the damage caused by trying to bring him to book was extensive, perhaps the burning of the sty to dine on roast pork.

I stared down through the bubble. The East River was the brimming gutter below, a traffic of aphids along its near curb, a smoking chip or two on its flood. The immediate question was: where did Ted head? To some Fire Island fastness of inversion, there, confirming Boris' theory, to attempt to breach, by brutality or blandishment, my heterosexual defenses? Before I played Lawrence of Arabia to Teddy's Turk, I would cook both our geese! I made feral claws of my hands and moved them slowly towards his nape, but to throttle him effectively I should have had to lift my hands farther than the seatbelt would tolerate.

I dropped them to the buckle, but as I freed its grasp

Villanova put his machine into a swinging turn and directed it back towards Manhattan. Centrifugation hurled me from the seat.

When I had remounted and belted again, we were near the place whence we had risen and losing altitude, so that I could identify the rooftop elevator-shack on my building, the incinerator-exhaust stack, the pimpled terminations of other ducts, the unfoliated TV tree, and a congeries of human beings, among whom I first recognized the most and the least: giant Bakewell and the tiny Hindu, the latter from his turban, looking at my range like the bulbous eraser on a pencil stub. The other recognitions came between these extremes: Boris' shako, Peggy's wig, Washburn's fair head, Zwingli's crown of Brillo, Calvin's white Stetson, the slouch felt of Hus, Natalie's pigtails, and a half-dozen lavender discs of schoolgirl hats. The principals were assembled, but director Teddy kept the *mise en scène* aloft while they practiced stage businesses, in the main thrust fingers and shaken fists.

For a moment I thought Villanova might cause his machine to sink farther, perhaps continue on to the very roofful of his enemies and ruthlessly sweep it clean with his broom of wind. But in fact he did nothing in the nature of assault, swinging rather, as if on an invisible cord attached to their pivot, he and I inclining in unison with the craft's new attitude towards the horizon, in a great encompassment of not only the appropriate building but some of its neighborhood, including Christopher Columbus' hospital, Washington Irving's place, and the little private park that exemplifies Milton's "What gramercy to be sober, just, or continent," being ever kept locked against all strangers and denied even to locals who carry bottles, air a dog, or walk seminude.

Teddy's purpose in tracing a circle in the nullity was unknown to me, whether in salute, taunt, or, in perverse kindness, to dissipate the suspended soot and make the atmosphere more salubrious for his adversaries. He looked down, but, I thought, idly, his trace of lips available to my vision being of a repose that indicated nothing, and when we had come round to point northwards again, he corrected our obliquity, and levelly we moved towards Twenty-third Street, leaving the convocation of constables, *et al.*, to their bootless fury—if such it was, and not now, with me a *de facto* prisoner of Teddy, the expression of the greatest ruse of all.

Indeed, as paranoia came like a plow to my momentarily fallow fields of emotion, recently overfarmed, I could not even exempt Peggy Tumulty from complicity in my complex confounding of the past twenty-four hours. How did that wardrobe of bawdy underwear happen to fit her so snugly? How had Natalie so quickly escaped the patrolmen, and why were Washburn & Bakewell back so soon from Teterboro? And it seemed only by chance that Teddy's ladder had swung near just as the vice-squad Cossack forced me through the window: Boris was would-be assassin, whether for hire or because he could not endure my breath—for his was a personality that tended towards hysteria—remained to be proved. I also came to entertain a belief that Calvin and his blanched bitch had intended to shotgun *me* on Union Square, not Pete & Tony, whose fortuitous intervention proved their own ruin. Even Natalie's claim to the Lesbian persuasion, whether sound or in mere bravado, was a kind of attempted homicide, given my previous association with her. As to those depraved school-girls, memory seemed insistent to the effect that their visages were unduly wizened for the tender-aged: could this have been the result of mere vice, too much too soon, or were they really a troop of midget policewomen, like Calvin equipped by Nature to work under cover as reputed rogues?

Notice that I now accepted the law-enforcement credentials of the entire rooftop lot, and placing these in conjunction with their various performances, had been captured by that terrible nightmare of the sensibility founded on the arts called liberal: cynicism; though common sense to any unlettered rustic. Had all this learning led only to the simple apprehension of the peasant on seeing a neighbor filch his flitch of bacon, *viz.*, that man is ineluctably incorrigible?

Or was this the moment for the formulation of general principles, with the helicopter in descent? In fact, in a trice, landing—on what would appear to be the narrow roof of the building in which I maintained my office.

The great fan overhead made one last lazy *swish* and came to stasis. The engine sounded a few gasps and mumbles and expired. Teddy's seat squeaked and the buckle of his safety belt snickered and then clattered. I made mine do the same. His black leather hand threw a lever, and an oval door broke the wall of the bubble.

I was nearer the exit than he, and had more need to leave first, too much to offer courteous deference in departure.

I grasped the Lucite edges of the opening and hurled myself out. My exertion, evoked by a need to relieve psychic strain, embarrassed the requirement by excess. I took one step on the tarred roof; the next, impelled into a spring by irresistible impetus, inertia's lackey, took me over the low parapet, and I plunged . . .

15

. . . Fetching up, however, in another embarrassment, not far below, for the contiguous building rose to within two feet of that from which I had leaped, and its roof was a roosting place for pigeons: guano abounded, too little gone to powder, much yet as slime. My landing was three-point and sliding, and a pretext for the unseating of a parliament of fowls, who fled with a feathery commotion which, along with the mess on my left hand and both knees, diverted me from a surveillance on Teddy.

When I clambered across to the heliport he was gone, though his machine remained. Obviously he had lifted the trap door at the roof's rear and insinuated himself into the building like a virus in a vein.

Another reversal of relative roles: I was pardoned as prisoner and once again he was prey. I opened the hatch and more slid than stepped down the fixed iron ladder so revealed, precipitating myself into a crepuscular corner of the fifth-floor rear, opposite which was a battered door labeled 5B. Behind this, if memory served, the rock-music group called Custer's Last Dance practiced their apishness, the none too distant howls of which could often be clearly heard at my own third-floor front.

All was silent now. My polite knock was simultaneously delivered with my rude turn and thrust of knob. An empty chamber yawned before me, from scarred threshold to windows filmed with filth, beneath them what close inspection proved a raisin heap of dead flies. No Teddy Villanova, and no hairy, guitar-clutching epigones of that craze of my later youth or, as it now seemed, my earlier middle age.

I flung out into the corridor and pelted to the entrance to 5A, for which I could remember no tenant, and appropriately so, for the door stood open and there was no one within, nor by the look of the old lesions on the walls, the newspapers gone tobacco-brown and brittle on the floor, and the skeleton of a rat, scoured by the teeth of its pragmatic brethren (like *Homo sapiens,* a cannibal breed)— but I shrink from the lavishness of saying since Peter Stuyvesant had toured the Bowery on silver peg leg: it seemed, anyway, ever so long.

I used the stairs to inject myself headlong into the fourth floor, of which the rearmore door bore the rubric *B* and beneath it, from a runny heliotrope stencil: FUN THINGS INC, so often mischievously misrepresented on the lobby directory board, if you can remember, as "Fucing," and pronounced by Sam Polidor according to its altered orthography. I took an instant to think of that banal, venal man and sigh at all that eluded his simple philosophy of leases. A helicopter now sat on his roof, an archcriminal had penetrated his building.

"Foosing," then, was gone, leaving no more souvenirs of its tenancy that had Custer and Anonymous above, and the same fact was soon established for Corngold & Co., late in costume-jewelry findings, fleeing from whose 4A former space at the dash I finally remembered who, before the ossified rat, had occupied the office directly overhead: Natural Relations, either marriage counselors or computerized panders.

Well, the third floor was mine own and immune to alteration. Ganymede's closed door faced me as with imaginary poles I made a skiless *Geländesprung* off the last step. Teddy might well have taken refuge in the pots and pans within, and I hesitated briefly for loin-girding before breaching the portal and battering him from the *batterie de la cuisine*.

Three deep breaths, mouth-taken, nose-expelled, an aspiratory technique recalled from some adolescent manual on bully-trouncing, and I was ready. I twisted the knob and hurled myself in, knowing as I did that were the woman there, and not Teddy, I should have added another gaffe to that of helping myself to the second brownie.

Perhaps you are now too blasé, as I was not yet, to be startled by my assurance that no person was in the Ganymede outer office, no furniture, no wall-to-wall carpeting, and in the rear showroom, to which I next repaired through an empty rectangle in the partition, the blond door having vanished as well, neither pot, pan, table, nor fluorescent fixture!

I discarded all thought of Teddy at that moment and sped through the hall to my own office.

If the disappearances had become routine, I hope to shock you now with an existence *in statu quo*: my rooms were precisely as last seen. Peggy's crumpled Blimpie bag lay yet on her desk, guarded by the sentry wearing the regimental colors of Tab. In my inner sanctum, in memoriam to the working over at the hands, and feet, of Pete & Tony, since smithereened on Union Square, the desk drawers and their former contents were still floor-bound at random. The blue towel lay where it had fallen when, after washing the paw that had struck my frontal bone, Bakewell had flung it into my face. How long ago that seemed; yet, contradictorily, in time's perverse fashion, how recent as well.

I flung myself from the third floor to the second, conscious of touching no stair en route, and burst into what had ever been the Wyandotte Club, which, had it been occupied, might have earned me at least a merciless hiding, at worst a concrete burial. But I was back again in the old series of voids: gone were staff and members and whatever furnishings they had sported amidst, bar, machines of chance, gaming tables, perhaps curtained alcoves in which to sluice their molls: of what had gone on there I was, and to remain forever, innocent.

I had no hopes for the final enclosure, 2A, once the home of Alpenstock Industries: whatever they had been, they were gone, lugs and luggage.

I went to the ground floor and squirted through the lobby like Rioja from a skin squeezed by a Spaniard, debouching onto the sidewalk, from which I wheeled and re-entered, not without noticing on my old adversary, the directory board, that no names remained but my own. Sam Polidor would have much to elucidate, but first I was faced with the bearding of Teddy, who, unless he had fled the building, abandoning the expensive aircraft on the roof, must be cornered, fangs bared, in the cellar.

No doubt he had maintained his stronghold there throughout, with God knew what armory, to the total ignorance of heedless, myopic Polidor, so sensitive to petty irregularities, so oblivious to enterprises of great pith and moment.

I ripped open the door and confronted the garbage cans and, beyond, the strait, precipitous stairway. So framed, I should be an irresistible target to him who stood below with firearm, crossbow, sling, or assagai. Fortunately, no such figure could be seen on the oblong of cracked concrete. I scampered down the splintery treads.

A shadowy, inclined element against the bulky boiler seemed a crouching man. I addressed it—"Swine!"—and regardless of such weapons as it might bristle with, advanced with balled fists, receding navel, and jellied knees, until I was sufficiently near to fetch it so savage a loafered toe as almost to disable my poor foot.

It was Sam's baseball bat, and it went hurtling into the

dark recess behind the furnace, where, if Teddy hid there, he must now be felled. Stepping into this place, however, I heard only a smaller rat, skittering away from which evil sound I barked my pate on a booming duct of galvanized metal.

The remainder of the basement, stalactited with valves, festooned with loosened insulation and the corroded metallic tapes that once had snugged it, showed nothing of sufficient bulk to hide a man, and in the interests of continuity I shall not here catalogue Sam's cellar, an inventory of which would interest only the antiquarian of that which never had recommendation: disemboweled Morris chairs, ocherous newspaper pages advertising Nehru jackets, etc.

I toiled back to the lobby and stared into the elevator. It had not been used during my search, else I should have heard it. The car was grounded and open, and I stepped within. The slow ascent was appropriate to my ratiocinative mood, and when I emerged on the third floor I knew the signal failure of my previous tour: I had neglected to examine the water closet in each hallway.

As if on cue, at my approach, the one at the end of my own hall now swung back its door and . . . Sam Polidor emerged.

He was in the act of grossly zippering his trousers. His carnelian necktie was a loose noose around the white collar of his ultramarine shirt. After closing his fly, he tightened his tie.

He stared at me through his horn-rims. "So Ran I see ya still here no matter what you sonofagun you."

"I advise you to take cover, Sam," said I. "A desperate man is at large in the building."

He was unmoved. "So that's New York for you. I wouldn't never had a tenant if I wouldn't rent to schmucks."

"You don't seem to have any at the moment but me,"

I said. "But time for that no doubt fascinating explanation anon. A master criminal, a fiendish fellow, lurks in some cranny of this edifice. I should ask you to call the police, but they have proved inept, if not impotent, in their previous efforts against him. Like all contemporary art-forms, theirs is in its decadence, occupied solely with structure and not substance, more ritualistic role-playing. A vice-squadder, for example, speaks like a character from *Euphues*—"

Sam pawed the old boards with his shoe of dark patent leather, from which the highlights winked in ruby; across the instep stretched a golden horse bit, a chain between two rings.

"Know," said he, "these woods are good yet dating from the first Rusevelt probably. Real lead in the plumbing, solid doors. Scratch the paint off the switch plates, you find pure brass. Used to do things right, Rone, before the world turned to shit."

Did I see a tear behind his refracting lenses? I was touched, suddenly, by his feeling for quality. The man had a dimension I had never discerned. "Yes, Sam, book-binding, engraving, and the lost-wax process of molding bronze are also dying crafts."

Sam winced hatefully. "Don't talk like a prick, Run. This breaks my hot."

I was not offended. I saw his authentic distress, though I knew not its pretext.

"Well," said I, "all this is but the masochist's flight forward. The old place has a good many years in it yet." However, this might be a bit too far to go with a New York landlord, and I quickly added: "Not that certain improvements would be unwelcome. The full flood of my faucets seldom exceeds the trickle; the rubbish of a fortnight past can usually be found in the garbage cans; the super has been an utter stranger on my floor since his

Xmas collection from me of sufficient funds to buy a pint of Twister. . . ."

Sam was surveying the length of my person. Tarrying at my forehead, he told me: "Rin, you got me beat, I'm man enough to admit. So gimme your proposition."

"Proposition?"

"Your run-around awready cost me a fortune." He showed his teeth in an evil smile, very like the expression of a dog suffering an unwanted snout at its hind parts but restrained by its master's ukase against combat. "I been through a lot, Rum. My brother-in-lore a cocksucker sold me a Valiant once that was a lemon." He glared while I tried to puzzle out whether his relative and the fellator were one and the same, then went on before I succeeded. "I gotta kid, you know. He went bad for a while, lived with a lotta hoors and hopheads on some reservation or whadduh yuh call it where all they do is take dope and play the banjo. He finally straightened out, thank God, though didn't go inna business but went for sociology professor in California. I guess he's a bigger Commie than ever but don't knock it he earns a good living the little mumser."

"Sam," I said gently, "you are somewhat overwrought. It touches me to be so taken into your confidence, and these incidents from a life as valuable as any are eloquent. But I doubt your motive is purely to supply fragments of a great confession. I suspect you are somehow putting an onus on me."

Sam was not deterred by my speech, throughout which he continued to list the ailments incurred in his passage through the years, the betrayals, the miscarriages, and eventually fetched up at: "But you take the cake, Rain."

I sighed. "What is your point?"

"The Wyoming guys never cost me a penny!" Sam cried. "They said they was moving anyhow, on account of they didn't like the neighbors." He guffawed in a style that partook of desperation, gloating, and malevolence. "Meaning *you*, haha! Shooting people upstairs what a schmuck!"

I said schmugly: "They're involved in a gang war with black rivals. Good for you they've gone."

"Don't talk to me about niggers," Sam said, sea-gulling his arms. "Don't think I wanted to sell out to them. They're the only ones with money in this derecession."

In confusion my incisors momentarily detained my tongue on the terminal word: "You've lost me further, Stan."

"Sam's the name," he said, not, however highly exercised, missing a trivial lapse.

"What's this about selling out?"

"Maybe you been shrewd befaw," said he, "but now you're dumb. If I was to tell them you alone was holding up the deal, you find yourself with the throat cut inna garbage can in Hollem, and how police would trace it to me they couldn't, and I'd save myself a lot of trouble and more money. Know what I spent on you so far? A bundle. For what? For shit. I was wrong, and I admit it. I thought you was some *fegeleh*. So you turn out a tough cookie. O.K. You can't be bought off, you can't be scared off. So you wanna be killed by some big bastard black as tar?"

"No," I confessed, "certainly not. Though neither do I share your bias against the African-derived. Timbuktu in its golden age may not have been Periclean Athens, but then what was? And did they poison their dusky Socrates? And, in the most extravagant fantasy, engendered by racist paranoia, would New York suffer morally, culturally, or aesthetically if replaced by a cluster of huts woven of wattles and cemented with cowdung?"

Sam made a glottal sound that suggested the flush of the water closet from which he had lately emerged (incidentally, without such sound of flush).

"My final offer take it and leave," said he. "Four-five, you got it."

"Offer? Four-five? I got?"

"Not a penny more, Rind." Sam slapped his forehead. "Awright, *five*, you hustleh. But that's tops, and next is some big coon with a switch knife. I don't want no blood on my hands." He turned, walked rapidly away, returned to breathe stertorously at the banister, peering at me from time to time and moving his lips as if a fragment of nut were trapped in a nook of gum.

"Sam," I said, "I know that it will violate the most cherished principle of yours and your milieu, namely: the total disregard of other human beings except as objects to be manipulated or eluded, but I ask you now to consider an unprecedented experience: not merely listening, but hearing. *I have no clue as to the subject of your remarks.*"

And then, detecting no evidence that he comprehended my incomprehension, and being furthermore at the limits of my patience, so sorely tried these twenty-four hours by a raft of rogues, I unleashed the animal from the cage of culture and cried: "What the fuck are you talking about?"

Sam whipped his glasses from his face. For an instant I believed this the preface to belligerence, but soon saw it was rather the reverse, displaying a nudity much more shocking than the exposure of Washburn's bare pelt or even the show of Peggy confined by two ribbons.

"You're crucifying me is what you're doon!" he wailed from this parody visage of defenselessness.

Saying, "I cannot minister to a mind diseased," I side-stepped the man and went along the hall to my office, entered the inner chamber, and hurled myself into the swivel chair behind the desk, forgetting its spring was feeble and would not sustain a backward thrust. Fortunately, the wall behind was near enough to catch me at an angle, feet in air, sight line below the surface of the desk, in fact going into the aperture left by Pete & Tony's removal of the central drawer. An object was secured therein, Scotch-taped to the underside of the desk top.

I rocked and toed myself down, reached in and plucked the thing away, examined the cold metal rectangle so procured.

It was a cartridge clip for an automatic pistol. It was in fact very like *the* cartridge clip for *my* automatic.

Sam entered during my examination of this object. "Sure," he said, "I hid it so nobody would get killed with these shenanigans. That big schmuck Bakewell has to make it look good, so before laying down like a corpse he shoots the gun inna wall so one bullet would be gone and the barrel would stink. He could of killed somebody next store but he don't think of that. I tell you, this is the last time I work with actors."

I lowered the clip to the desk and said slowly: "It went into a brownie."

"What a buncha bums!" Sam sighed. He had seemingly spent his passion. He fell onto the couch. "They couldn't make a living in any other line, I tell you that. I'm paying the son of a bitch, but he gets a chance to play a corpse in some show called *The Reformers* and he takes off."

"A Ziggy Zimmerman film," I said. "They shot the scene in my apartment, which no doubt was rented to them, in my absence, by that swine of super or dog of doorman."

"Him and the other one, their asses are out most of the time," said Sam, as usual ignoring what I said and pursuing his own sequence. "That Washburn had a bit part once on 'Kojak,' he played a fag bartender, but he's on unemployment all a time, on account he wants to stay in this Shitville and not to go to California. Can you beat that? You know this town is fulla assholes."

"One of whom is me," I said. "You're Teddy Villanova, aren't you?"

"You!" he exclaimed. "You're some kinda real smart apple. You saw through it right away, you sonofagun." He wore his glasses again and used them to produce a leer of admiration. "Know what it costs to hire a chopper?"

"Neither do I have any idea of how an urban slumlord could fly one."

"Rusty! I tell you that, and they changed some since Korea. I had a real bitch with the thermals over ya house, maybe you noticed how I hadda swing over the river to turn?"

"Korea?"

"I was young once," said Sam.

"I thought it would have been much longer ago than that."

"This city takes a lot outa ya. I still got lead in the pencil, though." He patted his belly, with an index finger thrown crotchwards. "I don't wanna speak out of turn, but when your girl says come around, I'll give you a good jazzing, the old soldier stood right up at attention."

"She released an alternative version," said I. "Her stated purpose being, taking you as archcriminal, to lure you to capture—perhaps hitting you with a paperweight at your instant of maximum vulnerability, for she was unarmed."

"Got some pair, that cooze," said Sam. "I envy you, Ram. You're a winnah."

"So Bakewell and Washburn are professional Thespians—"

"You're talking about them girls, Nat and Al, and it's funny, ain't it, so good-looking, could get alla guys they wanted. Whatinhell they *really* do, Rome? Muff one another? I can't see it."

"—and Zwingli, Knox, and Calvin are genuine police-

men. What of Hus and Boris? . . . Just a moment, who
really is Natalie Novotny?"

Polidor moued lavishly. "Uh nairline stew with a great
sensa yooma. I met huh rin a singles place, name of Big
Dick's Pub, Second Avenue inna eighties."

"She did this in malicious japery?" I asked, and then,
to rout his frown: "A practical joke?"

Sam's thumb and forefinger felt whether he had grown
a mustache. "Hates men. You know the type."

I could manage my sweep of reason only by assembling
a broom straw by straw. "Hus and Boris are what they say
they are? . . . Your irresponsible scheme, for which I trust
you will soon explain the purpose, unwittingly brought
many forces into play, Polidor. Unruly man! There may
well be international reverberations. Do you know of the
Hindu?"

"He's the pal of them actors, runs a yoghurt gym where
they go to keep in shape. A Jewish kid from the Grand
Concourse," Sam added with the usual contempt he displayed towards his ethnic fellows. "Little pisspot! I used to
rent to him here. Had to throw him out. All *fonfing*, he
didn't pay a nickel."

The yoga wallah's authenticity as native Indian having
been the only identification I accepted as unquestionable,
I fled to another theme, though not forgetting I owed him
a return for that savage *zetz* to the head that he obviously
had himself given me on his threshold. The only remaining character to deal with was the main, the grand, the
motive for all this play of passion and volition, to which
the other performers were but supernumerary: Teddy
Villanova, also known as Sam Polidor.

"*Why*, Sam?" I asked quietly. "Why Teddy?"

Polidor was dumfounded. "I tole ya! I thought I'd save
a buck by scaring you out. You wouldn't listen to them
other offers."

"Just a moment. Defer telling me Why and explain What Other Offers. You said nothing, before a few moments ago, about any offer for whatever."

Sam winced. "So I tole Big Boobs to tell *you*. That's the way it works, professional dealing. Like these niggers, see, they dint come to me direct, went through my wife's nephew. 'Got some buyers for your dump,' he tells me. He never mentions their color, the two-timer, till I heard the price. So to take it I got to buy out the leases, the ones that still got time to run, right? Gimme Meat is leaving anyhow, going outa business; nobody cooks any more when you got Kentucky Fried Chickens on every corner: makes the home cleaner. Custard Stand owes six months' rent; should of evicted them long ago. Jack Alpenstock, that chiseler—"

"Mine still has fourteen months to go," I said.

"Thirteen plus a matter of days," said Sam.

"You assert that you offered to buy out my lease, submitting such offer to Peggy Tumulty?"

"More than once!" cried Sam. "You know that, Rissel Run, you fucks."

"Fox? I hardly deserve that honorific," I said. "As it happens, she never passed those offers on." I picked up the cartridge clip and in fancy pumped the remaining slugs, through the barrel of my index finger, into Peggy's navel. "I'll get her for that."

"Come *awn*," said Sam. "For what, if you're telling the truth? For making me up the price?"

"I took a lot of abuse because of her fecklessness."

"So what!" He threw his arms aloft and followed them with his body. "Take my word for it, you don't come into a buck in this day and age without getting a little shit on your hands. I'll tell the lawyer to make the papers and fix you a check. That was four?"

"It was *five*, but not accepted," said I. "It's *six* now."

"Six thousand dollars!"

I confess I was even more incredulous: I thought he had meant hundreds. He went into a howl of exquisite agony, maintained it throughout the handshake, his half of which was insubstantial as that of the victim of a mortal disease, continued howling as he left, went along the hall, and entered the elevator. And even above the hoarse moan of the motor, the cacophony of cable, I could hear the thrill of his keen as he sang earthwards.

But we seemed to have a deal, and I was rich. I decided impulsively to abandon the squalor of the office as was, leaving behind even the complete, boxed Plato, along with the files on white adulterers, for the edification of the black newcomers. I could now afford to return to my play, which Zwingli had been good enough to admire, and he was a movie star. The work of a moment would convert it to film script, and already my imagination had begun to roam in the wider scope thus offered. . . . This might well be Ziggy Zimmerman's next vehicle. He anyway owed me a favor for the scene I had, unwittingly and unwaged, played in *The Reformers.*

I rushed to the window that gave on Twenty-third Street, raised the sash, and put my head into the noisy, noisome atmosphere without. Soon seeing the sheen of Sam Polidor's bald spot emerge from the building, I eventually succeeded in catching his ear and, subsequently, under an Indian-scout hand, his eyeglasses.

The following dialogue consumed more time than can here be represented conveniently, having to wait as it did for the rare interstices in an all but solid wall of din.

"*Where did you get the name Teddy Villanova?*"

Explosive flatulence of bus.

"*Teee-Veee!*"

Teddy's initials. "*News or play?*"

"*Police show.*"

Thunder of jackhammer.

"Major character or minor?"

"Walk-on!" shouted Sam, lowered his face, and walked on, leaving me with all I needed. I adored that name and would pluck it from the public domain for my title, *Who Is Teddy Villanova?*

I had no further business in the building—the razing of which, to go beyond the temporal range of this narrative, was begun a fortnight hence: the great iron orb swinging on its cable, succeeded by the voracious bulldozer, and secreted within the resulting rubbish, hauled away to make new land of some old swamp or bay, were my grayed T-shirts, unpaid bills, a Blimpie bag, and a Tab can. The new owners of the property, will, I have been apprised— by Sam, who has with their money purchased three tenements in Spanish Harlem—erect thereupon an "automated garage," a jargon title I interpret to suggest that·the churlish fender-smashing, bumper-bashing attendant of yore will give way to a courteous robot-mechanism, and thus one more bit of the inhumane is replaced by the nonhuman.

I used the water closet for the last time ever—finding Sam's helmet and flayed flying suit on the floor: what a fanatic he had proved; though justifiably enough, the motive being purely mercenary and not ideological—and then voided the building. My progress was jaunty along Third Avenue, but was given pause when, between Twentieth and Twenty-first streets, I was passed, at great speed, by the mauve minibus of the Stavrogin Academy for Young Ladies, and saw serially through the windows headgear of fur, felt, lavender, and cocooned silk, a pigtailed wig, Washburn's blond hair, and the great sphere Bakewell carried on his redwood neck.

Seemingly they did not see me—they looked as if in some intestine squabble, competing no doubt for exotic pre-eminence—and though I might in my projected screen-play have roles for them all, I did not yearn for their present company.

With the sight of my doorman, my stride became a stalk, but he soon became foremost an obsequious display of teeth. "Ziggy showed us the rushes last night. You're terrific, Mr. Wren, a real sta."

Anything but a show of modesty here would have been infra dig. "Thanks," said I. "It was a piece of cake, once I had worked out the motivation. The character is essentially a moral leper, yet human like us all, *mon semblable, mon frère.*"

I swept into the elevator, mounted to my floor, and, remembering that I had not seen Peggy among those in the Stavrogin bus, worked out, on my progress through the hall, a technique for dealing with her should she be yet in the apartment.

She was. She wore her office attire and her quotidian hair and eyes. The familiar quarter-moons were in the armpits of her off-white blouse, her ankles were wrinkled, and the zipper of her skirt lay in front of her hipbone. She sat on the couch, sucking the chromium push button of a crimson Paper-Mate. What appeared from its size to be a copy of *TV Guide*, opened to the crossword puzzle, lay in her rumpled lap.

"Say, Russ," she said, without looking up, "who's that Frenchman does the stuff on the ocean?"

"Peg, I haven't watched TV religiously since 'Speed Racer' went off the air."

"What?" She counted squares with a cracked fingernail.

"Saturday morning kid-cartoon. I was an addict. Hero had a remarkable car, used it to rout those who sought to control the world, generally porcine types with guttural accents. . . . Fantasy has its uses, Peggy. In dreams begin responsibilities, according to your countryman Yeats."

"Jacques!" she screamed, and her pen began to hop the scotches.

"Whose Crazy Jane poems I can recommend whole-heartedly," ᴛ added.

Completing the puzzle with one final extravagant uncial —upside down, the page, in red ink, had a medieval look— she closed the magazine with a *slap* of covers and hurled it away as an offensive thing. Like all grand masters at such terminological games—at which I am hopeless—she despised words.

I surveyed my quarters. "I see you have disposed of the unmentionables."

She pointed at the window, through which I saw a lowering pall.

"Yes," I said stoically, "that super burns rubbish at any hour he has a savage's whim to make fire. Santayana says the 'barbarian believes that the outflow of energy is the absolute good, irrespective of motives or consequences.'"

"That's *them*," said Peg, "all that dirty stuff. I threw it down the incinerator."

"No, Peggy," said I, sinking to a seat alongside her on the sofa. "It's not 'dirty.' That's a received idea, engendered by grim-lipped, icy-veined Calvinists. Nothing's wrong with pleasure—unless of course it's imposed against one's will. The cult of underwear may not be one which I would join—for me, much sistered in my youth, it is even a repellent association—but I cannot see it bringing social harm. In fact, taking sexual enterprise, as we must, individually, such fetishism may well be healthy." I raised my chin. "Let me explain, dear Peg, old comrade—"

"Partner!" she corrected me.

I fluttered my lashes. "In my former business, now dissolved."

"Sam met your price."

"For a few sous, scarcely enough to pay the costs of moving."

"Don't give me that bull. I'd say he went as high as four, maybe five. If you had let me handle it, he'd of paid through the nose. Know what he's getting for that firetrap? A million-two. And we alone were holding up his deal—which if he didn't take it right away might of blown up in his face. You know how *they* are." I had never heard Peggy refer to Afro-Americans except pronominally.

That I had settled for six was small satisfaction. However, I had a thousand to which she could never, being ignorant, lay claim. Which theory was immediately exploded.

"Whatever you got—and I'll find out from Sam—half belongs to me."

I moved my head from one shoulder to the other. "Since when are you so close to that shark?"

"He's sweet on me," said Peggy, reminding me, with a nuance of trunk, of the opulent body beneath her rumple.

"But did you know he was Teddy Villanova?" I asked triumphantly.

"Don't be ridiculous."

"You didn't figure it out, did you? And you wanted to be a private investigator."

"You mean to sit there and tell me Sam Polidor owned that filthy junk, those whips and chains and helmets and spurs—"

"Oh, stop! Don't get too *Mitteleuropäisch* with your Queens fancy," I warned. "There was a bra or two and a vulgar garter belt, et cetera." I put up a finger. "Because you see, Peggy—and I say this sympathetically—on my route down the hall just now I *understood*. That accounts for my foregoing comments on fetishism. I see they did not penetrate. I'll be frank, then: you've lived a sheltered life, while all around you are unrestrained animals, spending their spirits in a waste of shame. You've looked in a book or two, contemporary trash that exalts the passions while jeering at every stern tenet you learned from the nuns, and you've stared with open mouth at movies that do worse. Even popular TV shows, far cries from 'Speed Racer,' now accept sexual irregularities as inconsequential under the aspect of the social moment. Yet an untarnished maiden at the ripe age of twenty-nine—"

"Twenty-eight, ten months, and three days!" Peggy shouted.

"—you wonder whether," I proceeded doggedly, "you are withering on the vine. Somewhere you come across Pierre's catalogue, see therein what in your innocence you assume arouses male ardor, and in a desperate stroke, purchase by mail a shipment of naughty underclothes, which you don in a private place, unwittingly provided by me, my apartment being unoccupied. You secretly borrow my keys and have copies made. Owing to your series of wigs, the doorman believes you a sequence of different harlots."

I must announce that *in medias res* Peggy had got up and gone into the bathroom, and I had spoken the several latter sentences to the closed door.

"Believe me, I don't condemn you," I continued. "It was a necessary rite of initiation, harmless to your fellow man. It was the first giant step. But sexuality at its best, Peggy, is sharing, and not what the French call solitary pleasures, valuable as they are to introduce a new state of mind."

I feared I was going too far, and left off. Perhaps she merely adorned herself and paraded around the apartment. Whatever, I never sneer at the fantasy-prone.

I had left the immediate vicinity of the door but quite clearly heard her quiet question within.

"Russ, underneath it all, are you saying you are really queer?"

Before I had time to fashion an answer that would meet my needs, the telephone rang. I loped to the kitchenette, removed the wall-hung instrument, and supported myself with the other hand, fisted, on the lip of the sink.

"Wren?"

"Who's this?"

"Villanova."

I lowered my voice: "Say, Sam, do me a favor: kindly don't mention to Peggy Tumulty the price at which you are buying out my lease. And forget about your aspiration to know her in the Biblical sense." I peered towards the bathroom door and spoke behind a clamshelled hand. "She's of the other persuasion: same breed, I'm afraid, as Nat and Al, Gertrude Stein, and—"

"Delphine and Hippolyte?"

This was not Sam Polidor. Washburn was given to hoaxes, if paid, and Boris like all czarists was a Francophile, but the steely ring of derisive insolence did not quite suit either of them. Nor did the voice, a mellifluous baritone, resemble Zwingli's hoarse whisper. But I answered as if to another of the drug-dick's literary quizzes.

"Racine, surely?"

"*Sot!*" he crowed. "*Dummkopf!* It is of course *Femmes damnées: Delphine et Hippolyte.*"

"You caught me off guard, whoever you are. And I know Sade only in translations; the French texts are rare birds over here."

"That's Bawdy Liar, you ass."

"You couldn't be—?" No, my old French teacher at State, Hyacinthe Greuze, whose acerbity was here being brought to memory, had long since chain-smoked himself into the grave.

"Look here, you are a droll type, but there is no Teddy Villanova. The name was an invention of Sam Polidor's or rather lifted from some TV trash."

"Speaking of trash," said the voice, "while I used your flat, I perused your fragment of play."

Obviously this was a cunning fellow, who hoped to trap me in an extravagance of spleen.

"No doubt its wit is too keen for your coarse sensors," I said. "But Ziggy will be mad about it. I'll admit, though, it is yet imperfect and needs a few dotting of *i*'s to work on the big screen." I jeered. "My flat, eh? You lie. A hysterical friend stored that underwear here."

"And the implements of discipline?"

"There were none such. And besides, they weren't mine."

"No," said he, "they are mine."

"You're Boris, aren't you, speaking through a scarf?"

"I keep a keep in Bavaria, one of the few castles built by Ludwig the Mad that are not tourist attractions, but mine is isolated, and protected by a private guard of husky brutes recruited from the local peasantry. However, having business in New York and needing a discreet hideaway, there to pursue the peculiar pleasures that I find, haha! I cannot long deny myself"—he struck a petulant note—"and why should I?, I came upon your abandoned apartment, admittance to which I gained by flinging a few sovereigns to a servitor."

"What *is* your business?" asked I, tongue in cheek.

"Obscene art-objects on classical themes, opiates: poppy, mandragora, wolfsbane—"

"It's too late in the game for me to be gulled again," said I. "I no longer believe in archcriminals and polymorphous perverts. Quixotism cannot long survive among the Panzas of Manhattan."

The voice took on what sounded very like a timbre of compassion. "Wren, I am in your debt. I have been called a fiend, but no man can charge me with a failure to meet my obligations. I left behind some delicacies, as well as certain pieces of armor and the like. Do consider them your

own. Still, that's small compensation. There is no doubt
certain visible wear and tear. Alas, your suede chair was
besmirched by one of my unguents."

"Anyone could have made that stain. The place was full
of film crew."

"I rang you up now—my private jet is warming its after-
burners on the runway—to make amends. Kindly state a
sum that would compensate you for particular stain and
general strain, double it to represent a certain affection I
acquired for you while roaming your pretentious little library—I have a weakness for the intellectual poseur—and
soon you will be the recipient of a package of banknotes
in some stable currency, suitably disguised of course and
unrecorded by any tax bureau."

"I still would like to find the scoundrel who inscribed
false *ex libris* in my books or who replaced my identification with a license for a great Dane."

"Ophelia's head is at my elbow," said he. "You may discard her lingerie and wigs." I heard a basso bark, but he
could have made that himself.

I had enough of this. I still had to answer Peggy's insult-
ing question. "Well, 'Teddy,' you are a raffish fellow indeed, but my presence is required elsewhere."

"If it's with those Stavrogin tots, be careful: they're police plants, old boy. If you crave green fruit, come visit me
in Bavaria." He proceeded to specify certain amusements
that I could not entertain even in joke.

I hung up, went to the bathroom door, and cried: "No,
I'm not homosexual, nor zoophile, pederast, pedophile,
flagellant, nor fetishist!"

I went across the room and, in defiance, sat upon the defaced suede chair; my trousers were anyway streaked with
pigeon dung.

"Glad to hear that," said Peggy, opening the door and
emerging in my old mulberry bathrobe.

"I received a preposterous telephone call," I said. "Some movie mountebank, with execrable taste, pretending, at this thirteenth hour, to be Teddy Villanova."

Peggy went to the couch and began to remove the pillows.

I frowned. "I didn't recognize the voice. . . . No, it couldn't be. Everyone knows of the series of fantastic Bavarian castles built by Ludwig II, surnamed *der Verrückte*."

Peggy's forthright forearm levered open the concealed bed. She removed my old robe. She was nude. Her mode of entering bed was as kneewalker. She was not of the school who sit down and swivel, with thighs adhesively paralleled. Show me how a woman approaches the horizontal, and I will tell you her philosophy. —A useless prescription, like most that address themselves to moral variations. I assumed that Peggy, as worn as I by the cares of this case, had climbed on the train for a nap.

"I've given this a lotta thought, Russ," she said from the supine. "I think it's the only thing will make a man of you."

I remained obtuse. "Obviously the man is ᴜ charlatan. He has all the earmarks: arch idiom; strained and impertinent references to the higher culture; a pose as being, at once, all the kinds of degenerate I confessed to you, just now through the door, that I am not—"

I halted, carrying an imaginary pinch of snuff towards my nose. "But did he or did he not display those necessary evidences of deviation, identified by Sergeant Boris, an authority in this area, as symmetry and precision . . .?"

"Come *awn*," Peggy complained, horse blinding herself with her hands. "I've got a Mama Celeste Deluxe pizza in the oven, and it's done in twelve to fifteen minutes, depending on if you want the crust crisp or chewy."

"Still," I said, "I wonder whether I should cable Interpol's office in München? By no means have all the *bizar-*

reries of the past twenty-four hours been explained. Despite his motley, Boris was not playing a role in a motion picture—he seethed with envy at Zwingli's new career as cinemactor. And those schoolgirls are obviously unregenerate miscreants. There *was* a dog answering the description of Ophelia. It might well be that Natalie's masks are layered: first, Sapphic stewardess, then fake government operative—to further Polidor's scheme against me—but finally, *real* Treasury agent in pursuit of an actual archcriminal. The voice on the phone just now spoke suspiciously of currency, and made references as well to a commerce in what could include heroin on the one hand and the Sforza figurine on the other."

When I removed my speculative fingers from the division between my nostrils I smelled singed mozzarella, tomato sauce, and oregano. I had fasted since devouring the second brownie a sun and moon ago.

I ravenously changed the subject: "The Deluxe, unless I miss my guess, has sausage *and* mushrooms *and* peppers *and*—"

"For crying out loud, Russ," Peggy howled, exposing her eyes. "Here I am finally letting you have what you hired me for in the first place and have been trying to get ever since by hook or by crook. Come on and get it over with, because if we go to Bavaria there's no sense in paying for two rooms."

But for the horrible grimace with which she concluded this speech, she was more comely than I had ever seen her —as I now, tardily, realized.

I draw the curtain across the episode that followed—requiring neither the huzzahs nor the jeers of a bawdy audience—except, perhaps ungallantly, to lift the fringe and reveal the only absolute fact (as it was the most startling) yet established in the Villanova case: Peggy was not, as the pizza went to cinder, serving her novitiate in venery.